BURDEN OF TRUTH

A Cass Leary Legal Thriller

ROBIN JAMES

Burden of Truth

A Cass Leary Legal Thriller

By

Robin James

For all the latest on my new releases and exclusive content, sign up for my newsletter.

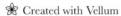 Created with Vellum

Prologue

Delphi, Michigan
The first day of spring
Three months ago ...

RAIN PELTED MY WINDSHIELD, leaving thick streaks in my field of vision where the wiper blades caught. I should have replaced them before I made this drive. But I never did things like that anymore. Not for ten years.

Since the day the Thorne Law Group hired me as a junior associate, I had my own driver if I wanted it. Company cars. A Lexus. No need to do mundane tasks like oil changes or even pumping my own gas. By the time I made partner three years ago, I had a corner office in one of the most coveted office buildings in Chicago. Now, with each mile I put behind me going east on I-94, the trappings of my old life slipped away.

Two hundred and fifty-two miles. The distance between my old life and my new. No ... that wasn't it. Chicago had been my new life. My second chance. My flipped script. Or at least, that's what I'd told myself all those years ago when I severed the ties that threatened to drag me down.

The green-and-white road sign for Exit 159A loomed to my right, the left corner chipped off and rusted. I could keep going. Ann Arbor, Detroit, maybe even further east or over the Ambassador Bridge into Canada. It didn't have to be this way.

Except I knew it did. As the pieces of my life shattered and reformed, I recognized the shape almost instantly. There was only one place left for me to go. I took the exit to the old highway that would bring me back. Gripping the steering wheel, my heart flipped as my headlights caught the big green sign on the side of the road.

Welcome to Delphi – Home of the Class B State Championship Men's Basketball Team:

2005, 2006, 2008, 2009, 2011, 2013, 2014, 2016 – Go Fighting Shamrocks!

I smiled to myself. Fighting Shamrocks. Everyone in the town just accepted that like it was normal. To me, it had always seemed as absurd as saying the Mighty Ferns or the Menacing Dandelions. But at least it was memorable.

The rain let up some as I took the turn to Main Street. My stomach clenched as I headed into town. Nothing had changed. I should have found that comforting. When the ground beneath me had just shifted to quicksand, maybe coming home was just what I needed to feel safe again.

Downtown Delphi consisted of two main intersections and a quaint town square complete with a water fountain and old-fashioned storefronts. The Town Beautification Committee had fought and lost the battle to keep the big box stores from moving in a half mile to the east. But they'd kept this little corner of the world looking like it had for the past seventy years or so.

I kept on going. My muscles seemed pre-wired to go east and turn down Trumbull Avenue. But I kept heading south to the lake. What little civilization Delphi offered faded away and the woods grew thicker along the winding business route.

Ten minutes later, I'd made the sharp curve and the lake view opened up before me. Finn Lake seemed so much smaller than I remembered. But I'd spent the last decade staring out at the vast blue waters of Lake Michigan from my office windows. Endless. Fathomless. And now, unreachable.

Gravel crunched beneath my tires as I pulled into the tiny driveway next to the little yellow bungalow. Well, it had been yellow once. Now the siding faded to a sort of rusted beige.

Grandpa Pat's ancient pontoon still sat at a tilted angle up on cinder blocks across the street. Three of the windows on the south side of the house were boarded up. My heart lurched as I saw the dock sinking into the water at the front of the house.

I gripped the steering wheel one last time and took a steeling breath. I was here. This was real. I cut the engine and got out. A dozen smells hit me as I made my way around the house, keys still dangling from my fingertips.

Boat fuel. Trees. Wet grass. Fish. I was twelve years old again. It hit me like a gut punch as I gingerly stepped down the crooked paving stones to the edge of the water. Just one section of the dock looked stable and I took a chance, stepping onto it. Minnows darted away as my footsteps echoed across the placid water.

A strange sense of calm came over me as a bullfrog made his rubber band chirp somewhere in the weeds.

I caught my reflection in the water. My blonde hair fell forward. My blue-gray eyes looked cold and dark. Just forty-eight hours ago, I'd stared at this same reflection from the waters of Lake Michigan off the deck of a yacht. Only then, my hands and feet had been tightly bound with zip ties as they'd pulled that dark-blue pillowcase off my head. I rubbed the raw skin on my wrists now, trying to push the pain away. I hadn't cried yet. Not once. I couldn't now. I had to rebuild my life again from scratch. This was my second chance. I straightened my back and turned toward the house.

Chapter 1

Present Day

"ALL RISE!"

I nudged my client with my elbow. Sandy York was a pleasant, fifty-year-old woman with wiry hair that went prematurely gray. She let it and that was one of the many things I admired about her. With no small effort, Sandy hauled herself to her feet.

For a moment, she looked like she might keel over. Sandy had Parkinson's disease. She didn't have to stand. No one in the courtroom would have demanded it of her, but Sandy York wanted no special treatment.

Moira Pierce, my favorite judge of the Woodbridge County Family Court so far, took the bench. She peered at Sandy over her half-moon reading glasses and she pursed her lips into a thin line. Moira knew how hard it was for Sandy to get to her feet these days too.

"Counsel, are you ready to proceed?" Judge Pierce addressed Bill Walden to my right. It was his client's motion today. He wanted to increase his parenting time to every

weekend and half the summer. Sandy planned to fight him with all the strength she had left, which was considerable.

"Yes, Your Honor," Bill said. He'd been practicing law in this county for over forty years. Longer than I'd been alive. I'm pretty sure the blue seersucker suit he had on was just as old. Bill had an unruly mass of white hair that stuck out in peaks and cones. He had a habit of brushing it over to the side, Kennedy-style, when he talked.

"If it pleases the court, my client seeks an increase to his previously court-ordered parenting time. Under MCL 722.25, we believe this request will serve the best interests of the three minor children he shares with the plaintiff by a preponderance of the evidence ... to wit..."

I winced. Bill was already stumbling out of the gate and it was in me to interject, but one look at Judge Pierce's face told me that wouldn't be necessary. I've seen hundreds of other lawyers walk into that mistake. There was no need to pounce when a judge was paying attention like Moira Pierce was.

"Mr. Walden," she said. "Let me stop you right there. I've read your motion and brief. I'm not interested in a rehashing of the law. I know it well. You have anything to add, Ms. Leary?"

She looked at me over those reading glasses. I half wondered if they weren't an affectation. Moira was young enough not to need them. But wise enough to know they might lend her a certain air of wisdom for the closed-minded good old boys that ran rampant in my hometown. God. This was one of the reasons I left in the first place.

"The plaintiff stands on our brief and the Friend of the Court recommendation filed last week. We see no reason for this change. It's not broken, Your Honor. There is no need to fix it," I said, knowing Judge Pierce hated having her time wasted. Walden was about to read his brief verbatim to her.

6

"Though I would like to point out that opposing counsel has just recited the wrong standard of review for the type of relief he's requesting."

"Thank you," she said. "I'll make this short and sweet. Mr. Walden, your client has been here a few times before on this request. Twice with my predecessor and now twice with me."

"Now hold on," Bill said, standing up again. My heart lurched. His client had just whispered something in Bill's ear that made his face turn purple. "These boys need more time with their father. They're of an age now. And I'd like to point out that the referee assigned to this case is also a woman."

Sandy rolled her eyes beside me. I knew what this was about. Sandy knew what this was about. Everyone in this *room* knew what this was about, probably even Bill. Colby York was sick of paying child support. He probably read on the internet somewhere he could only get a reduction if he had more overnights with the kids. It had nothing to do with their best interests.

Judge Pierce nodded and shuffled the papers in front of her. "I agree with the plaintiff on this one, Mr. Walden. You haven't met your burden. I'm not mucking up the custody arrangement."

"Your Honor!" Bill Walden actually tried to shout the judge down.

"I've made my ruling," she said. "Ms. Leary, if you have a proposed order I'll sign it now."

"I do," I said, giving Sandy another squeeze on the shoulder. I walked around her and handed my order to Bill. He grabbed it out of my hand. A rude gesture that wasn't lost on Judge Pierce or her bailiff.

"We'll need time to review this," he said. "Counsel for the plaintiff can submit it under the seven-day rule."

Judge Pierce's eyebrow went up. "Excuse me? Who's

wearing the robe here, counselor? Defendant's motion is denied. Is that what Ms. Leary's order says?"

"It is," he grumbled.

"Perfect," she said. "You may approach the bench with it."

More grumbling from Bill Walden. His client whispered something behind my back that rhymes with shunt. I felt my blood turn to lava, but kept on smiling. The sooner I could get Sandy out of here, the better for all of us.

Judge Pierce's bailiff stepped between the bench and Bill Walden. His name was Ted Moran and he was six foot seven, easy. He graduated with my younger brother, Matty. He'd been captain of one of the Fighting Shamrock's basketball state championships, if memory served. A big, burly guy with hands roughly the size of dinner plates. I remembered Ted with dark, curly hair once upon a time. Now he shaved it completely bald, Dwayne Johnson-style.

As Ted took my order and pivoted on his heel, I noticed something else about this two-hundred-and-fifty-pound giant. He had tears in his eyes and his hand shook as he brought that single piece of paper to Judge Pierce's side.

She noticed it too. She gave a quick scan of the order, signed it and put it in her outbox. Then, before anyone else could figure out what was going on with Ted, she banged her gavel and adjourned court for lunch.

"Thank you," Sandy said. She gave me a hug and got back to her feet. I knew she wouldn't want to be anywhere near her ex. She had family in the gallery and I made eye contact with her brother, Rob, sitting behind us. He'd make sure Sandy got out of the building without incident.

Rob's color had turned to ash. He wasn't crying, but it looked like he was about to. Hushed murmurs spread through the gallery in a rolling wave. A few sobs broke the silence but I couldn't see who made them.

"You just let me know if there are any other issues with Colby or the kids," I said to Sandy. "Hopefully he got the message this time." She hugged me, still oblivious to whatever news had gripped what looked like the entire population of Delphi.

"I knew I made the right choice with you," Sandy whispered. "Rob tried to talk me out of it. Hell, a *lot* of people tried to talk me out of it. But I had a feeling, Miss Leary. I don't care who your family is. You shouldn't either."

Her words stung but I'd heard ones like it my whole life. Until I left town, that is. I'd been gone for ten years but some things would never change. In the three months since I'd come back, I found that equal parts irritating and comforting. But it wasn't like I had any other choice.

"Thanks," I said. Sandy York meant well. She overcame plenty of her own baggage to get where she was in life. Besides, other than my court-appointed work, she was currently my only paying client. I needed her good graces and word of mouth if I was ever going to get my feet fully back under me.

"We'll talk soon," I said.

"Not *too* soon, I hope." She shot me a wink. "Colby's had his wings clipped good today. It won't last though. Especially if I *do* go after more child support. You really think we can get it?"

"It's basic math," I said. "Just give me a call when you know for sure where he's working now."

Sandy finally caught her brother's eye and realized something was off. I excused myself from the pair of them. I had an early lunch planned with a potential new client with a property line dispute. General practice might be the death of me and it was something I swore I'd never do. I suppose that should teach me about swearing.

I stepped out in the hall. Three other lawyers stood

huddled near the vending machine. One of them let loose a stream of obscenities that damn near blew my hair back. A door slammed beside me and Ted Moran came out. He was full-on crying now.

"Ted!" I went to him. His shoulders quaked and his color deepened from red to purple. He swayed on his feet.

"Come here," I said, reaching up to touch his shoulder. He let me lead him to the little law library adjacent to Courtroom 5. The books in the stacks were outdated now as the county long since stopped paying to update them. They did spring for two computer terminals against the wall. Ted sat down on a mismatched office chair at the end of a long conference table.

"Put your head between your knees and breathe," I said. "Are you lightheaded?"

Ted let out a choked sound that cut through me. Something had happened. Something awful. My heart thundered and for a moment I was about to take my own advice.

"Coach." He managed that single word before he broke down again and sobbed into his catcher's-mitt-sized hands.

"Ted, what's going on?"

He looked up at me. I took a seat across from him, sliding it so our knees touched. Ted Moran was one of the good ones. He grew up on the east side of the lake like I did. He'd been a good friend to Matty when my mother died and lost his own a few years earlier. Back in the day, I made just as many school lunches for Ted as I had for my own younger siblings.

"C-Coach D," he said, sobbing. "I can't believe it. I just can't believe it."

My phone vibrated from the outside compartment of my leather messenger bag. I let it go but something told me I should answer it.

"Coach D," I repeated. "Coach Drazdowski?"

Larry Drazdowski was the high school basketball coach. In Ted's case, I knew he'd become somewhat of a father figure. He was a legend in this town ... hell ... maybe in the whole country. The team had won their eight state titles under him.

"I can't believe it. I just can't believe it."

"Ted. Teddy ... is he ... what happened to him?" I asked, but of course I already knew. Ted Moran was broken from it.

"He's dead. Oh God. Cass, he's dead." Then Ted got up. The thing seemed to happen in slow motion but still too fast for me to stop it. Ted Moran curled his giant fist and drove it straight through the wall.

"Shit," I shot to my feet and went to him. Ted crumpled against me, curling in half to rest his forehead on my shoulder.

"What was it?" I asked, as if it mattered to Ted or any of the boys that man had coached. "His heart?"

Ted gasped against me. My spine creaked as he rested his weight against me then sank back into his chair. "No," he said. "Cass. He was murdered. Gutted like a fucking deer. They found him last night but the news just came out."

The air in my lungs turned to ash. Murdered. That didn't happen. Not here. Not in Delphi. Not to Larry Drazdowski. The coach. My phone buzzed again.

"There you are!" A female voice cut through the noise in my head. I turned. Ted turned. It was Nancy Olsen, the deputy court clerk. She knew my family and was one of the few people who didn't hold it against me.

"I'll get out of your hair," I said to Ted, thinking Nancy was here for him.

Nancy's face fell. She came further into the room. Ted straightened. "Maybe give us a minute," Nancy said.

I stood. "Of course. I need to get back to my office. Gosh, I'm so sorry, Ted. I can't even ..."

"No, honey," Nancy said to me. "I was looking for you."

"Me?"

She lifted her hand. She held a thin green file in it. Under the county's filing system, green was reserved for criminal cases.

"Your name came up," she said.

"My name," I repeated. It was all in my head, but I swore I heard the sound of a freight train coming straight for me.

"Criminal court appointments," she said. Nancy gave a pained look to Ted, realizing how lousy her timing was right now.

"Nancy ... I ..."

She handed me the file as Ted let out a garbled cry. He straightened his shoulders and gave the room to Nancy and me.

"This isn't ..." I said, shaking my head. It couldn't be. Not this soon.

"I'm afraid so, honey. I mean ... you can decline, of course ... but they've made an arrest already. That poor, poor man. But, like I said, your name came up."

She handed me the file. I squeezed my eyes shut, not needing to even read the charging document inside of it.

It would be murder. The victim's name would be Coach Larry Drazdowski.

Chapter 2

THE WOODBRIDGE COUNTY JAIL is housed in a three-story brick building kitty-corner to the courthouse. I'd learned that on any given day, you can be treated to the thunderous rattling of the windows from the second-floor common area while crossing Main Street. That was the men's side.

I walked in through the Clancy Street entrance, away from the visitors' area, otherwise known as the lawyer's entrance. Two deputy sheriffs manned the metal detectors. I put my black pumps in the plastic bin and slid my messenger bag and cell phone down the conveyor. The sheriffs knew me, of course. From the glare I got from both of them, they'd already figured out why I was here.

The younger deputy looked me up and down as if I were covered in dog shit. I took a breath and grabbed my shoes from the bin, sliding them back on. The second deputy shoved my messenger bag down the conveyor belt. It would have fallen off the end if I hadn't been quick enough to catch it.

"Really?" I turned back to him. The man's eyes were red-rimmed. Chances were, he was also one of Coach D's all-stars.

"You want the door to the left of central processing," he said, taking at least a small degree of pity on me.

I thanked him and checked in with the desk clerk. She too was someone I knew though I couldn't place her name. She gave me a kind smile when she signed me in.

"Nancy called ahead," she said in a whisper. "They're bringing your client up. She and I didn't think it was a good idea for you to have to wait around here too long. Best get you in a private room so you can talk."

"Thanks," I said. "It seems there are a lot of people jumping to some pretty big conclusions already. I'm just doing my job. And I'm not even sure if this *is* my job yet." I don't know why I felt the need to explain. I'd spent the last ten years doing business litigation and white-collar criminal defense. This was something altogether different. This was murder and the victim was someone I knew, at least in passing.

A female deputy poked her head around the corner. She looked familiar to me too, but a few years younger than me. Maybe just out of college. My sister Vangie's age, maybe. I felt a little sliver of ice low in my gut thinking about her. I wouldn't let my mind go to how long it had been since we'd last spoken.

"I've got you set up down here," the female deputy said. Her badge read "Carver." Familiar, yes, but only just.

The kind clerk shot me a wink and I slid the strap of my messenger bag over my right shoulder. Deputy Carver led me down a long hallway. Carver opened the door. The room was small, maybe twelve feet by twelve feet. There was a long metal table in the center and a two-way mirror taking up one whole wall. The lights were on though. The room behind us was empty.

My would-be client sat with her wrists shackled, the chain threaded through a metal loop in the center of the table. She wore an orange jumpsuit that was easily two sizes too big on her. Her head was down and I couldn't see her face through the stringy blonde hair that hung in front of it. She was crying. Sobbing, actually. And she was just a tiny little thing.

My trial lawyer brain was already filing things away. Larry Drazdowski was huge. A basketball coach. Fit. Well muscled. Close to six foot five.

"Thank you, Deputy Carver," I smiled back. She cleared her throat and shut the door behind her.

"Aubrey?" I said, my voice soft and gentle. I took a seat across from her.

Aubrey Ames slowly raised her chin. She had big doe eyes filled with tears. They streaked down her cheeks and the chains binding her rattled as she shook in her seat. God, she was skinny. Her skin was pale, nearly translucent so I could see tiny blue veins running up her arm.

I saw no track marks. Though puffy, her eyes looked clear, focusing with laser-like precision straight on me. It didn't mean she wasn't on something, of course, but it was at least a positive sign.

I'd had all of fifteen minutes to read through the thin green file Nancy Olsen gave me. There wasn't much to it. A preliminary police report and the criminal complaint. They were charging this nineteen-year-old girl in front of me with first-degree murder.

"You're the lawyer?" she asked.

"I am," I said. "My name is Cass. Cass Leary."

It registered on her face with the flicker of her eyelids. Her mouth turned down. I had to bite the inside of my mouth to keep from letting out an ironic laugh. This girl was chained to a table facing life imprisonment. But *I* was the one with the shitty family name. Welcome back to Delphi. The signs were all around.

"Wow," she whispered. "I heard about you. You went to law school and everything?"

"I did," I said, hoisting my messenger bag to the table. I slid Aubrey's case file out of the side pocket.

"Why in the world did you come back here?" Aubrey asked. Her words seemed more steady now. Good. The girl was starting to get a grip. Still, she'd just asked the million-dollar question and this meeting wasn't about me. Plus, we didn't have a whole lot of time.

"I'm your court-appointed lawyer," I said. "Well, if I agree to take this case, that is. I'll be honest, I haven't decided that yet."

What little color she had drained even more. "You have to!" She almost screamed it.

"Listen," I said. "Let's just focus on what comes next. Do you understand what they've charged you with?"

A single tear fell down Aubrey's face. I knew the Ameses too. On the status ladder of Delphi, Michigan, the Ames family was maybe only half a rung above the Learys. To be honest, it's the second reason I took that file from Nancy.

"They want to fry me for what happened to Coach D," she said.

I raised a brow. "Well, first things first. There's no death penalty in Michigan, Aubrey."

She blanched. It hit me this really was news to her. Her shoulders dropped. For a moment, she looked relieved. Then she slowly closed her eyes.

"It doesn't matter," she whispered. "They'll want to kill me anyway."

"Listen," I said. "Let's just take this one step at a time. That's how you're going to get through this, okay? You're scheduled for arraignment and a bail hearing first thing in the morning. Now, I'm going to ask some questions. What you *do* tell me needs to be the truth, okay?"

"You'll help me though?"

"One thing at a time. You're being charged with first-degree murder. Tomorrow, during your arraignment, they're going to ask you if you understand that. And they're going to ask you to enter a plea."

"This isn't what anyone thinks!" she shouted.

"Great," I said. "Now that we have that out of the way, that's the last time I want you to answer a question you haven't been asked. The police read you your rights when they arrested you. Use them. You are not to say anything to the police outside my presence. You are not to discuss this case with *anyone* but me. Ever. Not your parents, your friends, your priest, no one. Do you understand what I'm telling you?"

Aubrey nodded. "You want me to keep my mouth shut."

"Tightly," I said. "Now, have you said anything to them so far?"

I cringed waiting for her to answer. Any statements she made would be in the full police report. I was picking that up before I left the building. What they had so far was sparse. Her cell phone was found at the scene near the victim's body. I didn't yet know what was on it, but it was enough to give them probable cause to arrest her. That was ominous.

"No," she said. "My dad ... he was there when they came to the house to arrest me. He told me not to say anything else."

"Smart man," I said. "Now, what am I going to find when I look up your record, Aubrey? I need to know everything down to the last parking ticket."

"Nothing." She started to cry in earnest. "I swear. I got a speeding ticket two years ago over on Waverly. It's a speed trap down there. But that's it. I promise."

I sat back in my chair. I'd handled plenty of felony cases in my life but only a few involving teenage girls. Usually I'd been asked to take care of Minor in Possession charges for the sons and daughters of the Thorne Group's biggest clients. But I'd handled enough to know most people lie about their records.

"He was alive when I saw him last."

My head spun. I was nowhere near familiar with the timeline the prosecution was building. I almost didn't want to go too much deeper with Aubrey before I had that solid.

"When was that?" I asked.

Aubrey sniffled. "A little after ten o'clock at the park."

"You were there alone with him?"

She nodded, her expression growing more dour. Things looked bad enough already.

"Where did you go after that?" I asked.

Aubrey shrugged and, if it was even possible, managed to make herself look smaller in her chair. "I drove around. I knew my dad was going to be pissed I missed curfew."

Oh boy.

"Okay," I said. "Let's table the bigger talk we'll need to have and focus on tomorrow's procedure. I'll talk to your parents next. You're going to spend the night in here and there's nothing I can do about that. But with any luck, the District Court judge will set a reasonable bail and you'll be back in your own bed by tomorrow night. In the meantime, your main job is to just keep quiet."

She nodded and wiped a tear from her eye. I reached for a tissue from the cardboard box at the end of the table. Aubrey blew her nose into it, looking every inch the little girl she was so close to being.

"I can't believe this is happening," she said, crushing the tissue into her fist. "Miss Leary. You don't know me. You have to be thinking all sorts of awful things about me."

It hit me then. I *did* know this girl. She was an Ames, of course, not a Leary. Her grandfather worked with my dad a million years ago on the line at the spark plug plant on the west side of town that wasn't there anymore. She had an uncle in prison for dealing ... at least, I thought so.

She reminded me of me in a way, once upon a time. And I knew it was dangerous for me to think that. She was vulnerable, but tough in the way she kept her back straight even as she fell apart right in front of me.

"Will you help me?" she asked, meeting my eyes. "They're going to want me dead."

"We're going to have a lot to talk about, Aubrey," I said. "One step at a time. Focus on your hearing tomorrow."

"Aren't you going to ask me?" she said, holding my stare.

The weight of her question hung between us. It was one I never asked of criminal clients. In a legal sense, the answer didn't matter. That's not what this was about. It was about the prosecution being held to its burden of proof. It was about upholding a system designed to protect all of us.

In the space of those few seconds, my world seemed to shift on its axis. The haunted, hopeless look in Aubrey Ames's eyes cut straight through me. It was like looking in a mirror in a lot of ways.

"Aubrey ... it's better if ..."

"No," she said. "It's not better. Not for me. It matters. I didn't kill that man. I did *not* kill that man."

The thing was ... at that moment, God help us both, I believed her. And she was right. It did matter.

"Okay," I said. "So let me get to work."

Chapter 3

I GOT AS FAR as the parking lot before it started.

"You must be trying to tank your law practice before you get it off the ground."

I stood next to my newly leased Ford Fusion with my keys in my hand before I turned. Bill Walden stood next to Deputy Ron Tucker. Tucker was twenty years older than me and moonlighted as a driving instructor. He'd helped me get my license. He stared me down with cold, dark eyes, his keys jangling from his belt as he approached.

"Boys, I'm not in the mood," I said.

"You see the crime scene photos yet?" Tucker asked. I was about to ask him how the hell he had.

"I'm not going to discuss this with you. Either of you."

"Larry Drazdowski was gutted like a damn deer, Cass," Bill said.

So *he'd* seen the crime scene photos? Jesus. No matter what else happened, this case was already getting out of hand.

"You take court appointments too, Bill. Why are you giving me asses and elbows on this?"

"Just giving you some friendly business advice," he said, taking a step toward me. "You've been away for a long time. Maybe you've forgotten a few things. But you're going to want to stay away from this one."

They weren't overtly threatening me, but they stood shoulder to shoulder and didn't back up. Tucker's eyes were puffy. He'd taken the coach's death just as hard as Ted Moran had.

"I'll mind my own business, Bill. I know you'll do the same."

"This is open and shut," Ron said. "You get in the way of this, you might as well pack your shit back up and keep heading east."

"Is that a threat?" I said. I'd had enough of those to last me a lifetime and from far bigger and badder characters than Ron Tucker. Sometimes at night, I could still feel those zip ties cutting into my wrists and ankles as two goons threatened to throw me into Lake Michigan.

"Ron!"

A deep voice came from across the street. I couldn't place the face at first but knew instantly it was another cop. This one in a suit hustling his way across Main Street and coming straight for us. Great.

He was tall with black hair and the first touches of gray peppered his temples. He slid his hand in his pocket and his jacket spread, revealing his sidearm and badge clipped to his belt.

"Perfect," Ron said. "Maybe Wray can talk some damn sense into you."

Wray. As the detective approached, recognition came. Eric Wray. He'd been captain of the football team my freshman year when he was a senior. Eric still had that athlete's swagger as he crossed the street. He stood nearly a head taller than Bill Walden and had several inches on Tucker.

"Everything okay out here?" he asked, his blue eyes darting from Ron to Bill then back to me.

"Why don't you fill Ms. Leary in on what they've got on her client," Ron said.

Eric Wray at least had the decency to look shocked. "And I'm pretty sure Ms. Leary can figure out how to do her job without any of our help. Now, I'm heading over to Mickey's. I could use a beer. You assholes plan on hogging your usual spots over there?"

He put a heavy hand on Ron Tucker's shoulder and shot me a glance. He kept his eyes on mine as Bill and Ron turned, grumbled, and headed back toward the courthouse. I mouthed a quick thank you to Eric Wray. He lifted his chin and turned his back to me.

I sank against my car knowing this would be just the first of many encounters like this if I agreed to defend Aubrey Ames. Letting out a hard breath I hadn't realized I'd been holding, I slid behind the wheel and headed back for the lake.

Chapter 4

A PERFECT ORANGE sunset melted into the lake as I pulled up the gravel driveway. My brother Joe stood silhouetted against it, casting his line with a fluid zip at the end of the dock. He'd managed to salvage most of the planks of wood I'd found sinking into the sand the day I came back. He was the only member of my family willing to talk to me since my surprise homecoming.

I walked out to meet him, peering over the side of the dock. Joe had constructed a live well using chicken wire and two-by-fours. It was empty now, which meant he hadn't been standing out here very long. He reeled his line in.

"I take it you've already heard," I said, crossing my arms. Late June and it was above eighty even with the sun setting.

Joe turned to me. He was just a year and a day older than me at thirty-five. He had thick, light-brown hair he wore cropped close to his head. He rarely smiled, but I could always read his emotions from those deep-set brown eyes that cut right through me. Joey had devastating good looks. Rugged, well-muscled. And his utter lack of interest in it made him that much more irresistible to the women of

Delphi. Today, he wore his typical uniform: a plain white t-shirt, faded, loose-fitting jeans, and tan work boots.

He was a house painter by trade, but Joe Leary Jr. made a small fortune doing odd jobs around town. He could fix anything ... build *anything* with his hands. He'd also been the one person in my life I knew I could depend on. My leaving had hurt him the most, though it would kill him to say so.

Joe cocked his head to the side. "I didn't come here to get in your business."

This got a full-throated laugh out of me, loud enough to scare away a pair of mallards a few yards to the left of us.

"Come on," I said, turning. "It's been a long damn day and I need a glass of wine. There's probably a beer in the fridge if you didn't already drink it all."

The dock creaked beneath my feet as we made our way back up to the house. Joe didn't come in. He took a seat on the wooden porch swing at the back of the house. I tossed my suit jacket over a chair on the way to the kitchen. I took my time pouring a glass of Riesling for myself then grabbed a Bud for Joey. Hiking up my skirt, I took the seat next to him as he started to swing.

"Awful thing," he said, peeling at the label on his beer bottle. "Em said they found his body in the middle of Shamrock Park."

I nodded. There was no preamble with Joe and me. Even after ten years of living apart, we still had a sort of shorthand to our conversations. It drove Joe's first wife crazy. His second, Katy, hadn't been around me enough to get there yet.

"What else does Emma know about it?" I asked, wincing. Emma was Joe's oldest daughter. He'd been just eighteen when she was born. Her mother, Josie, was from the affluent, west side of town. She'd been the homecoming queen, class president, town darling until the night she soiled herself and screwed Eastlake trash, Joey Leary. At least, that's the story everyone liked to tell that wasn't us. Six months ago, Emma moved out of her mother's place and in with Joey.

"Her phone's been blowing up all day," Joe said. "Started out people said it was some kind of satanic ritual with a pentagram and the body all carved up. Then they said Coach D's head was blown off with a shotgun."

"Jesus." I took another sip of my wine. I had to be careful what I said. The truth was, Larry Drazdowski was stabbed once in the kidney and bled to death. That was awful enough, but the rest of these rumors wouldn't do my case any good.

"Did you know him?" I asked. "I didn't really. I was what ... in ninth grade when the high school hired him? Sports weren't my thing."

"Mine either," Joe said, downing his beer. Of course I read the irony in his words. My brother was actually a gifted athlete. He could have excelled at nearly any sport he chose. In another time, another place, maybe he was even good enough to get a baseball scholarship to the University of Michigan or somewhere far away from here. But Joe and I didn't have the luxury of extracurricular activities growing up. By the time we both hit our teens, we had to work to keep the lights on and food on the table for my younger siblings.

"You really going to do this?" he asked. There was no judgment in his tone. Not yet. But I knew my brother well enough to know he was really saying *you know you really shouldn't do this.*

"I don't know, Joe. That's the God's honest truth right now. I'm mostly just trying to keep my head above water just like everybody else."

"Let somebody else take Aubrey Ames's case," he said. I squeezed my eyes shut and exhaled.

27

"Yeah? Who?"

Joe set his beer on the ground. "Anyone, Cass. Literally anyone. I'm telling you. Don't touch this one."

"I'm not afraid," I said.

"You just got back," he said. "I wish I could tell you things have changed around here since you left but you know they haven't. People still judge us by our last names."

I raised a brow. "Really? You think that's all they judge us by. Come on, Joe. Dad's been the town drunk since before we were born. He's got to own that. I don't. Matty's no better. He's thirty years old and can't hold a job. I've seen where they live. And Vangie ... well ... who knows. Maybe she's the smartest one of all of us after all. Have you heard from her lately?"

He looked down, his silence giving me my answer.

"If we worried about what everyone else thought about us, we'd never have the strength to get out of bed on any given day," I said. "But what if it were me. Or you? Tell me. If you'd been falsely accused of killing somebody, you think anyone would believe you?"

"Is she?" Joe asked. "Is she innocent, Cass? You sure about that?"

"It's a figure of speech," I said. "She's entitled to a defense lawyer. My name got drawn. That's it."

Joe shook his head and pulled himself off the bench. It swayed wildly backward without his weight to keep it straight. I dug my heels into the ground to stop it.

"You just got back, Cass," he said again. "They can't force you to represent someone. I know that much."

"And the town can't force me *not* to represent someone, Joey. In my opinion, that's even worse. I don't care what they think. I can't. This is my job now."

He hopped off the porch and started walking back toward the lake. I hated when he got like this. Just like our

28

dad. He'd leave in the middle of an argument I was winning. And *I'd* always chase him down and keep going until I felt like I was losing. I went after him.

"What are you afraid of?" I asked him, putting a light hand on his back. Joe stiffened. Then he picked up his pole and cast another line.

"They're going to come after you again if you do this," he said. "It's not about Aubrey Ames. I know her too. She's just a skinny little kid. She was on Emma's cheerleading squad when she was a senior. I've driven the two of them to get coneys and ice cream after practice. I can't wrap my mind around it and I know more than anybody how this goes if the people around here think she did it."

"You don't, do you?" I said it more as a statement than a question.

His shoulders dropped as he let out a sigh. "She's just a kid," he said. "She can't weigh more than a hundred pounds soaking wet."

"Hmm. Well, it's nice to know somebody around here has an open mind."

Joe put the pole back in the holster. "I *don't* care what they think, Cass. Not about me. I don't even care what they think about *you*. But *you* do. It's why you left Delphi in the first place."

So there it was. I saw the fear in my brother's eyes plainly. It snaked its way around my heart and squeezed so hard I could barely breathe.

I went up on my tiptoes and kissed my brother's cheek. "Is that your way of telling me you missed me?"

He rolled his eyes. "You've never told me why."

"Why I left?" I asked, knowing full well that wasn't what he meant.

"Why you came back," he answered, not letting me off the hook any more than the fish he was trying to catch.

29

In the three months since I left Chicago, it's the first time Joe had even asked. I knew he figured I'd tell him in my own good time, except I hadn't. I didn't know how. A shiver went through me as I remembered bits of that last day again.

"I heard rumors they were about to disbar you in Illinois," he said.

"No," I answered. "That's not true. It's just ... the big firm life just wasn't for me anymore. That's all."

I couldn't tell him the truth. I'd gotten in over my head with one of the firm's most lucrative clients. I'd made a series of decisions that could have landed me in jail, the morgue, or witness protection. No, I couldn't tell him any of that. But I wouldn't lie to him either.

"Fine. I'm worried the heat from this murder case is going to be too much for you. I'm worried you're going to leave again."

I couldn't help the bitter laugh that came out of me. "Well, the good news is, I've got nowhere else to go, Joe. I'm making just about enough to pay the tax lien on this property and for my malpractice insurance. Court appointments, even murder cases, only pay about fifty bucks an hour. I have a grand sum total of one paying client and three other cases I took on contingency. It's going to take me about fifty grand to fix up this dump even with you doing a ton of it like you offered. And I know damn well that Dad, and Matty, are pissed Gramps left this place to me instead of them. Damned if I know why he did!"

"Isn't it obvious!" Joe yelled. "He knew you were the one who had your shit together." His eyes twinkled in the moonlight and he let out a great big belly laugh. It struck me speechless for a half a second before I laughed with him. It was enough to tell me we were done arguing for now.

"Come on," I said, looping my arm through his. "The mosquitoes are coming out and I need a good night's sleep if

I'm going to have to face all those torches and pitchforks in the morning."

Joe grumbled, but he walked up the dock with me. In spite of it all, I missed him. I missed this. And I knew no matter what else happened, Joey was still the one person in my life I could count on.

Chapter 5

ON TUESDAY MORNING, murmurs rumbled behind me in the courtroom when I entered my appearance for Aubrey Ames on the record. "Cassiopeia Leary on behalf of the defendant." There were a few snickers as well and I heard my last name whispered more than once. It made me stand taller.

Aubrey stood beside me, a full two inches shorter than my five foot three. Still shackled and wearing her orange jumpsuit, Aubrey barely got the words "not guilty" out when Judge Colton asked how she pleaded She needed to do better. She was on trial every second from here on out.

The benches were filled with former team members from Coach Larry Drazdowski's eight state championships and more. Some were in their mid-thirties, closer to my age. Some looked just out of high school. All of them wore their green-and-gray varsity letter jackets in solidarity.

At the table near the empty jury box, assistant prosecutor, Jack LaForge, puffed out his chest as the judge rifled through the file in front of him.

I made my pitch for bail. "Your Honor, my client has strong ties to the community. She still lives with her parents.

She has no prior record other than a speeding ticket two years ago. She makes minimum wage at Dewar's Bakery ... she hasn't ..."

"The hell she does!" A deep male voice shouted from the gallery. "That trash doesn't work for me anymore!"

I turned. Ed Dewar had risen to his feet. He pointed a shaky finger at Aubrey. She stayed quiet, stoic.

Judge Colton banged the gavel then pointed it at Ed Dewar. "That's enough out of you, Ed. Show yourself out of my courtroom."

The damage was already done. Ed's outburst riled up the rest of the gallery. Coach D's players cheered Ed on as he turned and headed for the double doors.

"That's it," Colton said. "I'm not concerned about Miss Ames skipping town. I'm setting bail at two hundred and fifty thousand. She'll be released to her parents' home. Standard bond conditions apply."

Aubrey finally exhaled.

Two female deputies came up on either side of the table to escort her back to the jail for processing. She gave me a panicked look.

"It's going to be okay," I said. "I'll make arrangements with your family to get you safely out of here." Aubrey's parents and brother hung back. They'd been lost in the crowd in the corner.

"You should be okay to go here in a few minutes, Ms. Leary."

The voice came from behind me, deep, commanding. It was Detective Eric Wray. "Thanks," I said.

"If you need someplace to talk, jury room four is open. I checked with the bailiff."

"Thanks, Eric," Dan Ames said. He stepped forward looking haggard. His eyes were puffy with dark circles and his hand trembled as he extended it to shake Detective

Wray's. I did a mental count. Eric graduated two years ahead of Joe. Dan was probably in the same class.

Diane Ames clung to her husband's arm. Their younger son stood behind her wearing a suit that was two sizes too big. I was a little surprised his parents dragged him into court today. He had to be still in high school. There was no way the poor kid wouldn't get bullied during this.

"I really appreciate it," I said.

"Cass!" Jack LaForge caught up with me as I tried to usher the Ames family to the relative privacy of the adjacent jury room.

"Detective Wray," I said. "Do you mind showing these folks to the jury room?"

"No problem." I knew it cost him something too. Two deputies waited in the hall, glaring at us. Eric Wray was with the city of Delphi P.D., not the sheriff's department. They had control of the courthouse and even this seemed to be turning into a turf war.

Wray never flinched though. He walked to the end of the aisle leading the Ames family behind him. He stuck his chest out and blew right past the deputies, alpha male-style. Now I had the courtroom alone with Jack.

He held a file out for me. "Detailed police report. Crime scene photos. I should have the complete cell phone report by morning."

I raised a skeptical brow. "Don't give me that, Jack. You've got it now."

He didn't deny it, but neither did he offer to get that report to me any quicker. "I'd appreciate a gentleman's agreement regarding talking to the press," he said.

I bit my lip past the automatic retort that popped into my head, misogyny aside. "I'm not interested in trying this case in the media, Jack. There's no way my client can get a fair trial in Delphi. Today was a freak show."

"File whatever motions you want," he said. "I will *not* agree to a transfer of venue. Larry Drazdowski deserves his justice right here in Delphi."

"Just get me the cell phone reports, okay?"

I knew he was waiting for me to open the file. The edge of one of the color photos stuck out the side. I could just see an ash-gray hand laying flat on the ground, palm up. I would not do this in front of him.

"Call my office in the morning," he said.

"Fine."

Jack already had his back to me. He lifted his briefcase in a sort of dismissive wave as he left the courtroom.

Though I didn't want to keep the Ames family waiting any longer, I knew I had to see those pictures before I went any further. If this case went to trial, I'd try to keep as much of them out as possible, but the jury would see them. No question.

I let out a hard breath and spread the color photos on the table. The crime scene investigators had taken about fifty-odd pictures from every angle and distance. The worst were the full body shots. Larry Drazdowski lay face up, his hands spread over his head as if he were stretching. His brown eyes were open, frozen in shock as the life had drained out of him.

He wore a white t-shirt with Delphi High School written across his chest in green letters. Below that was a green shamrock.

"Fucking perfect," I muttered, in case the potential jury pool could ever forget who this man was and what he meant to the town.

The bottom front of his shirt was soaked in dark-red blood. You could just see the knife wound beneath the hem of his shirt on the left side. He'd been stabbed just under his rib cage, likely straight through the kidney, though the autopsy report wasn't ready yet. If Jack's behavior was any indication, he'd probably try to delay getting that to me as well. Rumor was, he was planning to run for his boss's job the year after next.

"Oh Coach," I whispered.

I pulled out the police report. I already knew the gist. Aubrey had been seen leaning into the window of Coach D's car just outside the park. Her cell phone had been found two feet from his body. Blonde hairs matching hers had been found on him. Aubrey hadn't denied she'd been with the man. I slid the photos and the pages back into the thin file folder and stuffed them into my messenger bag.

I walked into the hall, looking both ways. The sheriffs had done a good job ushering out any angry spectators. There would likely still be some on the courthouse steps. I made a note to ask for an escort for the Ames family and myself. Then I walked into jury room four and faced Aubrey Ames's devastated mother and father.

Diane sat with her face buried in her hands. Dan was more stoic, sitting straight-backed against the wall. Eric Wray was long gone and I couldn't blame him. He'd gone over and above on this one.

"Okay," I said. "We got through the first hurdle. If you can swing the ten percent surety, you can have your daughter back home by tomorrow."

Dan nodded. "Twenty-five thou. Eric kind of explained that part. I can drain my retirement."

"We can't go home!" Diane shrieked. "We've already had a brick through our front window right before we came."

Shit. It's exactly what I feared. "Right. Well, you'll have to go there, at least temporarily. It's one of the conditions of Aubrey's bond. But under the circumstances I think we can see about getting some extra patrols in front of your house. Did you file a report about the brick?"

"Not yet," Dan said. "We were going to do that when we got done here today."

"Good. You need to talk to the clerk about bonding Aubrey out anyway."

"She didn't do this ... did she?" Diane asked. Her question gutted me. Her eyes widened with sheer terror.

"Diane, please," Dan said, snaking an arm around his wife. "This is Aubrey. *Our* baby." His voice was a soothing whisper. Though the man looked like he hadn't slept in two days—and likely hadn't—he was remarkably calm.

"We've had Coach D to our home," Diane sniffed. "At our dinner table. He's been working with ... he *was* working with Sean." She looked over her shoulder at her son. Sean had practically blended into the wall. The ill-fitting suit he wore looked even bigger on him now.

"Look, I'm going to need to talk to you about all of this. In detail. But not today. Now, I've filed my appearance as Aubrey's attorney. She's my client. I'm going to do everything I can for her. But you need to be prepared. This is going to be a slow process. And right now, it appears the entire town thinks Aubrey's guilty. They're grieving. This is a shock for everyone. To get through this, Aubrey's going to need your strength more than anything. I need you to resist the urge to talk to the press. To anyone about this case. I don't have to remind you how small a town this is. People might try to goad you into reacting to ... whatever. You can't. Not once. Do you understand what I'm telling you?"

Dan nodded. "We can keep things under control from our end. Just ... just get our baby girl out of that hellhole and back to us."

I nodded. "I'm working on that. You've got your homework on it too. I'll let you get to it."

No sooner had I said the words before we heard a soft knock at the door. A young female deputy stood at the door.

"I'm really sorry to interrupt, but the judge is going to need this room soon. And ... uh ... the coast is more or less clear now. My boss arranged to have us walk you to your cars."

"Thanks," I said, finding a polite smile. I stepped to the end of the table and put a hand on Diane Ames's shoulder. She rose in unison with her husband. Young Sean filed in right behind them.

He hung back a moment as his parents stepped into the hall. He looked so scared, so broken. I had no idea what all this must be like for him. He loved his sister, of course, but he probably idolized Larry Drazdowski like everyone else in that courtroom today. His grief was his own.

"Hang in there, kiddo," I said, squeezing his shoulder.

I expected Sean Ames to look back at me near tears. He didn't. His face was stone cold as he gave me a nod. "You gotta know they're going to kill her for what she did."

Before I could so much as react, he scooted past me and caught up to his parents.

Chapter 6

I COULDN'T SLEEP. Larry Drazdowski's frozen face seemed
to float through my thoughts. As crime scenes went, his
wasn't even the most grisly I'd ever seen. But the man had
died terrified. He would have felt the knife go in and each
beat of his heart after that until blackness came.

I curled on my side, wrapping my arms around a pillow. I
couldn't breathe. Larry's face wavered in front of me and
became my own.

*"It won't hurt. Much. At least ... not for long. I can make it go
quick or slow. One turn of the knife, or I can just let you fall over the
side. It's about three hundred feet deep here. You might even live long
enough to feel your feet touch the bottom." He pressed his lips against my
ear, his Irish brogue thick and dark.*

*His fingers dug into my arms as I struggled against the bindings on
my wrists. My lungs burned. He shoved me forward. I couldn't get my
feet to work. I flailed backward, panicked. He would do it. He would
kill me.*

*I felt the churning waters coming at me. I hated bridges. All my life
I'd had this phobia of driving over the side of one. Sinking to the bottom*

of the lake, trapped in my car. To me it was the most horrible way a person could die.

I screamed. My captor just laughed. Then his phone vibrated in his back pocket and Killian Thorne's familiar ringtone became the lifeline I never thought would come.

I sat bolt upright, covered in sweat. I clutched the pillow to me, trying to convince myself it was real. I was here. This wasn't the deck of the *Crown of Thorne* in the middle of Green Bay. I was home. Safe.

My phone rang again. Maybe I *had* been dreaming just now. I reached for it.

"Hey, Cass." Miranda Sulier's usually bright voice was off. This was bad news and it wasn't even seven o'clock in the morning.

"What's going on?"

I rented office space a few blocks from the courthouse. The rent was dirt cheap but I didn't need much. I shared the space with one of the larger P.I. firms based in Southfield. They had a satellite office here in Delphi and Miranda actually worked for them. But she answered my landline for me and referred any walk-ins I got.

"Honey, I'm so sorry to bug you. I know you've got a lot on your plate. But ... it's just ... well ... your brother ..."

Before she could get the words out, I heard a loud banging on the other end of the phone followed by some slurred, indecipherable words from a voice I recognized well enough.

"Rich bitch!"

"I'm so sorry," Miranda said, clearing her throat. "I'd normally give a shout out to one of the deputies, but I figured you'd want a heads-up first."

"Thanks," I said, sliding out of bed. I tried to finger comb my unruly hair. It stuck out at wild angles. I needed to find a new stylist. I had an inch of brown roots sprouting and the honey-blonde I preferred had started to fade. "Can you give me just ten minutes and I'll be there? Hand him the phone."

Miranda let out a sigh. I heard muffled voices and more banging before my brother Matty took the phone from her.

"Rich bitch!" he shouted into my ear as if I hadn't heard him the first time. "Just waltzes back here and takes everything away from me."

I pressed my phone to my forehead and took a long, deep breath, steeling myself for the next bit. "Matty ... you're loaded. Have Ms. Sulier let you into my office. There's a couch in there. Crash on it until I get there, okay?"

"You'll see," he said, but his tone had already softened. He handed the phone back to Miranda. I heard one last loud bang as my younger brother must have found his way to my office door.

"Fifteen minutes," I said. "And I'm so sorry, Miranda. I'll be right there."

I didn't give her the chance to change her mind. Instead, I vaulted out of bed and ripped through my closet. I had no idea if I'd end up in court today but I dressed for it just in case. I pulled on a pair of black dress pants, a white shell, and swung a red blazer over my shoulders. My black pumps were still scattered somewhere in the living room. I twisted my hair into a top knot and brushed my teeth.

It took me closer to twenty minutes before I pulled into the lot behind my downtown office. Gripping the steering wheel as if it could give me a shot of strength to face the day, I flipped the visor down and applied a coat of nude lipstick. It would have to do for now.

Miranda waited for me in the lobby, arms crossed, tapping her foot.

"I'm so sorry," I whispered, hoping to get a few sentences

in with her before Matty came barreling back out. With any
luck, he'd passed out by now.

"He was propped up against the dumpster when I came
in," she said. "Doesn't look like he tried to drive anywhere, so
that's the good news."

It was great news. I knew Matty had two DUIs under his
belt. A third would finish him.

"You didn't call anybody else, did you?" I asked.

Miranda smiled. She had a kind face with an upturned
nose, drawn-on dark eyebrows, and high cheekbones. At
sixty, she'd come out of retirement at least twice to work for
various lawyers. Her current job was easy as these things
went. She was a whip-smart legal secretary who had probably put many a young lawyer in their place over the years.

"I know the drill," Miranda said. "You know your
mother was one of my best friends." She reached behind her
and handed me a steaming cup of coffee she had waiting for
me. I gave her a disapproving brow raise. She knew I hated
her getting me coffee unless she was getting some for herself.
Miranda was a tea drinker.

"Thanks," I said. I wouldn't deny how badly I needed
caffeine right now.

"You seen Matty yet since you got back into town?"
Miranda asked. She knew the answer already and it wasn't
the first time she'd asked.

"He doesn't return my calls these days," I said.

"Well, he's been sniffing around," she said. "I wasn't
going to mention it, but he stopped in last week pretending
like he was looking for somebody else."

I shook my head. "There's nobody else in here and my
name's on the door. Smooth. So much for his second career
with the C.I.A."

Miranda laughed. We heard a thump from inside my
office. Matty had probably rolled off the couch.

"He's sure mad at you," she said. "Maybe he needs me to remind him how much you've looked after him all these years. Since …"

She couldn't finish the sentence. Since my mom died.

"My brother is under the impression our grandparents owed him something I got instead."

"That dump on Finn Lake," she answered, then had the decency to look chagrined. For a moment, she'd forgotten I was currently living in said dump.

"Right. Anyway, I've got this. Thanks for not calling the cops. My schedule is clear for the day. As long as he's quiet, Matty can just sleep it off here for a while. Then I'll figure out how to get him home."

"He's got a wife, hasn't he?" Miranda asked. "Shouldn't we call her?"

"He and Tina aren't on good terms," I answered. I hated this. Even though it was Miranda, I felt protective of my family. They were a shit show, but they were my shit show. But there was no judgment in the look Miranda gave me. The phone on her desk began to ring, saving me the need for any more explanations.

Reluctantly, I walked into my office.

Matty was on his back. He lay sleeping with his hands folded on his chest as if he were praying. It squeezed my heart to see it. He'd slept like that since he was a little baby. He had a thick shock of black hair that stuck to his forehead at the moment. Of all of us, he looked the most like my mom with penetrating green eyes and a ready smile.

I stepped over him and threw my messenger bag on a chair. The thud was just loud enough to make Matty stir. His eyes fluttered open. Before he could register where he was, Miranda knocked softly on my door.

"Sorry," she whispered. "I forgot to tell you. A courier dropped this off about an hour ago." She held a white envelope in her hand. I took it from her, noting the return address on the label. It came from Jack LaForge's office. My missing cell phone report on Aubrey Ames. Matty rubbed the sleep from his eyes and sat up. I wasn't sure whether I dreaded the contents of that envelope or Matty's wrath more.

"Thanks, Miranda. Is there any more coffee left in that pot?" I asked, eyeing my brother. It occurred to me it might do more good to throw whatever was left in Miranda's coffee pot on him rather than in him.

I made a move but Miranda gestured for me to sit. "I've got this, Cass. You know I don't mind."

"I mind, Miranda. It's not your job to fetch things for me."

"Well, I appreciate your enlightenment. It's refreshing. Truly. Except haven't you figured out by now I don't do things unless I want to?"

She was joking. Partly. But her point was made. I mouthed thank you again as she popped back into the hallway.

Matty found his way to his feet. I set the envelope on my desk. It would have to wait.

"Fancy office," he said staggering sideways. Gravity won and he plopped back down on the couch. He reeked of bourbon all the way from here. It broke my heart. Matty had been off and on the wagon so many times. He'd been just six when our mother died. He had only fleeting memories of her. Then there was Vangie, the baby of the family. She'd only been four when Mom died. I felt that hollow ache again at just the thought of her and where she might be now.

"Cut the shit, Matty. You're lucky Miranda likes to get in this early. Were you planning on breaking down the door if she hadn't answered?"

"Maybe I was," he said. "Would have served you right."

46

"Jesus, Matty. For what? Huh? Exactly which of my million sins are you trying to punish me for today?"

I knew better than to try to argue with him when he was drunk. I'd had years of practice when it came to our father.

"Dad was right about you," he said. Oh boy. There it was.

"You think you're too good for all of us. Fancy cars. Fancy office."

"Fancy? Matty, this is Turner Street. I park next to a dumpster and I'm next door to a laundromat."

"Left!" he shouted, pointing a wavering finger at me. "Gone. Just like Mom. I needed you, sis. All the time."

I let out a hard breath. I couldn't do this with him. Not today. Maybe not ever.

"Well," I said, stepping around my desk, I went to him. Matty hiccupped as I sank to the cushion beside him. I ran a hand over his head, smoothing his hair back like I used to do when he was little. "I'm here now. And you still need me. I need you too, Matty. But sober. Not like this. I won't watch you turn into Dad."

He dropped his chin to his chest. God, I knew that gesture too. I'd give him about ninety seconds, tops, before he'd be snoring loud enough to shake the walls. Thirty seconds later, he was out again.

"Well, shit, Matty. That's just like you to fall asleep when I'm winning the argument." I stood up, guided his head down and grabbed his ankles, swinging them over the arm of the couch. He might be out for a couple of hours. I could figure out what to do with him before lunch. In the meantime, I had a murder case to figure out.

Matty's rhythmic snoring gave me a strange sense of comfort as I went back to my desk. I connected my phone to my Bluetooth speaker and picked a classical music playlist.

Then I slid my finger under the seal of Jack LaForge's envelope.

The bulk of Aubrey's cell phone report dealt with pinpointing its location in the hours before Coach D's death. Most of it tracked with what Aubrey had already told me. She worked at Dewar's until they closed at ten that night. It pinged the tower nearest Shamrock Park at ten thirty. That fit with a witness from the police report who said he saw Aubrey leaning into Coach D's driver's side window around that time. Coach D's body was found a few minutes past midnight by some late dog walkers.

Ninety minutes. What happened in those ninety minutes was the key.

I flipped to the last few pages. These contained the record of texts and calls Aubrey made. There was one call to her father at 10:05 that night. It lasted three minutes. She'd received incoming calls at 10:22 and another at 10:41. The latter was a telemarketer. The 10:22 call came from a local number. The police traced it to her friend, Kaitlyn Taylor.

There was a series of texts earlier in the night between Aubrey and Coach D himself. They started at eight o'clock while she was still at work. The transcript of them was on the very last page. As I read it, my heart stopped cold.

Miranda poked her head in. "Here's that coffee for Matthew," she said. Her step faltered as she read my face. She set the coffee on the edge of my desk.

"Thanks," I managed. My heartbeat thundered in my ears.

"Oh," she said. "There was a call for you. I figured you wouldn't want to be disturbed. It was the clerk's office. Just an F.Y.I. The Ames girl posted her bond. She's on her way home with her parents as we speak."

My eyes went back to the transcript of Aubrey's texts.

"Can you track down their home number for me?" I asked. "I need to meet them there as soon as possible."

Miranda pursed her lips but didn't pry. "I'll be back in a sec." She gave me a slow nod and slipped back to her desk. Now I just had to figure out how to explain to them all that Aubrey's case was sunk before it started.

Chapter 7

AUBREY AMES LIVED with her parents in a home built at the turn of the last century on Mancy Road. Mancy was one of the busiest streets in Delphi as it ran north to south and ran straight into U.S. 12. The speed limit was forty-five but people rarely heeded that.

I pulled into the long gravel driveway shaded by maple trees. The Ames family had two acres of woodlands in front of their house and an acre in back. Dan Ames had a horse farm on one side of him, and an archery center on the other. I saw a trail camera set up on one of the trees as I rounded the last curve. If he had to, he could set a silent alarm out here for even further protection.

I parked the car and cut the engine. Two huge Labs bounded around the side of the ranch house, wagging their respective chocolate and yellow tails. Their deep barks would let anyone inside know I was here as well as an alarm system. By the looks of these two, I was in more danger of being slobbered to death.

I grabbed my messenger bag from the passenger seat and hauled it into my lap. This would be a hard conversation. I had tough questions to ask and everything I thought I knew about the case turned upside down once I'd read Aubrey's texts.

Dan Ames stepped out onto the porch. He waved as I got out of my car and slid the strap of my bag over my shoulder. The two Labradors circled around me, yipping with glee.

"Molly! Desmond! Leave the lady alone!" he called out to the dogs. I reached down and pet ... uh ... Molly on the head. Desmond, the yellow one, was easy to pick out as he was still rather well-endowed.

"Sorry I'm running a little late," I said. Dan ushered me through the front door into the living room. Aubrey was sitting on the paisley-patterned couch with her hands in her lap and her hair still wet from showering. She wore ripped jeans and the same Delphi High t-shirt that Larry Drazdowski had been murdered in. Good God, my first order of business may be to tell her never to wear that thing outside the house again.

"Hi, Aubrey," I said. "You settling in okay?"

She tucked a wet strand of hair behind her ear and nodded. I didn't like her posture. She slouched and drew into herself as her eyes flicked to her father then back to me. Dan stood behind me, his arms crossed.

"I'm fine," Aubrey more or less whispered. "Good to sleep in my own bed."

"Diane's packing some things," Dan said. "I think it's best if she and Sean go stay with her mom in Chelsea for a few days. In fact, I wanted to ask you if it's okay if Aubrey went with them."

"No," I said. "I'm afraid that's a horrible idea where Aubrey is concerned. She needs to stay in the county at a minimum. She was released on the condition she'd be living here. No matter what else happens while this case is pending, we *will* be following court orders to the letter. Even if you don't agree with them."

"Right," Dan said. "Oh ... uh ... can I get you something to drink before we get started?"

I turned to him. "I'm fine. Thanks. And I need to speak with Aubrey somewhere private. This isn't a family meeting. Not right now. I hope you understand."

Dan creased his brow and his face flushed with color. He recovered quickly though. "Er ... yeah. Of course. I'll just make myself scarce and see if I can help Diane back there."

I kept a polite smile on my face as Dan disappeared through the back of the house. For her part, Aubrey had sunk even further into the couch. I did *not* like the vibe at all. But I reminded myself she was still a nineteen-year-old kid. And she was scared to death.

I sat down beside her and pulled out my file. There was no good way to do this. The prosecution would be tougher on her than this conversation. We had to face the elephant in the room, and fast.

"Aubrey," I said. "I need you to come clean with me on the kind of relationship you had with Coach D."

Her fingers shook as she smoothed that same strand of hair behind her ear. "I didn't ... we didn't ..."

"Stop," I said, opening the file. I flipped to the last page of the cell phone report with the transcript of her last few texts on the night of the murder. She took them from me, trembling. Her eyes darted over the words I had already committed to memory.

7:52 p.m.

Aubrey to Coach D: I'm ready to talk.

7:53 p.m.

Coach D: Glad to hear it. You can stop by my planning period on Monday.

7:57 p.m.

Aubrey: No. Now. Tonight.

8:03 p.m.

Coach D: I have a life, Aubrey. Anything school-related can wait for school hours.

8:03 pm.

Aubrey: Stop it. I can't take another second of this. You know what I told you. I wasn't kidding around.

8:04 p.m.

Coach D: You need help, Aubrey. I'm not the person qualified to give it. Have you talked to your parents?

8:07 p.m.

Aubrey: Are you serious with me right now?

8:07 p.m.

Coach D: Absolutely. I'd be more than willing to meet with them too. I just don't want you to do anything you can't undo.

8:07 p.m.

Aubrey: You're unbelievable. Pick up your damn phone the next time I call. I hate texting.

8:07 p.m.

Coach D: Under the circumstances, so do I.

8:09 p.m.

Aubrey: I get off work at 10. Meet me then.

8:11 p.m.

Coach D: I'm not sure I'm comfortable with that. Let's set something up on Monday.

8:11 p.m.

Aubrey: You know exactly why this can't wait until Monday. Come to Dewar's. We'll go to the diner across the street. Bernadette's.

8:20 p.m.

Aubrey: ??

8:25 p.m.

Coach D: I'm not coming to Bernadette's.

8:27 p.m.

Aubrey: Then where?

8:28 p.m.

Coach D: Why don't you swing by my house on your way home?

8:28 p.m.

Aubrey: No way.

8:31 p.m.

Aubrey: Fine. Shamrock Park. I think you know where. That stupid shamrock statue.

8:41 p.m.

Aubrey: I need an answer.

8:45 p.m.

Coach D: Fine.

Aubrey was in tears beside me. Her normally pale color had drained even more. She let the papers fall to the floor.

"Do you need me to explain the case they're building against you with this?" I said.

"No," she whispered. I plowed forward anyway.

"Your phone was found a few feet from Coach D's body. You were seen leaning into his car in the park, right by that stupid shamrock statue you mentioned in your text, at ten thirty. Coach D was found dead at midnight. The blonde hairs they found on his chest were yours. These texts ... Aubrey ... they paint a very disturbing picture. At a minimum, there can be no doubt that you lured Coach Drazdowski to the park that night."

"Lured?" She broke, sobbing. "Lured? I didn't lure him. He was a grown man."

"What was your relationship?"

She drew her knees up, hugging them in front of her in a defensive posture. This girl was a contradiction. In those texts, she sounded forceful, desperate, but absolutely in control. Now, the mere mention of any extracurricular relationship with Larry Drazdowski had her unhinged and trembling. It could just be her natural fear at the charges she faced, but every instinct in me told me there was much more going on. Only one thing was crystal clear to me. I could never call her to the stand if this thing went to trial.

"First-degree murder," I said. I'd explained all of this to her in our first jailhouse meeting, but she needed to hear it again. "Premeditation. That's all the prosecutor has to prove. Those texts are why they went with that charge over second-degree murder."

"Isn't it hearsay or something?" she said, her voice cracking. "I thought ..."

"Stop it," I said, putting a hand up. "No. It's not hearsay. These are your words, Aubrey. Or are you trying to tell me you didn't send these texts?" The instant I said it, I regretted it. Aubrey's eyes lit up.

"He had my phone," she said. "Maybe ..."

"Again, stop it. I need the truth from you right now. Every bit of it. The rest of these records pinpoint the location of your phone every second up until it was dropped near Coach D. You were texting him from work. From Dewar's. There will be witnesses that saw you there. Your time card."

"I didn't *do* this," she said, turning every bit into the little girl I knew she still was. "Ms. Leary ... I know what this looks like. I'm scared. Not stupid. I know what you think those texts mean. But you're wrong. I wasn't trying to lure the coach into anything. And he was *alive* when I left that park."

"What do you think I think those texts mean?"

Aubrey dropped her eyes. She hugged her knees even tighter.

"What were you angry about?" I asked.

She shook her head no. Aubrey Ames was shutting down on me. With each second, I felt this case sinking fast.

"Those texts don't prove you murdered him," I said,

changing tactics. "But they're damaging. No question. Right now, our best friend is the timeline. Aubrey, is there someone ... *anyone* who can testify to where you were from ten thirty on? You didn't have your phone at that point. Did you go home?"

"No," she said. "I just ... I drove around after that."

"Why? What was going on? What were you so desperate to meet the coach about?"

She ran a hand over her face and then rested her chin on her arm. "He was ... I was going through some stuff."

"Was he helping you with that? What stuff?"

"I didn't think I could keep going."

And we were talking in circles. "He was guarded in that conversation," I said. "That's what it looks like. If I'm being honest, without the greater context, those texts sound like the kind of thing I'd tell a client to say if a student contacted him like that after hours. He didn't want to meet with you alone. Why?"

She let out a bitter laugh then wiped the tears from her cheek. "I was just freaking out, okay? I got into a fight with my dad. Sometimes Coach D ... other kids think he's easy to talk to about stuff like that."

I sat back hard. There was movement from deeper in the house. I didn't like it. Aubrey stiffened as she heard it too. I leaned in.

"Aubrey ... was there something going on at home you wanted to talk to him about?"

She quickly shook her head no. "No. No! It was just me. I get overwhelmed sometimes. My parents don't like to hear that. Maybe no parent does. They want me to be fine and not worry. Coach D just ... at first he ... I just needed to talk. That's all. I was blowing things out of proportion."

It made a certain degree of sense. Larry Drazdowski had a reputation of savior to a lot of the troubled kids in Delphi.

But by all accounts, Aubrey Ames hadn't been one of them, from what I'd been able to gather. And she was over a year out of high school.

"I think Aubrey needs a break."

Dan Ames's voice startled me as he appeared in the hallway. I leaned down and picked up the cell phone records then shoved them back into my bag.

"Yeah," Aubrey said, her eyes fixed straight on her father over my shoulder. She dropped her knees and let her feet hit the floor. "I'm sorry. I didn't mean to get so upset."

Her entire demeanor changed. One quick nod from her father, and Aubrey's tears dried up. Just how much had he overheard? How much had Aubrey told him before I got here?

"Fine," I said.

"I'll try and think of someone I might have seen after I left the park," she said.

"I'm sure there's someone," Dan chimed in. "She hasn't been sleeping since all this started. You understand."

"I do," I said rising. "But you both need to understand how serious this is. I need complete honesty. No surprises. I can't sugarcoat things. I'm not your enemy. Whatever you think you have to protect, it can't be from me. I need to know it all."

"You do," Dan said. Aubrey folded herself against her father as he wrapped his arms around her. She looked so small.

"I'm going to need access to your medical records, your school records. You made a phone call to a friend of yours earlier in the night. Who was that?"

Dan and Aubrey exchanged a glance. "Kaitlyn," she said. "Kaitlyn Taylor. She's my best friend. I swear I don't remember what we talked about."

"Fine," I said. "I'm going to talk to her too. I'm waiting

on the medical examiner's report on Coach D. We'll have more to talk about when that gets back. In the meantime, anything I ask for, you need to get it for me. No questions. No arguments. This is the rest of your life we're talking about, Aubrey. Not your mom's. Not your dad's. Yours. Do you understand?"

She nodded but dropped her head again.

"Good," I said. "I need to be one step ahead of the prosecution at all times. Is there anything in those records I just mentioned that's going to make me unhappy?"

"Aubrey was seeing a therapist a little while back," Dan said. "Your basic teenage drama."

Aubrey didn't make eye contact with me. Teenage drama, my ass, I thought. *Something* was going on with this girl. Something tricky enough that Larry Drazdowski was bothered by it. And I was starting to believe with all my heart her father was at the center of it.

Chapter 8

SOMEONE WAS LYING. Someone was always lying. In Aubrey's case, it was more a lie of omission. And her father was a problem. Instinct told me he'd been coaching her all along. She still trusted his advice more than mine. While I understood it, I had to figure out a way to get her past it.

I sat at the light at Granger and Main Street. It was Wednesday, garbage day for the west side of Delphi. The truck ahead of me blocked traffic through the intersection. My phone rang and I hit the Bluetooth button on my dash. It was Miranda.

"Hey, there," I answered, hoping to God she wasn't calling about Matty again. He'd sobered up by noon the other day and I drove him back home with his promise he'd lay off the hard stuff for a while. I texted Tina, his estranged wife, to tell her what happened. She took it fairly well, considering, and promised to check in on him and call if she needed me. I didn't even bother calling Joe about this one. He'd been handling Matty's crises solo for plenty of years.

"Just checking in," she said in her bright, cheery voice.

Miranda had offered no judgment or probing questions about Matty. She just handled everything like the unflappable pro she was. Whatever Bennett and Cooper, P.C. was paying her, it wasn't nearly enough. I knew she wanted to retire for good within the next year. I had plans to make her a different offer. I just needed the funds to make it possible.

"I'm on my way to interview a witness for the Ames case. I should be back just before two. Anything pressing?"

"Nope," she sighed. "You've got a pretrial on Lorraine Graham's DUI case at three thirty. Then the Delanceys are coming in at four thirty. You want me to push that back?"

"No," I answered. "Graham will likely plead out today. She's not eligible for diversion. She's got a drunk and disorderly from 2015 hanging out there. But I'm pretty sure I can get a reduction if she agrees to a ninety-day program. I should be out of there no later than four fifteen."

"Gotcha," Miranda said. "You just be careful out there. We've got some interesting voicemails this morning."

"I'm sure we do. Sorry things have been so ... interesting ... lately."

"Don't be sorry," Miranda said. I could tell she was smiling from the change in her tone. "I've got a feeling about this one. Keep digging."

"So do I," I answered as I finally got through the light and made the turn down Granger.

I parked the car and leafed through the police report as it pertained to Kaitlyn. She hadn't told them much. She'd merely confirmed she and Aubrey talked at 10:22 on the night of Coach D's murder. It had been brief. Just firming up plans to go to a concert the following weekend. Still, the contact happened within fifteen minutes of when Aubrey was spotted in Shamrock Park with Coach Drazdowski.

Kaitlyn lived in a three-story apartment building next to the busiest gas station in Delphi. Years ago, I'd helped Matty get a place here. Back then, the place was cheap but clean. I'd given him six months' rent while he looked for work. He'd lasted here a whole year before getting evicted for non-payment.

Kaitlyn lived in a first-floor, corner unit. I knocked softly on the door and watched the curtains ruffle before she answered.

She was pretty, full-figured with stunning red hair and soft green eyes. She wore a Mickey's Bar tank top and black skirt. I'd done my research. Her shift didn't start for another hour.

"Miss Taylor?" I offered her my hand to shake.

Kaitlyn gave me a deeply dimpled smile and met me with a formidable grip.

"You can call me Kaitlyn," she said. "Come on in. Sorry the place is kind of a dump. But ... it's all mine."

"It's okay. And it's fine. Thanks for meeting with me."

Kaitlyn had one of the single-bedroom units with the kitchen off the living room to the left when I walked in. She had mismatched, but comfortable furniture and a huge flat-screen TV on the largest wall. She gestured to the couch and I took a seat. She chose the futon right across from it and turned it so we were facing each other squarely.

"Oh ... sorry. Do you want anything? I've got some bottled water in the fridge. I can make you coffee if you don't mind K-Cups."

"Really, nothing. Thanks for the offer though."

"Have you spoken with Aubrey lately?" I asked. Her answer damn well better be no or it was something else I'd have to remind Aubrey of.

"Uh ... no. Not since ... I mean ... I tried calling her. Her dad got on and said it wasn't a good time. She doesn't have a cell phone anymore, I don't think."

I relaxed a little. At least Aubrey and Dan Ames were following the most important directive I'd given them.

"Gotcha."

"Is she okay? I mean ... this whole thing. It's been nuts. The shit people have been saying. People know we were friends. I might lose my job over that."

My heart sank. Kaitlyn seemed nice enough, but she was also not much more than a kid herself. With public opinion so firmly against Aubrey, no question Kaitlyn Taylor would face pressure to turn on her.

"I'm sorry to hear that."

"What did she say? I mean ... about what happened? No one will tell me anything."

"Kaitlyn." I sat back and crossed my legs. "I'm not really at liberty to discuss that. I just wanted to ask you a few questions, get some background information. Is that okay with you?"

"What? Er. Of course. Yeah, that was pretty dumb of me to ask. I'm just worried about her, you know? Aubrey's ... well ..."

"She's what?" I said. Her posture was telling. She sat at the literal edge of her seat, wringing her hands. She looked ready to burst. Whether it was with gossip or nerves remained to be seen.

"How close were you and Aubrey?" I asked. "I mean ... up until this ... did you talk daily?"

"Oh yeah. Like tons of times a day. She's one of the people I text constantly. And she does to me."

"Right. And can we just ... let's take away the last week and everything that's happened with Coach D. Before that, how were things with her? With the two of you?"

"What do you mean?"

"Was she acting normally? Was there anything bothering her that you could share with me?"

Kaitlyn's shoulders dropped. "Aubrey's Aubrey. She's always been kind of high strung. One of those people it doesn't take much to set off, you know?"

"Okay ... what about a boyfriend? Does she have one?"

Kaitlyn shook her head quickly. "No. No way. She dated one of the basketball players in high school. Ben Manning. But they broke up right after senior prom."

"Ben Manning," I repeated. I took out a notepad and wrote it down. "So he was one of the coach's players?"

"Oh yeah. Part of his fan club, for sure. He came into Mickey's the other day asking about Aubrey. He wanted to know what I thought. You know ... did I think she did this?"

"And what did you say?"

Kaitlyn shrugged. "I said no. I said I couldn't believe it. I mean ... you've met her. You've seen her. Aubrey's just a little thing and Coach D was ..."

Kaitlyn's color went paler. She clasped her hands together and rubbed her thumb against the palm.

"Kaitlyn, do you know if Aubrey kept in touch with the coach after high school? Or recently?"

Aubrey's texts hadn't been released to the press. I was doing my best to try to keep a lid on all of it, but Delphi was Delphi. That said, Kaitlyn Taylor's eyes went wide at the suggestion.

"No. God, no."

I believed her ignorance. Kaitlyn had no idea Aubrey had basically begged Coach D to meet her in that park the night he was killed. It didn't help her case one bit. If she kept something that important from her best friend, what else was she hiding?

"I heard someone saw her with him in the park. That was in the paper," she said. "But that's nothing. I mean ... she ran into him. So what? I just don't get it."

"Well, that's what I'm trying to figure out as well. You

said you usually texted with Aubrey several times a day. But on the night of the 22nd, there was just the one text from you at 10:22. Did you see her that day? Talk to her in person?"

Kaitlyn shook her head. "I saw her the day before. We went out to the quarry for a swim. Whenever we have a mutual day off in the summer and it's hot, that's where you'll usually find us. I worked a day shift on the 22nd. Aubrey goes in at two, I think. I just didn't have time to talk to her."

"How did she seem to you at the quarry? Was she normal? Was she upset about something?"

Kaitlyn put her hands on her thighs and rubbed up and down. She was nervous. It didn't mean she was lying. No matter what else was going on, her best friend was charged with murdering someone they both knew well. This had to be strange for her.

"I told you. Aubrey's high strung. She's always having a meltdown over one thing or another."

"Did she have a meltdown at the quarry?"

Kaitlyn bit her lip. If she was trying to protect her friend, she wasn't helping one bit. If a jury saw her like this, she'd do more damage than good.

"Kaitlyn, you have to be honest with me. And with the police and everyone else. If this case goes to trial, you'll have to testify. You were with Aubrey the day before the murder. You texted her within an hour of Coach D's death."

"I don't have anything to say!" she shouted. Just like that, she broke. Her eyes welled with tears. "I don't know anything. God. I wish I did. I wish I'd been with her that night. Then I could say I was. I should have texted her again. I usually do. Hell, we're usually going back and forth until after midnight most nights."

"But not that night," I said. "Why not?"

"There was no particular reason. I was just tired. I think

I was asleep by eleven. Miss Leary, she didn't do this. She couldn't have done this. But that's not what everyone else is saying. You do realize that, right?"

"I do," I said, reaching for her. I put on a kind smile and touched her knee. "And I know this is a lot for you to process and you're trying to help your friend. I also know that attitude puts you in a precarious position around town. You just have to tell the truth. That's all."

"That's *all*," she snorted through a sob. "That's really fucking easy for you to say. That man walked on water in this town. This is like somebody murdering Jesus."

I resisted the urge to remind her someone *had* murdered Jesus, but it seemed beside the point.

"They're going to kill her," she said. "If you can't help Aubrey, she's going to fry for this."

"Well, she's not facing the death penalty. Let's just clear that up right now."

"It won't matter," Kaitlyn said. She shifted her weight away from me. "If they don't catch who really did this, she'll go down for it. Even if you're really good at your job, Miss Leary. If you get her out of this mess, they'll come after her anyway. It's all over town. It's all over social. People want Aubrey to pay, one way or the other."

"You've seen actual threats? Online?"

"Hell, yes."

"Well, we'll do what we can to protect her ... if ..."

"You should have just let her stay in jail."

I blanched at Kaitlyn's harsh tone.

"I mean it. She'd be safer there. And it's not fair. She doesn't deserve this. Nobody's perfect. Nobody."

"I understand. I really do. And I am doing everything I can for Aubrey. In the meantime, if you think of anything that might help her. Anything. Another friend. A witness who might have seen her that night. If you hear anything that just doesn't sit right with you, I want you to call me. Can you do that for me?" I took out my business card. Kaitlyn took it and put it on the end table beside her.

"Yeah," she answered, calmer now. "It's just …"

"Just what?" I rose to my feet and slid my bag over my shoulder. Kaitlyn looked up at me.

"I just hope you're really, really good at this. You should also know what everyone's saying about you."

"Oh?" I raised a brow.

Kaitlyn stood up. "Matty and Evangeline were a few years ahead of me in school, but I know everyone thinks your family is trash. They're saying the county gave Aubrey the shittiest lawyer they could."

I put a hand on her shoulder. "Well, thanks for that. I stopped worrying about what people say about me a long time ago. It's good advice for you too." I shot her a wink but Kaitlyn didn't smile back. She showed me to the door and gave me a weak wave goodbye as I left.

I got to my car and sat in front of the wheel for a moment before starting it. Kaitlyn would be a neutral witness at best. But it would be months before this case went to trial. A lot could happen in that time and she already seemed to be buckling under the pressure. I needed something more concrete to help Aubrey and fast.

As I pulled out of the apartment complex back on to Granger, my phone rang. It was Miranda again. My pulse quickened. She wouldn't be calling me again so soon unless there was another fire I had to put out. I was about to find out this was a full-out conflagration.

"Hey, Cass," Miranda said. My phone dinged as texts came in rapid succession.

"What's going on?" I asked, stopping at the same red light.

"Honey, you're going to want to get down to the jail," she said. "Aubrey Ames is there. Her father just called."

"She's what?"

"It's bad, Cass," Miranda said.

Chapter 9

THE DELPHI P.D. enjoyed office space about four miles away from downtown. After some wrangling, I stormed my way to the second-floor detective bureau. Once there, I lost my shit.

The desk sergeant was Mark Ramos. I knew at least one of my brothers had had run-ins with him back in his beat cop days. His face fell as I cleared the elevators and headed straight for him.

"I need someone to produce my client, Aubrey Ames, now!"

Ramos put his hands up. He was in his mid-fifties with the trim build of a runner. As he rose from behind his desk, he towered over me. I said a small, silent prayer that he was too old to be one of Coach Drazdowski's players. He probably had a kid or two who worshipped the man though.

"Just hold on. No one's keeping you from her. If you give me two seconds, I can arrange for you to have a room."

"Here? Are you kidding?"

I was about to launch into a blistering rant about the Sixth and Fourth Amendments. Hell, I had my brief and motion already written in my head. But first things first. I needed to get Aubrey out of this building and put duct tape across her mouth if that's what it took.

Two detectives headed toward me from the hallway to my left. I knew one was Tim Bowman, the lead investigator in Coach D's murder. He shot me a smug look as he adjusted his tie and came straight at me. He held a thin file in his left hand.

"Was it you?" I asked. "Tell me you did *not* just interview my client outside of my presence."

He raised a brow and turned to his partner. More doors opened deeper in the hall. I looked over Bowman's shoulder, but Aubrey didn't appear.

Bowman smoothed a hand down his tie. He made the gesture twice in the span of sixty seconds. I filed that away in the corner of my mind. It was a tell, I just wasn't sure of what yet.

"Your client contacted *me*, Miss Ames."

"What the fuck, Bowman? Are you serious with this? She's represented by counsel. Pretty sure they taught you what that means week one in the academy."

His look turned smug. "She just confessed to murdering Larry Drazdowski."

He had the decency to lower his voice on the last part, but I knew it didn't matter. If the news got to Miranda, half the town already knew.

"Unbelievable," I said.

"Oh, she was pretty credible." He lifted the file in his left hand and held it out to me. "I've made you a copy of her handwritten statement. She signed a waiver of counsel. Twice. And I told you, she contacted me. It wasn't the other way around."

I took the file but didn't dare open it in front of him. "Where is she?"

"She's collecting herself."

"I'll bet. Goddammit. This is meaningless and you know it. Though I suppose I should thank you. You've probably blown your whole case."

"She wasn't coerced," he said, calmly. "You'll see on your copy of the tape we made. I asked her repeatedly if we should wait for counsel. She was pretty clear on all of it. You don't scare me, Miss Leary."

I hated the way he said my last name, as if it tasted bad in his mouth. I'd heard it like that before. All my life, really. Bowman was a good ole boy. Through and through.

"She's a kid," I said. "Where are her parents?"

Bowman got in my face. The move seemed to startle even Ramos. He came around the bench. I straightened my back and kept my eyes locked with Bowman's. He had a beefy face with a crooked nose with at least one old break through the bridge. His mouth turned down as he raked his eyes over me. Pure contempt.

He was a bully. He puffed out his chest and looked down at me, narrowing his eyes. Was it because I was a Leary? A defense attorney? A woman? Maybe all three.

I hate bullies.

It triggered something in me and I had to check myself. This wasn't about me. This was about Aubrey and a justice system that *had* to work in this case, no matter who the victim was. Every nerve ending in me simmered with rage.

"Your *client* is nineteen years old. An adult. She doesn't need her mommy or daddy here to hold her hand and she knew exactly what she was doing."

I went back down, flat-footed, and took a step back. "And I'm still her lawyer. Unless you're planning on charging her with something else, it's time for her to go home."

Bowman flinched. He shot a look to Ramos.

"Bring her out," Ramos said.

"No way she gets to leave, she just confessed to ..."

"She's been granted bail," I said. "Nothing changes."

There was movement behind Bowman. A female detective walked briskly down the hallway. She had her arm around Aubrey as the two of them made their way to the main bullpen.

Aubrey's face was purple and swollen from crying. She kept her head down and crossed her arms in front of her. It was the most submissive, defensive posture she could make short of curling up on the floor in a fetal position. What in the hell had happened back there?

Part of me wanted to shake her myself for the decisions she just made. But this was a broken soul in front of me. And if everything I'd just been told was true, she was also a killer. For now though, she was still my client.

"Aubrey?" I said, brushing past Bowman. He opened his mouth to protest, but a quick gesture from Mark Ramos stilled him.

"She's ready to go," the female detective said, her voice devoid of emotion. She was about my age. She introduced herself as Megan Lewis. She was tall, with sharp features and bleached-blonde hair pulled back into a severe bun. Aubrey leaned on her, practically curling herself against the woman. So this was good cop to Tim Bowman's bad cop.

"Come on," I said, putting an arm around Aubrey. "I'll drive you home."

Jack LaForge stepped off the elevator just as I headed toward it. His face fell when he saw us.

"Cass," he started. I held a hand up.

"Don't. Not now," I said. "I'm taking my client home. You can expect my motion to suppress just about immediately."

"It won't matter."

"Did you put them up to this?" I asked. I knew damn well LaForge was probably on the other side of the two-way mirror the entire time Aubrey was here. What I couldn't fathom was how he let it go on. No matter what they claimed about Aubrey waiving her rights, this was as messy as it got.

"I'm not going to dignify that with an answer, Cass. You may have been born in Delphi, but you're new around here as far as I'm concerned."

"Save it," I said, ushering Aubrey toward the elevator. I needed to get her the hell out of here and fast. Then I'd have to figure out what to do with her.

We got downstairs quickly. Aubrey folded herself against me just like she'd done to Detective Lewis. We made it three steps toward the curb and my waiting car before hell broke loose.

It came from three sides. Camera lights blinded me. Two live news trucks parked at odd angles further down the street. A handful of reporters shoved microphones toward us and barked questions.

"Is it true Miss Ames has confessed to killing Coach Drazdowski? Will you be making a statement?"

Son of a bitch. It felt like a setup. Surely Jack LaForge couldn't be that much of a dick. It could just as likely be the rumor mill always churning. I hugged Aubrey to my side and whispered in her ear, "Do *not* say a damn word."

The bigger danger came from my left. In a split second, I went from anger at the reporters to relief. If they hadn't been there, things might have turned out vastly different.

"Bitch!"

A rock sailed above my head and bounced off the building behind us.

"Fucking murderer!"

"Aubrey," I said, keeping my voice low and steady. "We have about thirty steps to take. You stay glued to my side and when I say, I want you to get into the back seat of my car and lay on the ground."

She nodded her understanding but her entire body trembled and fresh tears spilled down her cheeks.

Another rock flew over us. There were cell phones out, recording everything. Several police officers came running at top speed, pouring out of the building. A cup flew in front of me, spilling hot coffee at my feet. I jumped back but a few scalding drops hit my ankle. "Jesus!"

My car was maybe twenty feet away. Three uniformed officers threw themselves in front of us, trying to form a wall against the next thrown object and flying fists. I struggled to find my keys at the bottom of my messenger bag.

It was mob mentality. If not for those brave men and women in uniform, I have no doubt in my mind they would have ripped us to shreds. And it would all likely be posted to social media within the hour.

"Cass!"

A hand shot out, grabbing my shirt. I let go of Aubrey and flailed against it. Adrenaline shot through me and I shoved Aubrey toward my car, trying to get her out of the way.

"Cass!"

I stumbled, pitching forward. Two hands tightened on my shoulders and lifted me off my feet. I looked up.

Joe had me by the arm, sweat pouring down the side of his face. He looked just as terrified as I felt, but he moved with singular purpose. He grabbed Aubrey and shoved me down the nearest alley.

"No!" I shouted. "They'll corner us."

No sooner had I said it when truck tires screeched to a halt at the opposite end of the alley. My heart stopped for an instant, then blood rushed to my head as Matty threw open the passenger door and waved us forward.

I ran for all I was worth. Aubrey was right behind me. We threw ourselves at the truck. I scrambled into the passenger seat. Joe got in behind me and Aubrey got in next to him.

Joe slammed both doors shut as Matty peeled away from the curb and ran the light at the next intersection. I put my face in my hands, not brave enough to look back.

Chapter 10

MY HOUSE WAS the safest place to go. Matty parked the truck at an angle and was the first one to get to me, opening the door. I nearly collapsed against him. My whole body felt like rubber.

"You okay?" he asked, his eyes wild.

"Yeah," I said. "How in the hell did you know to come for me?"

"Rumor went down ... *she* ... was at the police department." Joe stepped forward. "I was over at Mickey's, working on an exterior paint job. Heard some of the loudmouths in there stirring up trouble. I knew you'd head straight into it."

"Thanks," I said, peering up at him. I went up on my tiptoes and planted a sloppy kiss on my brother's cheek. Feeling steadier, I slid out of his arms and did the same to Matty. My brothers. My protectors. Matty had been angry when I came back to town. But at the first sign of trouble, he had come running. My heart ached with love and gratitude as we went inside.

I didn't have to tell them. My brothers knew I needed a minute alone with my client. They made themselves scarce.

A myriad of emotions swirled through me as Aubrey sat down on the couch. She cried silently, worrying her hands together. She glanced out my front bay window as my brothers took positions up and down the dock. They were already laughing and easy with each other.

God, I'd missed them like that. A million years ago I went out there with them to keep the little ones out of trouble while Joe tried to catch dinner. Vangie had always been better keeping her line from getting tangled. Matty would bring his to me along with his sheepish grin. I'd unsnarl everything quickly before Joe even knew what was happening.

"I'm sorry," Aubrey whispered, pulling me out of my own head.

My hands were still shaking. I wouldn't be able to sleep tonight. The nightmares of that last blustery day on Lake Michigan were already starting to take shape. Would I ever truly feel safe again?

I sat down on the coffee table in front of her. There was something hanging in the air around her. The answer to a question I knew better than to ask. But as I sat there, still shaken from the trauma of shouted death threats and hurled rocks, my better judgment seemed to drift away.

"You went in there and told the cops you killed Coach Drazdowski?"

She didn't look like a killer. She looked like a victim.

"I don't want to talk about it."

"Tough shit," I said. "You apparently had no problems talking about it an hour ago."

She buried her face in her hands. God help me, I was either going to shake some sense into this girl or pull her into a hug.

"I did what I had to do," she answered. She raised her chin and met my eyes. She looked like a little girl, her lashes wet with tears. Her lips were almost purple, her face blotchy and red.

"That night in the park or today?"

Aubrey lifted her shoulders. "I don't know. Both, I guess. I just can't anymore today. I can't think. I can't talk. I just want to go home."

"Great. And what exactly do you expect me to do with all of this? Do you even want my help anymore?"

"Yes!" Aubrey found her voice. Her eyes widened with desperation.

"Yes," she said more softly. "Cass, I need you. Please keep helping me."

I let out a bitter laugh. "Then what was today about? Huh? Did someone put you up to this? You waived your right to have your attorney present. I'm sorry, Aubrey. I can't fix this. You just confessed to murder."

"They charged me with first degree. You said they'd have to prove premeditation. You said the other thing was better. Second degree. Can you get me a deal?"

I slowly rose. One minute, this girl was scared and vulnerable. The next, she was spouting sophisticated legal strategy. Did I have it all wrong? Was Aubrey Ames far more calculating than I gave her credit for? Than Larry Drazdowski gave her credit for?

"You want a deal. Great, Aubrey. Just, great."

"Second degree you said there's a possibility of parole."

"In twenty years maybe! I just can't even. I need some air."

"I did what I had to do. You don't have to believe me."

"A jury has to believe you!" I shouted.

"But now I don't have to testify. I've said everything I want to say. I just want this to be over."

I resisted the urge to tell her so did I. My gut told me this girl was lying about something. Maybe everything. I just couldn't figure out what.

"Cass!" Joe's shout startled me. At the same time I heard it, tires crunched on my gravel driveway.

"Wait here," I said. Then I ran upstairs to my bedroom. I kept a loaded .38 in a holster attached to my bed frame. I took it out and went out on the second-floor deck.

"Where is she?" The car door slammed as Matty threw his pole on the dock and ran up to join Joe.

I kept the gun to my side; my heartbeat hammered in my brain. Then the owner of the vehicle stepped into view. Dan Ames was red-faced and moving fast toward the house.

"Aubrey!" he shouted. Joe got to him and put two strong hands on Dan Ames's shoulders, shoving backward.

"You just hang on," he said. "You're not barging into my sister's house."

"I goddamn am if my daughter's in there! They told me she left with you three in a hurry. She didn't come home, she didn't go to Cass's office. And here you are."

"I'm here," Aubrey said, coming out the side door. I left the porch and went back through the bedroom, leaving my gun on the dresser. Flying down the stairs I met Aubrey on the back porch.

"Everything all right?" I asked. Dan Ames shook with rage. He curled and uncurled his fists, ready to punch something. At the moment, Joe seemed his most likely target.

"What the hell's going on?" he demanded. "I heard some crazy-ass rumors flying around town. And Aubrey's face is all over the news and online. Did you do it? They're saying you ..."

"Hold on," I said. "Let's just all calm down. Aubrey's okay. I'm okay."

I might as well have been invisible. Dan Ames charged the porch. Joe followed at his side, ready to shove him back again if needed. Dan put his hands on Aubrey's shoulders and shook her gently the same way I wanted to just a few minutes ago.

"What the hell are you doing?" His voice broke. "Is it true? Is what they're saying true? You told them you did this? That you killed that ... that ..." His eyes darted to mine. Some of the color drained from Dan's face as he tried to compose himself.

"Are you behind this?" he asked me.

"Am I what?"

"Daddy, stop it," Aubrey said. "Nobody's behind anything. I just want to go home. Can I do that? Will they take me to jail now?" She turned to me.

"Not directly," I said through a great sigh. "That is, your bail conditions shouldn't change after this. But ..."

"But, that's enough for now," Dan finished my sentence. "I can take my daughter home. That's all I'm interested in hearing right now."

"You?" I said, stepping off the porch. Dan was starting to remind me of Tim Bowman. "It's your daughter who needs to make some decisions."

"I have," Aubrey said. "I told you. I did what I had to do."

"Enough," I said. "Don't say another word. Not in front of my brothers. Not in front of your father. You've said more than enough for one day, Aubrey."

"You'll still help me?" Aubrey's voice was desperate, breaking on the last syllable.

I wanted to say a million things. Are you kidding me? Are you crazy? There's no help for any of this. But I wasn't sure which was true at the moment. Dan Ames threw an arm around his daughter and steered her toward his car. He threw a hostile glance at Joe. It seemed like they understood something with just that one look. My brother Joe was a father too. Joe put his hands up and backed off a few steps to let Dan and Aubrey by.

"Cass?" Aubrey said as Dan opened the passenger door for her.

"We'll talk tomorrow," I said. "I need to ... I need to think about it."

"Let's go," Dan said. Aubrey slid into the passenger seat. He climbed behind the wheel and slammed the car into reverse, kicking up more gravel along the way.

"What an asshole," Matty said. He stood in a ready stance, his fists curled at his sides.

"I don't know," Joe said. "I don't know what I'd be thinking or feeling in his shoes."

"Did she really confess?" Matty asked. "It looks bad, Cass."

"Tell me about it." I crossed my arms in front of me. I craved that bottle of wine chilling in my fridge. As soon as Matty went home, I had a date with it.

"What are you going to do?" Joe asked.

"What do you mean?"

"I mean ... you can't possibly still be thinking about representing her. After what happened today?"

I deflated. The adrenaline of the last hour sluiced off me. The weight of my exhaustion hit me. I sat down on the edge the porch and dangled my feet. A couple of power boats whizzed by, pulling skiers. Laughter filled the air. I, on the other hand, felt like I was in the Twilight Zone.

Joe didn't press. He saw the look on my face. Instead, my brothers traded insults as they made their way back to Matty's truck. I hugged each one of them. It felt good. It felt normal. Matty had a hard time with me being here. In this house. We might have our differences between us, but when someone came after any one of us ... hell was going to break loose.

Matty choked up a bit as I kissed him. "You come after one, you get us all," Matty said, giving voice to my thoughts.

"Yep," I said. "And you know I have your back. Always. Doesn't mean you're not going to get my foot up it when you need it. This is my house. But you know it's yours too. Don't forget that. And don't stay away because of stupid shit."

Matty climbed in the truck. Joe held back. "You sure you're okay?"

I nodded up at him and slid my hands into my back pockets. "I will be. Just need some wine. I didn't want …"

"Gotcha," he said. "I might swing back later this evening to stick a pole back in the water. Save me a beer or two."

"You got it." I also knew he was full of shit. If Joe came back tonight, it wouldn't be about the fish. He was worried about me.

"I just wish …" I couldn't finish the sentence. As harrowing as the afternoon had been, my brothers and I had reached a level of peace and normalcy. At least for us. There was just something … someone missing.

"I miss her today too," Joe said. "Vangie's always better at keeping Matty's shit together than we are. Plus, she's a better brawler than he is. She'd have drawn some blood today."

I burst out laughing. He was right. More than once, Joe had to drag Vangie off some hapless bully who tried to mess with Matty on the way to school. I hugged Joe again and it eased some of the ache in my heart. Vangie *should* be here today.

"I'll see you later tonight," I said. Joe gave me a wave and slid into the back seat of Matty's truck.

Chapter 11

MIRANDA WAS WAITING for me with another thick envelope in her hand. "LaForge's office just dropped this off," she said. "And you shouldn't be driving into town by yourself. Those videos from the police station were scary, Cass. They were trying to hurt you."

"Thanks," I said. I took the envelope from her and felt the outline of its contents. It was a DVD. My heart sank. Part of me was hoping the last twenty-four hours was a dream. That my most high-profile client *hadn't* just confessed to murder outside my presence.

"Already hooked up the cords in the conference room," she said. "Figured you'd want to run that from your laptop to the big screen. Nobody's coming in today. Your ten o'clock and your two thirty canceled."

"Rescheduled?" My morning appointment was a potential new client. A divorce case and the guy had money. Finally. My later appointment was with a new court appointment.

"Canceled," Miranda said, her expression grim. "I'm sorry, honey. Word's getting out about the Ames girl. Up until yesterday, I don't know. I think some folks were keeping an open mind. That's gone. It's making you radioactive."

"Just great. What, do they think I stuck that knife in Coach D?"

"Next worst thing," Miranda shrugged. "I've gotta love-hate relationship with this town."

"So do I. Thanks for thinking of me. I'll be in the conference room." Miranda gave me a motherly pat on the back as I moved past her.

I went to the conference room, clicked the remote and held my breath. The police camera produced a grainy, poorly lit image, like always. For the first few seconds, there was no sound as Detective Bowman adjusted the angle and pushed a microphone in front of Aubrey's face.

"God. She looks scared to death," I whispered.

She'd worn a gray hooded sweatshirt yesterday and her thin fingers disappeared into the sleeves. She started talking but too softly for the mics to pick it up.

"Speak up." Bowman almost shouted it. There was mumbling beside him and the back of Detective Megan Lewis's head came into view. Bowman cleared his throat and sat back down. His posture shifted and I could pretty much guess what Lewis might have said to him. *Back off, she's already given us what we need.*

"Can you state your name and the date and time?" Lewis asked, her voice calm, almost soothing.

"Aubrey Ann Ames. It's July 10th."

"And why are you here today?" Lewis prompted. When Bowman leaned forward, Lewis put a hand up, gesturing for him to be still.

"I have a lawyer," Aubrey said. "But I don't want her here today. I ... uh ... I waive my rights to have her be here. I'm doing this on my own."

Of course they would have made that clear. My blood boiled, but Aubrey was straight up digging her own grave.

"I just had to get this out. I did it. I killed Coach D."

"You'll have to be a little more specific," Bowman said.

"I didn't ... don't I ..." Aubrey shifted in her seat. She was crying. She put her head down, resting it on her arm. I peered closer, trying to look in her eyes. The video quality just wasn't good enough to read them.

"I killed him. I stabbed him. On June 22nd in Shamrock Park."

"What happened, Aubrey?" Megan Lewis asked.

Miranda came into the conference room bearing two steaming mugs of coffee.

"I went there, okay?" Aubrey's voice shook. "I asked him to meet me there. We talked. He made me mad. Really mad. I didn't plan it. I just wanted to talk. But I got angry. Really heated. I don't know what happened. I just snapped."

"Geez Louise," Miranda said.

"What did you talk about? What made you snap?" Bowman picked up the questioning.

"Forget it!" Aubrey was openly sobbing. She wiped her eyes with her oversized sleeves. "It doesn't matter. None of it matters. I just did it, okay? I confess. That's everything you need to know. I just want this over. Can it be over?"

"Aubrey ..." Lewis started again.

"No! That's it. That's all I have to say. I went to the park. I got mad. I snapped. I have a knife. You know ... for self-defense."

"Was the coach threatening you?" Megan Lewis was clearly as baffled as I was watching this.

"He wasn't. I don't know ... maybe. I was just mad. Really mad. I snapped. I stabbed him. I'm done now. I need to go now. Can I go now?"

It went on like that for another five minutes. Over and

over, Aubrey kept saying she snapped. She stabbed the coach. Toward the end of the video, Megan slid a notepad in front of her. Aubrey picked up a pen and wrote the statement I'd been handed just a few minutes afterward.

Someone came to the door behind Megan's head. The voices grew muffled but I could make out enough. "Her lawyer's here now. You're going to want to wrap this up."

Then that was it. The recording stopped. Eight minutes and thirteen seconds of complete what-the-fuckery.

I sat for a moment, dumbfounded. Miranda slowly raised her coffee mug to her lips. "Well," she said. "What'd you think, boss?"

I leaned back in my chair. "I don't even know where to start."

"Felt like she spent some time googling before she walked into that police station. She snapped. She didn't plan it."

"Right. Of course I covered the different types of murder with her. But yeah ... I think so too. And I think a few other things too."

"So do I. You go first."

I stood up and started to pace. Somehow, I always thought better when moving. "She keeps saying she wants this to be over. She's scared of something and I can't put my finger on it. It's more than just jail time."

"Do you really think she did it?" Miranda asked.

My answer hit me like a lightning bolt to the chest. I knew I was right. I just had no idea how I was going to prove it yet.

"No. Dammit. No. But I think she knows who really did kill Coach D. I think she's covering for someone."

Miranda's slow smile made deep lines at the corners of her eyes. "That's what I think too. And I think *you* have an idea who."

Chapter 12

THE EASIEST THING TO do was walk away. Aubrey wasn't interested in her own defense. She was lying to me. I believed in my heart she was lying to the cops too but I was nowhere on proving any of it.

I had the Drazdowski murder's meager case file spread out on the conference room table. Most damning of course, was Aubrey's own half-assed confession. If I took that out of the equation (laughable, I know), I could have built something.

There was no murder weapon. There were strands of Aubrey's hair on Coach D's shirt but that alone wasn't damning. Her cell phone records were. She was the last known person to see him alive and her texts to him were ominous. Threatening even.

But I could have knocked those down.

Aubrey was a scared, possibly troubled kid. Coach D had a reputation for counseling students in trouble. Even ones he'd never coached.

Then there was the murder itself. The full autopsy report

had come in the morning of Aubrey's ridiculous confession. Coach D was stabbed exactly once with a four-inch blade. The coroner's specs matched the kind of hunting knife that half the men in this town probably carried. The killing wound had been delivered forcefully by someone with at least a passing knowledge of human anatomy or unbelievable luck.

Coach D hadn't expected it. There were no defensive wounds. His killer had attacked him face to face. Instinct told me he probably knew him or her. Then again, just like me, the coach knew just about everyone in town.

"What are you doing, Aubrey?" I whispered as I hovered over the most disturbing crime scene photo. It would be the "money" shot if this case ever saw a jury. It was taken about two feet above the body, head on. Coach D's lifeless eyes seemed to stare straight into the camera, filled with shock. One look at that picture and anyone would understand that Larry Drazdowski knew exactly what was happening to him and felt every second of agony as he left this world.

"Jack's calling again," Miranda said, poking her nose into the conference room.

"I gotta admit, I'm a little shocked he's still trying. I figured he'd be waiting for me to crawl into his office on my hands and knees."

"Maybe you should take it."

"Miranda, I don't even know if Aubrey's still my client. I don't even know if I want her to be."

Miranda raised a skeptical brow. "The hell you don't. That girl needs you. She needs *someone*. I know you don't really believe she killed that man. If the people of this town would just come to their senses, they'd know it too."

"Except she just told them all she did. She made it easy."

Miranda pointed to the landline conference phone on the

table beside me. Line one was blinking. "Take that call. See what he says. Then call your client and figure out what you want to do. You've been staring at that table for two days. It's not helping."

"You sound like my mother." I meant it as a throwaway comment. The moment it was out of my mouth though, my heart clenched. Of all people to say it to, Miranda was one of the last to know if it was actually true.

"Thanks," she said softly, smiling. "And come to think of it, that's what she *would* say to you if she could. Maybe I just channeled her."

"No fair."

"Take. The. Call!"

As Miranda shut the door, I did.

"Hey, Jack," I said, wincing.

"'Bout time you answered your phone, Leary," he said. So I was Leary now. Did that make me one of the good ole boys?

"Things have been a little hectic around here," I lied, hoping he bought it.

"Yeah. I imagine. Look, I don't feel like dragging this out any more than you do. And I also don't feel like kicking someone when they're down."

"How am I the one down, Larry? Your office crapped all over my client's civil rights."

He sighed into the phone. "Yeah, and you and I both know that's bullshit."

"You should have *called* me the minute you got wind of this. I heard it from my secretary who got it from courtroom gossip. How long did that take to wind its way down Main Street? This is going to blow up on you. As far as I'm concerned, we really don't have anything to talk about unless you called to tell me you're going to do the right thing and throw out that coerced confession."

I was stretching the truth, I knew. What happened hadn't really reached the level of coercion, but I was mad as hell.

"That's not happening, Leary."

"And you can take whatever ridiculous plea deal your boss thinks will cover his ass on this and …"

"Stop!" he shouted. "Just stop right there. You really think I called to talk about a plea? I called out of professional courtesy and so you wouldn't do anything like embarrass yourself in court on this one."

I felt my ears get hotter by the second.

"There isn't going to be a plea deal, Cass. Your client's admitted guilt. She killed someone most people in this town consider a goddamn saint. Take it to trial if you want, but you know you'll lose. She's going to get life in prison. Full stop."

"Thanks, Jack. Good talk."

Miranda came to the door. She leaned against the doorframe and made a slashing gesture across her throat. Then she pointed behind her. I had no appointments, but there was someone out there she wanted me to know about.

"We done?" Jack asked.

"Yeah. We're done."

I hung up the phone.

"Sorry," Miranda said. "I knew that was going to be painful. There's someone out here who needs to talk to you. She doesn't have an appointment but I figured you'd want to give her a few minutes, all things considered. I'll set her up in your office."

I rose to my feet and stepped around the conference table. Kaitlyn Taylor sat in the waiting room just behind Miranda's shoulder.

"Yeah. Okay. Thanks, Mir."

I could still feel my heart thundering in my ears as I

grabbed a pad of paper and headed into my office. Miranda stood with a smile halfway out the door.

"Thanks," I said again. Without a word, Miranda reached for Kaitlyn and rubbed her shoulder before leaving the two of us alone.

"Sit down," I said, finding my own chair behind my desk. "What's on your mind, Kaitlyn?"

Kaitlyn wouldn't sit. She stood chewing her thumbnail. She had on a DHS Shamrocks hoodie and ripped jeans today. With her hair in two braids, she looked more like twelve than twenty.

"You have to do something," she said, her voice cracking.

"About what?"

"About *Aubrey*! You have to help her."

I let out a sigh. "She's making that pretty difficult, Kaitlyn, and you know there isn't much I can discuss with you about any of it. She's still my client ... I think."

"Yeah. Yeah. I get all that. Look, Aubrey's an idiot. But she's not stupid, you know what I mean?"

I folded my hands and rested them on my desk. "At the moment, I really don't."

"She didn't *do* this! She didn't kill Coach D. I don't know why she's saying it. You have to talk to her. Alone. And don't let her blow you off. I really think if you could just get her here and, you know ... be really gentle with her. She needs to know you're her friend. She needs to trust you."

"She's not my friend, Kaitlyn. It doesn't work like that. But I know she's *your* friend. So be one. She's in trouble. Big, serious trouble. If you know something, if you can help her, you have to do it. Now's the time. Hell ... now is about two days past the time."

Kaitlyn finally sat. Her brow knit in deep, roping lines. I'd thought she looked twelve when she first came in. Now she looked eighty. Tears played at the corners of her eyes.

"You have to talk to her again," she whispered. "Please."

"What is it you think she needs to tell me?"

"Everything. She needs to tell you everything."

"Kaitlyn, no more games. You're on the prosecution's witness list. Whatever you know, I need to know. If this case goes to trial, you're going to have to testify. Under oath. If you really and truly want to help your friend, I need to know everything that you do before you get up there."

She broke. Kaitlyn drew into herself in much the same way I'd seen Aubrey do more than once. She was a little girl again in the space of a second. Whatever secret she carried inside her was torturing her.

"Why don't you already know?" she asked. "I mean, you … of all people. When I found out who you were. Who your family is. I mean … you're *one* of us."

Her words shook me. "My family? What about my family?"

She wouldn't meet my eyes. Tears rolled down Kaitlyn's cheeks and she shifted her focus to a spot on the floor. "I just mean … they've always treated everybody who lives east of the lake like dirt, you know? Like it matters. There are just as many trailer parks on the west side. More, actually. I counted once."

"Really?" My whole life I'd never once even thought of that.

"Aubrey just needs … I don't know … like … a champion. Nobody's ever believed in her. People make assumptions over things that aren't her fault."

"What about her parents? She's got a solid family, hasn't she?"

Even as I said it, the scene from my driveway the other day replayed in my head. Dan Ames was scared to death. On the one hand, I knew he wanted to protect his daughter. On the other, I had sensed rage in him that seemed, I don't know, more deep-seated than just the events of the last few weeks. But it was so hard to know. These weren't ordinary events. Then there was her younger brother. The day I met him, he'd whispered that odd statement about how Aubrey would end up paying for what she did.

"Her mom's cool," Kaitlyn answered. "A pushover. But she doesn't really like to rock the boat, you know. And her dad ... well ... you've met him. Still, he's a prince compared to my dad. I know I shouldn't say this, but ... ugh ... my dad's drunk more than he isn't. You know?"

I tilted my head to the side. I felt my lips draw together in a line. "Yes. I know."

Shared pain flashed in Kaitlyn's eyes. Of course, she probably didn't *really* know about my own demons. She would have heard plenty of rumors. But it was enough to tell her her instincts were right. I just hoped it would be enough to get her to open up all the way.

"This secret you have," I said. "Kaitlyn, it's poisoning you. I can see it. It probably feels manageable now. And maybe it is something you can carry even for years. But if it's about Aubrey ... if it's something that can help her now, it won't do her any good in a few years, will it?"

Kaitlyn shook her head. She straightened her shoulders and I knew I'd already lost her. That small moment she felt connected to me had been enough to give her strength she hadn't walked in with. She was about to walk out with it though.

"It's not like that for every secret, Miss Leary. Sometimes the truth is much, much worse."

"Kaitlyn ..."

But she was already on her feet and headed for the door. She turned back as she opened it. "Just ... talk to her. Give her one more chance. If you don't, nobody will. It'll be just like she said, after all."

"Said about what?"

Kaitlyn didn't answer. Instead, she just left my office and closed the door behind her.

"Dammit!" I sat back hard in my chair. I'd had my fill of cryptic teenagers for one day. I grabbed my messenger bag and went out to the lobby. Miranda had her own office just off the waiting room. A glass partition separated her from incoming clients.

"I think I'm over it for today," I said. "I need sleep. I need to breathe in some lake air and watch the sunset. Tomorrow, I gotta figure out if I still have a practice worth saving."

Miranda came out from behind her desk and slid open the glass partition. Then she wrapped her arms around me. I needed that hug more than I wanted to admit.

"That's a great idea," she said. "Things never look so dire the next day. Trust me. It's a rule."

"I hope you're right."

Miranda always kept fresh flowers on her desk. Her husband sent them once a week and had since the day they married thirty-seven years ago. I leaned down and smelled them. This week he sent white and pink roses.

As I rose, I noticed a thin, shiny green book on the edge of her desk. It had gold embossed lettering. I picked it up.

"What's that?" she asked.

"I was about to ask you." I fingered the binding. It was a Delphi High School Yearbook from three years ago.

"Did Kaitlyn drop this off?" I asked.

"I don't know. I can't imagine. I didn't bring her through this way. I've never seen that before. I swear it wasn't there an hour ago."

There was no note. I flipped through the pages. One small scrap of white paper slid out. It was a Post-it note but the glue backing hadn't stuck. There was no writing on it except for a small arrow in blue ballpoint ink. Unfortunately, now there was no way to know what it had been pointing to.

Adrenaline shot through me. I glanced at Miranda.

"Go! Maybe you can still catch her!"

I ran through the front door, but Kaitlyn Taylor had already pulled out of the parking lot, her tires squealing as she hit the gas.

Chapter 13

AT TEN O'CLOCK two mornings later, I found myself walking into the one place I promised I wouldn't enter when I came back to town. The Maple Valley Rehabilitation Center. Built just four years ago, it was a high-end nursing care center. I found the reason for my oath in room 214 recovering from her third of a six-round chemo treatment.

"Son of a bitch," Jeanie Mills sighed as I walked into her room. I suppose I should have called. But I knew damn well she'd find a way to guilt me into *not* coming.

In her prime, Jeanie's appearance made most people do a double take. She'd been about four foot nine inches both tall and wide with true black hair cropped short, her bangs cut straight across her brow. Save for one black streak near her forehead, Jeanie's hair had gone completely white. Not even the chemo had affected that. Jeanie was battling stage two breast cancer.

"Hey, yourself," I smiled. My heart lifted as she gave me that laser stare from clear, blue eyes. Jeanie was down, but never out. Though, at seventy, there may soon come a point where even her brand of toughness would give out.

I grabbed a chair from the corner of the room and slid it next to Jeanie's bed. She erupted into a wracking cough, but soon recovered. I reached for her, putting my hand over hers. She'd lost weight. Her crepe-paper skin hung from her wrists and her normally round cheeks had hollowed.

"Should have known I couldn't trust you to do the one thing I told you not to, Cassiopeia. I didn't want you to see me like this."

I leaned over the bed and drew her into a hug. The hell with it all. "I tried. But I missed you. You can't fault me for that." I helped Jeanie adjust a large pink crocheted blanket around her legs.

"Fine," she said. "But don't you dare ask me how the fuck I'm feeling. And I'll kill ya if you offer to pray for me."

This got a deep belly laugh from me. "I told you. I missed you."

"Yeah, yeah. I'm not an idiot. I've been watching the news. I was expecting you to show up here about a week or so ago. What the hell happened, kiddo?"

I set my messenger bag on the floor. The Delphi yearbook poked out of the side compartment and I pulled it out.

"Well, let me first ask you this. You been paying your bar dues?"

Jeanie moved to adjust the pillow behind her. I reached over and helped. She shot me a withering glance so I sat back down.

"Yeah," she answered. "Extortion is what that is."

I had a fifty-dollar bill folded in the pocket of my blazer. I took it out and pinned it to the corkboard over Jeanie's left shoulder, right next to a couple of get well cards and her menu.

"Now that that's out of the way," I said. "You're officially of counsel."

"Sheeit. I wouldn't lower myself."

"Oh, yes you would."

Jeanie Mills was a pioneer in this county. She'd formed the first all-female law firm not long after she got her license. Jeanie focused on family law matters. And she was a bulldog. In those first few years after we lost my mother, it was Jeanie who'd kept my younger siblings out of foster care when my father couldn't or wouldn't step up. She was also the main reason I decided to become a lawyer.

"First things first," she said. "I want to hear about you. The truth. I've heard enough rumors over the last few months. And I know better than to believe most of them."

I flapped my hands in defeat and crossed my leg at the ankle. "I'm pretty sure you can fill in the blanks yourself. I've committed the cardinal sin of trying to practice law ... or do anything in this town with the last name of Leary."

Jeanie sank back against her pillows. Her right hand twitched and she kneaded a loose yarn on her blanket. She was itching for the cigarette she usually held there.

"So, you're going to be *that* way," she said. "Cut the crap, Cass. You know exactly what I'm talking about. It's not your name that's the problem. What the hell are you doing back here?"

I had a pat answer to that question for everyone. One look from Jeanie and I knew she'd never buy it. Hell. I knew that was the real reason I hadn't come to visit her sooner. Sure, she'd made me promise not to. But that had just been convenient for me.

"It's a funny thing when you sell your soul to the devil," I said, staring at a point on the wall. "Everyone thinks they'll be able to outsmart him when he comes to collect."

There was dead silence between us. Jeanie's face softened into a smile. She reached for me, gathering my hands in hers. "Aw, honey. I'd say you still have your soul."

I wouldn't do this. I would not cry in front of her. I came here for her help, but not with this.

"So," she said. "The rumors are true then. The Thorne Group really is into some shady shit. Didn't I tell you their offer was too good to be true ten years ago?"

"Jeanie ... I can't ..."

She put a hand up. "You don't have to say a word. I can pretty much guess. The world's not that big and I still have some law enforcement contacts in wider circles than just Delphi. What I *can't* figure out is how you didn't end up in witsec?"

I couldn't breathe. Jeanie knew me too damn well. I trusted her with my life and on more than one occasion, my brothers and sister's lives. But I couldn't trust her with this. If I let this go on too long, she'd figure it out all by herself and I couldn't live with myself if my demons came back to hurt her.

"Hmm," she said, settling back. "You've got a friend in high places, then."

"Let's not," I said, but as I closed my eyes to exhale, Killian Thorne's deep blue eyes swam in front of me.

"Fine." She doubled over, struck by another coughing fit. I reached for the pitcher of water on the table beside her. Jeanie put up her hand.

"Not that. God, I'm so sick of ice water. I don't suppose you've got beer in that giant bag of yours?"

"No such luck. I saw a vending machine down the hall. How about a pop?"

Jeanie gave me a snarling smile. "As long as it's not diet."

"You got it. Fully leaded. I'll be right back."

I was grateful for the respite from Jeanie's blistering cross-examination. The woman had a way of getting me to confide just about everything in her. And she'd saved my life in more ways than one from the time I was thirteen on. I gave her a peck on the cheek and headed down the hall.

Maple Valley was one of the "nice ones" as far as facilities like this went. Clean. Cheery, with colorful artwork on the walls and big, open hallways. Whatever they'd done to soundproof this wing was working. I felt reasonably confident Jeanie would be able to get a nap uninterrupted by voices and the constant hum of ventilators and other medical machines.

I found the vending machine and worked on straightening the dollar I'd brought with me. I'd walked out of Jeanie's room with the yearbook still tucked under my arm. I balanced it and fed the bill into the machine. It spit right back out. I smoothed it even more and tried again.

"That's a tricky one." A deep male voice came from behind me, making the skin prickle between my shoulder blades.

I turned and found myself face to chest with Detective Eric Wray. He was off duty, dressed casually in a plain black t-shirt stretched taut over hard muscles and faded blue jeans. He was handsome, still, but more haggard, with dark circles rimming his gun-metal gray eyes. His dark hair looked slept on. He handed me a crisp, new dollar bill.

"Ah ... thanks," I said, trading him for my crumpled offering. I fed Eric's dollar into the machine and got rewarded with the clunking sound as an Orange Crush dropped into the bin.

"Meeting with a client?" he asked.

I smiled and reached for the pop can. "You know I couldn't tell you that even if I was."

Wray cast a furtive glance over his shoulder and it was in me to ask him why *he* was here. I didn't though. "You know, I didn't really get a chance to thank you for your help with the Ames family the other day. At the courthouse."

Eric gave me a sad smile and slid his hands into the back pockets of his jeans. "I'm sorry about that, actually. The Woodbridge county guys should have had a tighter lock on things that day. We may not always be on the same side of things, but you didn't deserve that."

"Well, your Delphi city guys had an even looser lock on things the last time I was in your building." I winced after I said it. So did Eric. It probably wasn't fair of me. He hadn't even been there the day of Aubrey's confession. This wasn't his case.

Eric put his hands up, palms out, in a gesture of mock surrender. "Listen, I won't pretend we're always going to be on the same side of things, but I respect your job."

Now I felt like a total ass. I bit my lip. "And I respect yours. But you can't tell me what happened was above board."

"Truce," he said. "If you stick around long enough, I have a feeling we'll cross paths on other stuff. Why don't we save our battles for then?"

I let out a breath. He was right and I was touchy. I tried a different approach.

"Dan Ames," I said. "You're friends, right?"

Eric didn't let his smile fall but side-stepped, heading down a short hallway from the vending machine. Whatever he meant to say, he clearly didn't want to be overheard. I followed.

Eric turned. "You've been gone for a while, huh? Big firm in Chicago?"

I smirked. Smooth evasion. "I have."

Eric pursed his lips and nodded, satisfied with that dribble of information. "Well, I suppose you're finding not much has changed around here. Everybody knows every-body. So yeah. I know Dan."

"It wasn't an accusation. Honest. If memory serves, you

were on the football team. Captain, right? I was just a lowly freshman."

"I remember you." He smiled. "Had your nose in a book."

His answer shocked me. Guys like Eric Wray didn't notice girls named Leary. "Nice guess," I said.

"No guessing. You went through a blue hair phase right?"

Okay. Now I was floored. Eric Wray had been about as big a deal as a guy could be back then. Homecoming King. Scholar athlete. All of it. I was pretty sure he'd been recruited by U. of M. until he had some kind of knee injury.

"Right," I answered. "And you had a Wendy Maloney phase. She made my life miserable." Wendy had been queen to his king. I'd been a favorite target of her and her cheerleader friends. Westlake snobbery at its very worst.

Eric's face fell, but he recovered just as fast. It was then that I saw the flash of gold on the ring finger of his left hand and the pieces fell in place.

"Oh. Sorry. Apparently not a phase. Well, I suppose we all had our own personal high school misery. Congratulations. Er ... tell Wendy I said hey."

Eric raised an amused brow but didn't torture me anymore. He just let me pull my own fat foot out of my mouth with his merciful silence.

"Looking to relive your glory days?" he asked, gesturing to the yearbook under my arm.

"What? Oh. No. I'm just ... doing a little ..."

"Little after our time though," he said, turning his head sideways so he could read the date on the book's spine. "Aubrey's year."

"I think so."

All traces of mirth melted from Eric Wray's face. "She's always been a good kid," he said, his tone growing serious. "Nose in a book. Kind of like you."

"You really think she did this?" I asked, surprised at my own boldness. Eric's eyes flashed. Maybe I'd asked one question too many. Still, I had a feeling this man knew more of the town secrets than most.

"I think it's time for me to let you finish your visit. I don't like being on Jeanie Mills's bad side." He gave me a wink.

Dammit. And there I was thinking I'd been the smooth one.

"See you around," I said.

Eric nodded and turned on his heel. I watched him disappear down the hall before heading back to Jeanie's room.

Chapter 14

Jeanie was sweating when I got back to her as she tried to climb back into bed. I put the yearbook and the pop down and went to help her.

"I've got it!" she shouted. I put my hands out, framing the air around her as she heaved herself up. When I was certain she wouldn't tip out of bed, I went for the pop, opened it, and stuck a straw through the hole.

"Thanks," she said, taking big gulps. "I was starting to think you got lost."

"I ran into someone," I said. "Eric Wray?"

"Ah," Jeanie said, putting the pop can on the table beside her. "Fridays at four. You can set your watch to it. I know half the nurses on this floor do."

"What's Fridays at four?"

"Honey, Eric Wray is the most ineligible bachelor in Delphi. Didn't he tell you why he's here?"

"He did not. I got the impression he wasn't planning on running into anyone he knew."

Jeanie shook her head. "I don't know why he bothers.

She doesn't know he's here. If she did, she wouldn't deserve to."

"Who? His mother?"

"No." Jeanie shifted her weight. I helped her readjust her blanket to cover her feet. I caught a glimpse of her expertly painted red toes and gave her a raised brow. No way she did those herself. The vision of her letting someone else give her a pedi put a smile on my face.

"Honey, Eric Wray comes to visit his piece-of-work wife every Friday. She's got a room down the hall from me. She's in a coma. I hear enough gossip when people think I'm sleeping. The bitch is never gonna wake up."

"Wait. Wendy? I'm lost. He married Wendy Maloney, right?"

"Right. Blonde. Big boobs. Snotty as they come."

"Geez, Jeanie. This is harsh even for you. Wendy's in a coma? How awful. How long?" The foot in my mouth was apparently fatter than I realized. Good God. I'd just told Eric to say "hey" to her for me.

Jeanie shrugged. "I think the better part of a year. She was cheating on that poor bastard forever. If that wasn't bad enough, she cleaned him out. Managed to drain his retirement fund and run up his credit cards. She was bad news all the way around. Word is her last and latest boyfriend dumped her. It was some other detective with the D.P.D. Can you believe that? She couldn't just cheat on him. Had to humiliate him too. Anyway, she had one too many beers down at Mickey's one night and got behind the wheel. Only good part of this story is that she didn't hurt anyone else besides the telephone pole at Newcomb and Laredo Streets."

"Good lord! That's awful! Wendy? I mean, we weren't exactly friends but she was just so beautiful."

Jeanie reached for her pop. "Anyway ... why don't you get

down to it? Tell me what you need. You've been hanging onto that silly yearbook since you got here."

I let out a sigh. "Someone left this for me. I was going to end my story with it."

Jeanie flapped a hand in front of her face. "Save the story. The cops have been sloppy with the press. Until your brilliant client waltzed in and started singing, their case against her was Swiss cheese, right? Full of holes?"

"Well, yeah. She was the last person seen with Coach D. Her phone was found near him. Let's assume she did in fact lure him to meet her in the park the night he was stabbed. And her texts to him raise a lot of questions."

I reached back into my briefcase and pulled out a single sheet of paper with the transcript of Aubrey's texts. Jeanie read it. Her eyes were still sharp enough she didn't need glasses. I knew her mind was even sharper. I filled her in on the rest of it, including my odd meeting with Kaitlyn and the yearbook showing up on Miranda's desk. Then I opened it to the one page that finally caught my eye. Jeanie took it from me.

"It's the girls' track team, Aubrey's junior year. There are some girls circled. Aubrey's not one of them but her class picture is circled in the same color pen. I have no idea what it means. I don't even know if Kaitlyn Taylor left this for me. Miranda swears she never had access to her desk. And there's no name in it or any signatures. Don't kids still sign these things?"

"Fuck if I know," Jeanie said, handing the yearbook back to me. "Who are the girls?"

I flipped to the page I'd dog-eared. Chelsea Holbrook. Lindsey Claussen. Danielle Ford. Chelsea had been a freshman in this book. Lindsey a sophomore. Danielle a senior. One girl from each class, including Aubrey.

"I really don't know."

Jeanie took the book again and flipped through it to the back. Her mouth turned down as she settled on one page. "You missed one," she said.

My stomach flipped as I saw what she meant. She had it open to the faculty pictures. Larry Drazdowski's face was also circled.

"Well, I'll be damned."

"You came here for a reason but it wasn't advice, Cass. Your gut's telling you something. What is it?"

I let out a hard breath. "I think she lied to the cops. Aubrey Ames is trying to protect somebody with that confession of hers. I just can't figure who or why."

"Did you try getting a hold of any of these other girls?"

"And say what? Oh ... I'm investigating a murder and your picture showed up on my desk circled in a yearbook?"

"If that's what your gut is telling you to do, yeah? Start with the Claussen girl. But what about Aubrey Ames? Where does it stand with her?"

"At a standstill. She's shut down, Jeanie. It's like she has no idea how serious the charges against her are. Jack LaForge isn't even offering a plea deal now. I can try to have her confession thrown out on a Sixth Amendment violation but I'm on shaky ground with it. She signed a written waiver. She said it into the damn camera. And I've got an entire town out for blood, including probably half the judges on the bench."

"You gotta get out of Delphi with this one."

"I plan to try. But that's *if* I'm willing to even keep going with this. I've had enough death threats to last me ... well ... forever."

Jeanie's face changed. Her penetrating gaze split me wide open. I'd been careless. If she'd asked me about the Thorne Group at that moment, I knew she'd see right through any lie I told.

Jeanie leaned back and scratched her chin. The corners of her mouth twitched as she tried to hold back a smile. How the hell could she find anything amusing in any of this?

"You've bonded with her, haven't you?"

"Bonded? What? She's like a squirrel caught in headlights. Terrified. Docile until the one day she wasn't and she marched into that damn detective's office. She doesn't even read like a murder suspect, Jeanie. She reads like a ... a victim."

Jeanie put her hands behind her head. It seemed like a victory gesture. When I caught her eyes again, I knew that's exactly what she thought too.

"You have to come at her hard, Cass. She's scared, but not of the right things. You've been babying her. She's not Vangie. She's not Matty. She's not your mother. Get her away from her parents and *make* her tell you the truth. *Somebody* out there is trying to tell you something. Let it start with her. And if she won't, then you wash your hands of it. Stop acting like her mother or her protector. You may have to be her enemy for a little while before you can really be her champion."

I opened my mouth to clap back, then shut it. *Be her enemy for a little while before you can be her champion.* Twenty-odd years ago, that's exactly what Jeanie had done for me.

"You're right."

"Of course I am. Now write down two of those girls' names for me. And have Miranda call my secretary. I still pay one. I need my laptop. I'll work on tracking them down. You deal with your client. Let's go to work."

And just like that, for the first time in four months, it felt good to be home.

Chapter 15

RAIN FELL in sheets as I made my way up Dan Ames's long driveway. My windshield wipers made a wide streak, catching a maple leaf beneath them. It was green still, but summer would give way to fall in just a few more weeks. In three short months, Aubrey would go on trial for her life.

The front door opened and Dan stepped out. He saw me and his step faltered. I left the car running and stepped outside, snapping open my umbrella.

"What are you doing here?" he asked, still standing under the protection of the porch.

"I need to talk to Aubrey alone."

Aubrey came to the door behind him, her face drained of all color.

"Cass ..."

"I haven't decided whether I'm staying on this case," I said. "No one in this family seems interested in following my advice. That's pretty much a deal breaker for me."

"Cass ... you have to. The court said ..." I put a hand up, cutting Aubrey off.

"Look, this isn't charity work for me. Coming this far

with you has cost me. If you want my help, it's going to have to come with my terms. You're over eighteen, Aubrey. Time to act like it. Let's take a little drive. Just the two of us."

Dan stormed off the porch. I stood my ground. There was movement in the window behind him. A curtain flapped as Diane Ames peaked out to see what was going on.

"This is *my* daughter. This is her future."

"Yes. It is. *Her* future. I told you the first day we met on this case I wasn't representing the family. Aubrey is my client. If I agree to stay on. If you think you need legal counsel, then I can refer you. But I don't go one step further until Aubrey and I have had a chance to talk."

The front door opened. Diane was still wearing a pink terry cloth robe. She stepped out and put a careful hand on her husband's arm. "Let her go, Dan," she said. "You can't protect her anymore."

He blanched then did a double take. Something about his wife's words seemed to hit him like a gut punch. Aubrey stepped off the porch.

I leaned forward and shielded her under my umbrella as the rain fell down even harder. She crossed her arms in front of her and walked slowly to the passenger door of my car. She gave one last look at her parents, then slid inside the car.

Aubrey sat in silence as I drove away from her parents' house and back toward town. She didn't say anything when I kept on going. But when I made the turn to Shamrock Park, she sat bolt upright in her seat and smacked her palm against the window.

She gave me a panicked look as I drove to the east side of the park near the entrance to the running trails. I cut my lights and pulled up perpendicular to a single park bench. A few yards to our right, mounds of wilting flowers and home-made signs decorated a twenty-foot circle around a street lamp.

I brought Aubrey to the spot where Larry Drazdowski died. The signs were telling.

R.I.P. Coach D

The One True Hero I'll Ever Know

Never Forgotten

Justice

The shrine went up the second the police tape came down.

"Why did you bring me here?" Aubrey was crying.

"Because you need to see it. You need to understand what we're up against."

"Come on," I said. "Get out of the car."

"What? It's raining!"

"We've got bigger things to be afraid of than rain." I got out of the car and slammed the door. My umbrella fought with me for a moment. The wind blew the rain sideways, so it wouldn't be much use anyway. Still, I walked to the make-shift shrine and stood there, reading the cards.

There were pictures of Larry Drazdowski smiling, laughing, hugging his players. One of them had even taped his state championship ring to one of the cards.

I stood out there for maybe five full minutes before Aubrey finally came to join me. She was soaked to the bone, her blonde hair plastered to her face. I couldn't tell anymore if those were tears on her cheeks or just more raindrops. Probably both.

"Life, Aubrey. Your life. First-degree murder means no parole. You're nineteen years old. Healthy. You could be in there seventy years. Eighty. You'd hold the record for the longest sentence ever served by a female inmate. Maybe any inmate. If you lived. Most don't. Either way, you'll die in there."

"Stop," she cried. "Just stop it. I know all of this."

"If you know all of this, then what the hell are you

doing?" I turned to her. "This man? They love him. They'll love him even more once they hear what happened to him in every awful detail at trial."

"There won't be a trial," she said. "I don't want one."

"It's not up to you. The prosecution isn't offering a plea deal. So, unless you're just planning to change your plea to guilty, this is over."

"But it's not first-degree murder. I didn't plan it. You said …"

"Did you kill him?" I practically screamed it. "The truth."

Aubrey sank to her knees. Her white jeans were soon covered with dark mud. I leaned down and covered her as best I could with the umbrella.

"It doesn't matter anymore," she said.

"It's going to matter a hell of a lot to the people who came out here and signed these cards. Tell me the truth, Aubrey. You're dying too. I can feel it pouring off you just like this rain."

"Stop it!"

I set the umbrella down. I put a hand out, meaning to grip Aubrey's shoulder. She pulled away so violently it nearly knocked me back. It was a visceral reaction. When her eyes met mine, hers looked like a scared animal's. Her truth flooded through me. Except I still needed her to say it.

"Did he touch you? Aubrey? Did Coach D …"

She put her hands up to her ears and started rocking back and forth on the ground. "Just stop it. It doesn't matter. They won't believe me. They never believe."

I stood up and went back to the car. The DHS yearbook lay in the back seat and I brought it back to Aubrey, shielding the pages with my umbrella as best I could.

Lindsey Claussen, Chelsea Holbrook, Danielle Ford. "Did you do this? Did you tell Kaitlyn to bring this to me?"

Aubrey's eyes went wide and she stopped rocking. "She shouldn't. No. Kaitlyn doesn't. I don't know where that came from."

"Did you kill him?!"

"No!" Aubrey screamed. "No!"

I let out a hard breath I'd been holding for weeks. I hooked a hand beneath Aubrey's arm and guided her back to the car. It seemed like she had no more tears left as she sagged against the dashboard. I kept a roll of paper towels in the back seat too. They were woefully inadequate but I tried to at least wipe Aubrey's face.

"Why?" I asked. "Why did you tell the police you did this?"

"You don't understand. Those cards? Those flowers? They won't believe me. I just wanted it all to be over."

"He hurt you," I said. "That night?"

Aubrey shook her head. "No. I just needed somebody to talk to. I was a sophomore. His office was next to the cafeteria and I just had a few minutes between classes."

My stomach started to roil. Once she started, a dam burst in Aubrey. Her words came out of her in an unbroken stream of rage, sadness, terror.

"He didn't say things like most grown-ups say. He didn't say things would be all right. He knew sometimes they weren't. I trusted him. He let us hold student meetings at his house sometimes. One time my dad was late picking me up. It was just a back rub. He said I was tense and I was. It didn't mean anything. It wasn't supposed to mean anything."

When Aubrey finally paused, I spoke as gently as I could. This had to come from her. I couldn't force her to say things she wasn't ready to admit. She turned to me, her eyes going hollow.

"I told him no. He was so big. So much stronger. Then I

thought maybe if I just closed my eyes and pretended I was somewhere else it would help. It did. The first time."

The first time. There were others. God. Of course there were others.

"You were a sophomore," I said. "Aubrey ... when was ..."

"He liked me. He said I was one of the special ones. Everyone thought I was so lucky that Coach D stuck up for me. They're so stupid. They are all so stupid."

"Where did it happen, Aubrey?"

She drew her knees up to her chin. Her tennis shoes were caked with mud.

"Every day sometimes. In the beginning. In his office. Sometimes at his house. I tried to stop him. Cass, I promise. I couldn't tell anybody. They all love him. He knew I was east-end trash to everybody else. Nobody would believe me. And they didn't."

The air burned in my lungs like acid. "Aubrey, who did you tell?"

She squeezed her eyes shut. "I tried to tell Mr. Sydney." Kevin Sydney was the athletic director. From the new tears that fell down Aubrey's cheeks, I didn't have to guess how that confession went.

"I'm so sorry, Aubrey. It wasn't your fault. You know that, right? You were a kid. We're talking about a grown man in a position of authority over you."

She sniffled. "I know that. I mean, I've read all the stuff. It's just ... it's different when it happens to you."

"Did it ever stop? You graduated a year ago," I said.

She nodded. "Kind of. But he kept calling me. I even changed my phone. But he'd show up at Dewar's. He didn't come near me in the same way, but it was like he wanted to make sure I wasn't ever going to say anything."

"Did you tell Kaitlyn?"

"She knows," Aubrey answered. "I told her a few months ago finally. She's been on me ever since to go to the police."

Aubrey needed a different kind of help than I could provide. I wanted to get her into a professional who worked with abuse survivors as soon as possible. But there was still one last truth she needed to tell.

"Why did you have her bring this yearbook to me?"

Aubrey shook her head. "I didn't. I swear. I made Kaitlyn swear never to say anything. I didn't want him coming after her too."

"But you told someone, didn't you?"

She leaned back against the seat. "I told my parents."

I didn't need to ask her how they reacted. A final truth slammed into place. "Aubrey, do you know who killed Coach D?"

Silence.

"Why did you want to meet with him that night?"

"I wanted to get him to admit everything on tape. I started to hear some rumors that maybe there was another girl at school he was messing around with. I couldn't live with that and not say something."

"Did your father know where you were going that night?" Dan Ames's rage took on new meaning.

"Don't," she said. "I can't lose him. I can't lose my dad over this. My mom and Sean can't lose my dad over this." One more piece slammed into place.

"Aubrey, tell me the truth. Was this your father? Is it him you are trying to protect? Honey, you can't. Do you think it's okay if they lose you?"

That did it. Aubrey broke. She broke, sobbing, her voice rising to a high-pitched, hysterical level. She smashed her fist against the window again and again.

"Shh. Aubrey!" I wanted to hug her but knew better than to touch her without her coming to me first. I wanted to tell her it would be okay, but I knew in my heart it might never be.

Then she did come to me. Aubrey collapsed in my arms and started to shake. I smoothed the hair from her face and let her cry herself out.

"Will you help me?" she asked, her voice raw and cracked.

I smiled down at her. "Yes," was my simple answer. But, God help me, I wasn't sure how.

Chapter 16

AT FOUR IN the morning in the middle of Dan Ames's living room, I watched a grown man break. I brought Aubrey back there when she finally felt strong enough to face her parents again. Her words were slow and quiet as she told her father why she confessed to a crime she hadn't committed.

"Baby," he whispered as his tears flowed. Diane Ames stood behind him, leaning against the wall at the entrance to the hallway. It was as if she thought that little bit of distance and an out could protect her from the words her daughter spoke.

"It's all my fault," Aubrey said. "If I hadn't told you. If I had just kept the secret everything could have gone back to normal."

"No," he said, shaking his head. "No. No. It's my fault. Mine and your mother's. We should have suspected. I let that monster into our lives. This wasn't for you to make right. It was my job."

He lifted his head, focusing his red-rimmed eyes on me. "I'll do it. I'll go to the police. I'll tell them I did it."

"No!" Diane cried. She didn't move from her position in the hallway, but her face turned white.

"Dan," I said. "I need the truth. All of it. Before you do anything, I want you to talk to your own lawyer. I can help you find …"

"Enough!" Diane's eye twitched as she moved into the room and sank into the seat beside her husband. "Not one more word. Dan didn't do this. Tell her. She wants the truth. He didn't do this. He has an alibi."

Diane Ames was coming apart at the seams. She was torn between protecting her husband and her child and right then, it didn't look like she could do both.

"No more lies," I said. "Tell me what you know."

Dan punched the side of the couch. When he looked up, he fixed his stare on Aubrey. "I'm so sorry, baby. I wish I'd done it. I should have. I wanted to. Cass, I told her I would. She heard me swear it. Only, I didn't get the chance."

"Where were you on the night of June 22nd?" I asked. "The whole truth."

Dan's shoulders dropped. "I was getting drunk at Mickey's."

"Did anyone see you there?" I asked.

"Everyone saw me there. We were watching the playoffs. Half the damn town was there. I was so damn angry. It started off with beer, then I moved to the hard stuff. Scotty was working the bar. I stayed all the way until closing. They took my keys and put them on the wall. Scotty put me in a cab and sent me home. I think it was after two in the morning."

I let out a sigh. "I can check that easily enough. Mickey's has security cameras all around the bar. The cab company will have records. If you're telling me the truth …"

"I am," Dan said, defeated. "But I wish like hell I wasn't."

"Aubrey," I said. "Who else knew about you and Coach D? Who did you tell?"

"I told Kaitlyn earlier this year. I don't know if she told anyone else. I don't think so. I made her swear not to. I told you, I tried to complain to Mr. Sydney, but he wouldn't meet with me. I kept trying to schedule it and his secretary kept calling to tell me he had to cancel. Then Coach D found out I was trying. He went nuts. He made it pretty clear no one would believe me. He told me he'd ruin my family if I tried. I believed him. He had the means."

"The yearbook," I said. "You have no idea who might have dropped that off in my office? And the girls. Lindsey Claussen, Danielle Ford, Chelsea Holbrook. Did you try talking to any of them?"

Aubrey shook her head. "I heard rumors. I tried talking to Lindsey. She's the only one I knew a little bit. I barely got more than Coach D's name out. She shut down pretty quick after that. She said she couldn't talk to me and hung up on me. I knew a couple of those other girls quit the track team so I tried to connect the dots. But it was so hard to know who to trust. Coach D was right. He said it would be my word against his. But I never said anything to Kaitlyn about Lindsey or the other girls."

"Dan," I turned to him. "How long have you known about what Coach D did to Aubrey?"

He and Diane exchanged a glance. "She told us at the end of April."

"And you didn't tell anyone? Not the police? No one?" I knew it sounded like judgment. Maybe it was, a little. But I had to know who else might have a motive to kill Larry Drazdowski. If the police were no longer going to investigate, I had no choice but to try.

Dan hesitated. Something flickered in his eyes and I got the distinct feeling he was about to lie to me again.

"Listen," I said. "There can't be any more secrets. The weight of them has come pretty close to burying this family already. You're in a hole and I need you to stop digging."

"Nobody," Dan said. "We kept it in the family. And I know I've failed my daughter in every way a father can. If I could take the rap for this now, I would. But they'll know I'm lying."

"You're right," I said. "No more lies. For better or worse, we all need to live with the truth now."

"What do we do now?" Diane asked. Sean Ames appeared in the hallway. He too had been crying. He must have been listening in all along.

I paused for a moment. I'd just asked this family for the truth. I owed it to them to give mine. "I don't know," I said. "I need some time to try and track down some leads. I have to be honest with you. We'll face an uphill battle even getting a jury to hear all of the claims you have against Coach D."

"What?" Dan erupted. "They have to know what he was. What he did."

I put a hand up. "I know that. But the prosecution will have a pretty strong argument to keep it out. Coach D isn't on trial. No matter how much of a monster he was, the fact remains, he was murdered."

"Then he did it," Aubrey said. "He won. Just like he said he would."

I leaned forward and took one of her hands in mine. "I said it would be an uphill battle. I didn't say we'd lose it."

"But you'll help?" she asked, her voice wavering. "You'll stick with me?"

"You bet your ass I will," I said, giving her a wink. "I don't know how, but I'm going to find a way."

Aubrey crumpled with relief. She sank against her father's shoulder. He caught my eye. This family was broken and bleeding. I was the only thing standing in the way of them and hell. But I could feel Aubrey's strength as she looked at me. God help us all, we might go right off a cliff together. To save her, it looked like I'd have to catch a killer all by myself.

Chapter 17

FRIDAY MORNING, things got even worse. Judge Castor, the circuit court judge who would preside over Aubrey's trial, shot down both of my motions. He refused to remove the case to another county, and he wouldn't throw out her confession.

I didn't know how to read Felix Castor yet. Since starting back up in Delphi, this was only the fourth time I'd appeared in front of him. The words I'd heard used to describe him were things like sharp-shooter, no-nonsense, erudite. Also, that he hated lawyers and rarely took the bench without already knowing precisely how he would rule. In this instance, I was toast before I said one word.

Castor sat on the bench and twirled the ends of his handlebar mustache. He was deeply tanned from his weekend golf games. It was small comfort, but he did throw me one small bone as he glared at Jack LaForge.

"Jack, this is horseshit and you know it," he said. "You gonna stand there and tell me you couldn't figure out how to give Ms. Leary a call before all this went down?"

Jack's jaw dropped as he shuffled papers on the table.

Everyone in this room knew the answer, though I doubted
Jack LaForge would ever admit it. But the judge had already
ruled. The confession would be admitted at trial. The jury
would hear it all. Judge Castor's outrage was small comfort as
he banged his gavel and called his next case.

I got the hell out of that courtroom as quickly as I could.
Jeanie was waiting for me at my office. She took the news
about Castor's ruling in stride. Then she dropped a bomb of
her own.

"You're absolutely sure?" I asked her for about the fourth
time. She was getting annoyed with me, but I felt like I
needed to hear her say it again. Each time, it stabbed
through my heart just a little more and I hoped it wasn't true.

Jeanie coughed into her fist. She sat at the conference
room table. Miranda kept popping in trying to make her
drink water.

"Cass ... I'm sure. It's better you don't know my methods.
But yeah. This information is ironclad. And truthfully, it
wasn't that hard to find out. I just ..."

"Right," I said, holding a hand up. "Better I don't know."
Jeanie worked with an investigator who had less than scrupu-
lous morals. I only knew his name was Pete but that might
not even be true. She'd been looking into the names circled
in that yearbook.

"Chelsea Holbrook is in the wind somewhere; her family
moved to Tennessee right after she graduated. They won't
return my calls. Lindsey Claussen was a track star all through
junior high. She crapped out her Freshman year though.
Danielle Ford committed suicide two years ago. I've still got a
call into her mother. She moved to Florida to the Villages. I
know somebody close. But Claussen. That's the low-hanging
tree you wanna bark up."

I smiled. Jeanie certainly knew how to mix a metaphor.

"And she's at Mickey's," I said. "Aubrey already told me that."

"You still sure she isn't the one who left this book for you?"

"I don't know anything anymore."

"Well, it looks like you need to make a trip to Mickey's," Jeanie said.

"Looks like. You up for a road trip?"

"Wish like hell I could," Jeanie said. "I could use a beer. But no, I need to get on home."

Jeanie had just finished her last course of chemo and was discharged from Maple Valley last week. She was putting on a brave front, but I knew she was terrified about her scans in two weeks. Anyone would be. She didn't know I knew exactly when her appointment was. Like it or not, I planned to be right by her side.

"Just call me after you know something," Jeanie said, sighing. "I'm tired as fuck."

Chapter 18

LATER THAT NIGHT, I pulled into the parking lot of Mickey's Bar. The place was packed like always. There was an MMA on pay per view and Mickey's catered hard to that crowd. I checked Lindsey Claussen's yearbook picture one more time. She was sixteen in it. She'd be twenty-one now.

I spotted Lindsey right away. She'd barely changed at all from her yearbook picture except for one thing. As she whipped her ponytail around, I saw she'd dyed the end of it a bright blue against her dark brown hair. She served a tray of drinks to a booth near the bar. She was pretty. Stunning even, with wide-set dark eyes and a dimple in her right cheek. It struck me for a moment how much she looked like Aubrey. Tall, but reed thin with a willowy quality to her movements. A pit formed in my stomach. Was I looking at Coach D's type?

I asked the hostess to seat me in Lindsey's section. A booth had opened up in the corner. It would be perfect, far away from the big-screen TVs broadcasting the fight. No one would be paying attention to this part of the bar.

I waited a few minutes and Lindsey came by with a menu

and a glass of water. She had a bright smile but it faltered as soon as she met my eyes. She knew me. I thought I would have to work my way into a conversation with her. Maybe even use today as a sort of icebreaker. But Lindsey nearly dropped her tray before she got a word out. She tried to recover and plastered her smile back on.

"Hi," I said. "So I guess I don't need to introduce myself."

Lindsey looked over her shoulder. The undercard match was just getting started and this section of the bar had all but cleared out.

"Yeah. I saw you on the news or whatever."

Or whatever.

"Look, I know you're working. And I can see by the expression on your face how you feel about seeing me. But I'd really like to set up a time to talk to you."

Lindsey set my water glass down. "I don't ... there's nothing ... um ... why?"

Here was the thing. How to broach it. My lead as far as Lindsey was about as solid as asking a Magic 8-Ball. God, I wanted to be wrong. For the first time since Aubrey broke, I realized it would probably be a hell of a lot easier if Coach Drazdowski were truly just an innocent murder victim and Aubrey a dumb kid who'd made a horrible choice.

I went right in, knowing this girl couldn't hide anything from her eyes.

"I know you went to Delphi. And I know you ran for Coach Drazdowski when he helped out with the girls' track team. I just want to ask you a few questions."

One beat. That's all it took. There'd been a part of me desperately hoping I'd hit a dead end tonight. But Lindsey Claussen's complexion changed. Purple blotches spread over her collarbone, rose up her neck, and settled in her cheeks.

God. She shook her head rapidly then brought her tray up, holding it in front of her like a shield.

"I can't," she said. "You aren't ... there isn't."

Then Lindsey staggered backward, dropped her tray, and took off out the back door of the bar.

"Son of a bitch," I muttered as a cheer rose from the main crowd. One fighter was on the mat. The other, bloodied and smiling, rose his fist in the air. I got up and followed Lindsey outside.

I found her throwing up beside a big blue dumpster. She saw me coming and put a hand up, trying to ward me off.

"Lindsey, I'm not here to upset you. I'm sorry about that."

"Who," she asked, wild-eyed. "Who told you to come talk to me?"

"I represent Aubrey Ames. I mean, I think you already know that."

"Listen," I said. "I can file a subpoena. If Aubrey's case goes to trial, I can make you testify. I don't want to do that though. I just want to have a conversation."

"Look, I'm done with this. I don't know anything about Coach D. I barely knew Aubrey. Whatever happened. Whatever she's saying. It's got nothing to do with me. If you call me at that trial I'll plead the fifth. You can't make me say anything."

"Lindsey, I understand you're upset. You can't just plead the fifth to keep from saying *anything*. It doesn't work that way."

I approached her cautiously. She trembled, just like I'd seen Aubrey do a dozen times. If I was right, if Larry Drazdowski did something inappropriate with her, I didn't want to be ... *couldn't* be some other person trying to back her into a corner. But I saw it in her eyes. She was absolutely terrified.

Like just the mention of Coach D's name conjured some ghost for her.

"Who did you try to talk to?" I asked, pretending I knew more than I did. "Was it Mr. Sydney? The athletic director?"

Lindsey's eyes flickered. I sensed I'd hit the nail on the head. Her posture changed, becoming more relaxed, or maybe it was defeat.

"You have no idea what you're kicking up. I didn't either until it was too late. Do you know I had a full ride? To M.S.U.? And just like that, it went up in smoke."

I narrowed my eyes. Lindsey was talking two beats ahead of me. "You're saying Sydney got in the way of your scholarship?"

"Well, it happened the very next day after I tried to talk to him. Didn't feel like a coincidence. So here I am slinging beers, just like Coach said I'd be. He wins. Even dead. He wins. And I'm done letting him. I need you to just leave me alone."

"Lindsey, Coach D can't hurt you anymore. You know that, right?"

Her tears finally fell. "Yes. He can. They all still love him out there. Open your eyes, Ms. Leary. I can't help you. I'm sorry."

The door opened behind me and another waitress popped her head out. "Linds, you need to get back in here. You've got four tables asking for you."

Before I could stop her, Lindsey Claussen brushed past me. I felt like I'd just taken one step forward and one step back. But with just four months before Aubrey's scheduled trial date, time was literally running out.

I made my way back into the bar. The crowd near the flat screens roared as the main event got underway. They seemed unusually raucous. The sound of breaking glass came from my left. Then the sea of bodies shifted, pressing back against the bar.

Scotty Teague, the bartender, reached up and started ringing a gold bell suspended above him. Long ago, he'd been the one to call the house when someone needed to come and pick up my drunken father. More than once, Joe or I had driven the truck down here to pick him up even before either of us were licensed.

"Break it up!" someone yelled. It seemed the MMA bout had inspired a couple of the drunks.

"Kiss my ass!" A familiar voice rose above the chaos and my heart fell.

The crowd parted and two combatants stumbled out of the circle. One had a height advantage, but his opponent was more nimble on his feet. The tall guy took a hard swing, landing a blow straight across the shorter guy's chin. A string of blood arched from his mouth and splattered right across my chest.

"Son of a bitch," I muttered for the second time tonight. I looked up. It was my brother, Matty. Matty took a ready stance, fists up, ready to pound the other drunk right back to the ground. His eyes were glassy though, and he swayed to the side.

"You!" Scotty Teague held a baseball bat and pointed it right at me. "He's yours, ain't he? He's finished. I told him last week he was on his last chance."

Matty's opponent started to rally. He lunged at Matty, catching him square in the chest. Matty tripped over his feet and landed hard on his ass. I grabbed a pitcher of beer from a nearby table and poured it over both of them.

Matty tried to stand and slipped in the liquid. I pulled a fifty-dollar bill out of my wallet and flicked it at Scott. "This cover him?"

"For tonight," Scott said. "But I meant what I said. He

crosses that threshold again I'm having his ass thrown in jail. Probably do him good."

"Get up," I hissed at Matty. He was just now figuring out it was me.

"Hey, ssssiisss," he said. "I won!"

"I don't even wanna know." I tried to hook my arm under his and haul him up. My heel slid in the beer and I nearly went down in it. Another arm caught me just in time and pulled me back.

"Allow me." Eric Wray let go of me and grabbed Matty by the shoulder. Eric pulled him up like he weighed nothing. Luckily, Matty's blood alcohol level kicked in and he went from angry to mellow.

"You're a fucker," he said to Eric, pointing at his nose. But the fight was out of him. Matty shot Eric a lopsided grin.

"Yeah. You're not the first to point that out," Eric said.

"You okay?" he asked me.

"Yeah. I just ... can you help me get my brother's sorry ass to my car?"

"Don't plan on driving him home." A shout came from the bar. It belonged to one of Matty's high school friends, Chris Browning. He looked just about as drunk.

"Why's that?" Eric asked. Matty had more or less sunk into Eric's side and was letting him walk him toward the door.

"Tina threw him out again last night," Chris answered. "Lucky asshole, that woman is a cu—"

"Save it!" I yelled, cutting him off.

"Lead the way," Eric said.

I mouthed thank you as Eric dragged my brother out of the bar.

Chapter 19

MATTY DIDN'T struggle much as Eric slid him into the passenger seat of my car and strapped him in. By the time we shut the door on him, he was already snoring.

"Thanks again," I said. "You seem to have a knack for showing up at the damndest times."

Eric leaned against the car. A snort from Matty drew his attention for a moment, but when my brother slumped back against the window, Eric turned back to me.

"Small town. And I've noticed drama has a way of following you around." He ran a hand through his thick dark hair making the front stand up at a peak. I had the urge to smooth it over but caught myself. The last thing I needed was Eric Wray getting the wrong idea. Plus, regardless of his wife's medical status, Eric Wray was a married man.

"I suppose so. I'm not asking for it though."

The corner of Eric's mouth lifted in a smile. "You sure about that? I saw you talking to Lindsey Claussen. Then she ran out the back door looking pretty upset. Anything I can help you with?"

He was good. He *looked* harmless enough with that small-town charm and aw-shucks swagger. But Eric Wray had the mistrustful eye of a career cop, and he was pumping me for information. There was no such thing as innocent small talk where this guy was concerned.

"Nope," I said. "You've helped plenty. I better get my brother somewhere less ... uh ... controversial so he can sleep it off."

"Doesn't sound like you can take him home," Eric said.

This got my back up. It was an old defense mechanism. Matty could be a shithead, but he was my shithead. It may not exactly be judgment in Eric's tone, but my overprotective-big-sister instincts kicked in.

"Well, like I said, you've helped plenty. I can take it from here."

"He gets pretty rough sometimes," Eric said. "I'd feel better if you let me follow you."

I bit my bottom lip. I wanted to tell Eric to back off. Tell him he didn't know what the hell he was talking about. Hell, with the gossip mill running strong in this town, Wray likely already knew about Matty's temper tantrum at my office a few weeks ago.

"I appreciate you looking out. Really. But I've got this. I've been handling drunken Leary men since I was little. I'll let him sleep it off on my couch."

Eric chewed the inside of his cheek, considering my speech. Something sparked in his eyes, but whatever it was, he left it unsaid.

"Just ... have a care, Cass. I don't want to see you get hurt."

"We talking about my brother or something else?"

Eric shrugged. "He's a good man. Or can be. Matty. He sure tries awful hard. Did he ever tell you I tried to get him in with the D.P.D?"

"Um ... no. He didn't mention that. When?"

"Two, maybe three years ago. He got pretty far ... then ..."

Eric's voice and gaze wandered off. He didn't have to finish the sentence, I knew where it would lead. Where it always led with my dad and Matty. None of them could ever get past their demons long enough to change their lives.

"Thanks for that too, then," I said. I dug my keys out of my purse. "I really need to get him home. I'll see you around, Eric."

He nodded. "You let me know if you need anything." The front door of Mickey's swung wide open and the roar of the fight crowd rose.

"Better get back in there," I said. "Scotty might need more help than I do if that fight goes the wrong way."

"Yeah," Eric said, pushing himself off my car. I stuck out a hand to shake his. He smiled down at me and took it. Then he headed back into the bar, leaving me to finish cleaning up Matty's mess.

Chapter 20

I never even had to call Joe. It was like we had some sort of Leary family bat signal. By nine o'clock the next morning, I heard his truck door slam shut and he made his way up the stairs.

Matty was still sleeping it off on the couch. I had a pot of coffee brewing. I swung the side door open before Joe could knock.

"Shit," Joe said as he stepped inside and saw Matty face down on the couch. I meant to put him in the back bedroom but didn't quite have the muscle.

"Tell me it's not true," I said, pouring myself a cup of coffee. Joe stayed in the foyer, hesitant to come in all the way.

"Jesus, which thing?"

"Tina," I said, blowing over the steam in my cup. I held up an empty mug for him. He still hadn't come fully inside.

"You waiting for an invitation?" I asked. Joe gave a furtive look over his shoulder. I leaned down so I could see out the side window. His truck was still running and my niece Emma was in the front seat looking glum.

"Yeah. I know the timing on this sucks, but I was kind of

hoping I could drop Emma off to stay with you for the week-end." Joe looked back over his shoulder.

"Oh for Pete's sake. Tell her to come inside. You both look miserable and Matty's eventually going to wake up. Let's deal with one crisis at a time, shall we? Katy throw you out too?"

Joe shrugged. "Not exactly. She and Emma got into it last night. I got her out of the house to avoid the ultimatum I know is coming."

Poor Joe. I loved his wife Katy, truly. She'd helped straighten Joe's shit out and for that I'd be forever grateful. She was rigid though. He'd never had someone to help him set healthy boundaries in his life. But Emma was a problem between them. She reminded me so much of my sister Vangie. Stubborn, forceful. Moody as hell. But she was whip-smart and gorgeous. It would take everything Joe had to keep Emma straight. She was a master at playing her stepmother off my brother.

"I've got a job in Chelsea this weekend. I can't really take her with me."

I stepped around Joe and opened the side door. "Emma, come inside," I yelled. Emma's face brightened a little and I felt that same pang I always did when I looked at her. She was just like Vangie all right. And they were both the spitting image of my mother with dark-blonde, straight hair and eyes that burned emerald fire.

"Hey, Aunt Cass," Emma said, giving me a soft smile. She'd grown at least two inches taller than me in the last year or so. I eyed Joe over her shoulder. Emma went straight for the kitchen and poured her own cup of coffee.

We congregated around the kitchen table. "You gonna let him stay here?" Joe asked, tearing a donut in half. They were from yesterday. Miranda had brought them into the office and insisted I bring them home.

"Why not?" I said. "For a day or two anyway. You cool with that, Emma? Looks like we're going to have a little family reunion weekend. Something tells me you wouldn't say no to an air mattress either, Joe."

Joe froze, mid-chew, and I knew I'd hit the nail on the head. Well, shit. Whatever falling out he'd had with Katy over Emma was worse than he was letting on. I knew it would blow over. No matter what else happened, Katy was head over heels in love with my brother. In Matty and Tina's case, I worried his nine marital lives had probably run out.

"Yeah," Joe admitted. "Maybe."

"Don't blame me," Emma said, reaching for her own donut. "Katy's gone psycho this time."

"Enough," Joe said. "I'm so sick and tired of the two of you going at it. You might want to try meeting her halfway."

Emma let out a sound that cleared my sinuses and jarred her Uncle Matty awake. He tumbled off the couch, his hair sticking up at odd angles. "Halfway!" Emma screeched. "Halfway? She took away my phone and my laptop. How am I supposed to get any homework done?"

"School doesn't start for a week," Joe said. Emma turned away from him.

Matty walked heavy-footed into the kitchen. His eyes were bloodshot but focused. He sported dark stubble and his shirt was ripped from his little brawl last night. He leaned over Joe and grabbed a donut.

"Ugh," Emma said, "you stink."

My brother made a credible impression of a grizzly bear then promptly gave his niece a whisker rub. She squealed again.

"Coffee's fresh," I said. "And there's extra toothbrushes in the downstairs bathroom."

Our grandmother had always made a point of keeping travel toothbrushes and hotel soaps stocked in the guest bath-

ROBIN JAMES

room. She said she never knew when someone would want to spend the night at the lake house and she wanted to be ready. It was a hard habit to break.

"Got anything stronger than this?" Matty asked as he lifted the coffee pot and reached for a mug from the cupboard.

"Stick with the coffee," Joe said. "Give us all a break."

If Emma hadn't been sitting there, Matty might have gone at him. But she *was* there and even in his disheveled state, my brother knew to sidestep teenage girl drama when it was right in front of him. He poured his coffee and plunked down on the chair beside me, straddling it backward. He shoved another donut in his face.

"So," I said. "I don't suppose I could get you to fix the roof on the shed while you're here. The rain's coming in."

"Can I take the boat out?" Emma asked, hopeful.

"You're not on vacation," Joe said. "You're going to make yourself useful. Rake the beach after you finish your donut."

I drew my coffee cup up to my face to hide my smile. He sounded just like Grandpa. We'd all heard him say those same words to each of us when we came here looking to escape the drama at home.

God, it was good to have them here. I was sorry that Joe and Matty were having trouble at home. In Matty's case, he was heading at top speed for a wall that could destroy him. But right now, he was home and he was mine. I couldn't keep him out of trouble, but like my mother before me, I never stopped thinking I could try.

I wanted it to be easy. At that moment, I wished I could erase all the drama of the last month and the years before. We could just sit here, enjoying each other's company. The moment I thought it, I realized maybe it could be that easy. Just for one afternoon. Late summer and the sun was already

146

shining. It would be a perfect day on the lake and I craved the strength I drew from these boys. Emma too.

There was a thump at the front door as the mailman slipped my mail through the slot. Two dogs barked down the street. Emma got up and went to the door. She came back with a pile of junk and a small brown package that looked like the kind they send check refills in, though I hadn't ordered any.

"Ugh," Emma said. "Aunt Cass, this stinks."

She set the package on the table. The smell hit all three of us at once.

"Fuck!" Matty said as he scooted away from the table and retched near the sink.

Joe grabbed the package. It was addressed to me but my name was spelled wrong. "Cassie Leary." No one ever called me that.

"I'm going to open this outside," he said, plugging his nose. I followed him. He took out a pocket knife and opened the package.

"Ugh!" Joe dropped it to the ground. "It's dog shit."

A postcard fluttered to the ground beside it, landing face up. Written in a scrawling hand with a red sharpie, the note read, "R.I.P. Coach D. Die you piece of shit, bitch."

"Lovely," I said. I grabbed two garbage bags, picked up the offending package with one and shoved it all in the other, then took the thing to the dumpster on the other side of the house.

When I got back, Joe was pacing in the living room. "This is nuts, Cass. You've gotta get out of this. That girl confessed. It's over."

"Joe …"

"No!" he shouted. "How much more has to happen for you to get it?"

"Get what?"

Emma sat on the couch. She grew strangely quiet. Matty came out of the bathroom. He brushed his teeth and his color looked a lot better. Now I just needed to get some water into him.

"They love that man," Joe said. "Don't you get it? There's no win in this for you, Cass. Even if by some miracle you get that girl off, they'll crucify you. If she's convicted, they'll crucify you. You'll always be the bitch who defended Coach D's murderer. He's a damn saint."

My stomach turned. A saint. I wanted so badly to tell him what I knew. I couldn't. I could never reveal Aubrey's confidence.

"It's more complicated than you think," I said. "But you have to trust me. I know what I'm doing. And I'm too far in to back out now."

"For what? Fifty bucks an hour or whatever shit pay the county hands out? No, you're not too far in. You can back out. No one will blame you. Hell, they'll cheer you."

"I'll blame me," I said. "I'm doing the right thing, even if you can't see it. He was no saint." I muttered the last bit under my breath, thinking none of them caught it.

"Jesus." Joe shook his head. "What is it with the women in this family?" He shot a look at Emma. She'd gone sheet white.

It hit me like a ton of bricks. She caught my eye and her color drained even more.

"Emma," I said, ignoring my brother for the moment. "What is it?"

She lifted one shoulder and her gaze went out toward the lake.

"Emma?" I asked again.

Joe had finally stopped pacing.

"Honey," I said, my heart racing. I felt like she and I were on a different frequency than the other people in this room. "You can tell me."

"I don't know," she said. "It's just ... I don't think everyone thought Coach D was a saint, Dad."

"What are you talking about?" Joe asked.

Emma shrugged. "I don't know. I just ... you hear stuff. Especially now."

"What did you hear?" I asked.

"I don't know. He just ... I always thought he was kind of creepy. And I'm not the only one. It's just ... it's not the kind of thing anyone would ever say to too many people. You know?"

"Emma," I said, sinking down to the seat beside her. "Honey, I think it's time for you to tell me exactly what you mean."

Chapter 21

JOE SPENT the weekend on my couch. Matty took the back bedroom and Emma slept in the guest bedroom upstairs by me. By Monday morning, I was no longer just worried about Matty staying on the wagon. Joe tried to keep his anger from me, spending hours at the end of the dock and tinkering with the boat.

I put on my best navy-blue power suit, stuffed my laptop in my messenger bag and headed out to the end of the dock to join my brother. Matty and Emma were still asleep. Joe watched a group of mallards glide across the lake as he white-knuckled his coffee cup. He didn't say a word at first as I stood beside him.

"You're not going to let this go, are you?"

I had a speech all prepared. Now, as we stood together watching the sun come up, it all just went out of me. I settled for a simple, "No."

"Goddammit," Joe muttered. He threw a stone across the water, getting five perfect skips with an expert flick of his wrist. I could never get it to do that.

"This guy, Drazdowski. He was bad, wasn't he?"

I swallowed hard. Joe had sat patiently while Emma tried to explain the vibe she'd always gotten from him. There was nothing overt. But she said she didn't like the way he looked at her and some of her friends. One day when she was a sophomore, Coach D had come up to her in the hallway and asked her to meet with him during her homeroom. He'd caught wind of the fact she wanted to try out for the track team. She never went though. One of her other friends had quietly told her not to take the meeting but never explained why.

"I think he might have been, Joe. Yes."

Joe worked the muscles of his jaw. His face flushed. "Did he do something to that girl? To Aubrey?"

I adjusted the strap of my messenger bag on my shoulder. "You know I can't answer that."

He skipped another rock.

"I would have killed him," he said quietly. "If that asshole had ever laid a finger on Emma. God. Are you telling me that was what was going on?"

"I'm not telling you anything."

He kicked the dock post, making the whole structure sway. "This can't be happening. Jesus. That's why she confessed. I mean, if Aubrey didn't really do this. If Dan Ames found out that fucker was messing with his little girl ... it makes sense, Cass. I would have done the same thing. Except, why the hell is he letting her take the fall for this now?"

"Joe ..."

He put a hand up. "Yeah. You can't talk about it. But dammit, as much as I want to know the truth ... as much as I'd want to protect Emma ... I want to protect you too. The people in this town might never believe it. They'll keep coming after you."

"Maybe. But maybe that's also why I'm here. I don't

152

know if I believe in fate. But I *do* know I'm all Aubrey Ames has."

As we stood there looking out at the water, I felt like the lake itself was listening.

"It *is* going to get worse before it gets better, Joe," I said. "And it starts today. I've got an appointment to meet with Kevin Sydney."

Joe took a step back. For a second, he looked gut-punched. "The athletic director. Shit. He's probably the second biggest hero in this town for hiring that motherfucker, Drazdowski. He's going to push back."

"Maybe. Maybe not. But like I said. I'm going to go do my job. Wish me luck, brother."

I went up on my tiptoes and kissed Joe's cheek. He felt hard as granite. I loved him. We'd had each other's backs since the day we were born. It had cost us both plenty. As I turned and walked up the dock to my car, I knew the price of this case was about to get very steep indeed.

KEVIN SYDNEY HAD BEEN the Delphi High School athletic director for twenty-eight years. Two away from retiring. He wasn't from Delphi and a lot of the people in this town held that against him at first. Until Larry Drazdowski started winning basketball state championships.

The hallway to his office was lined with tournament championship plaques and the pictures of Hall of Fame graduates, almost all members of one of Coach D's teams. There were no Learys on that wall. No Ameses either. I walked outside Sydney's office door and cracked a smile. Eric Wray's senior photo smirked down at me. He'd made it up there for his football prowess and his spiky dark hair screamed mid-nineties cool kid.

The office door opened and I straightened my back. Sydney's secretary was about my age. Pretty, with a slim build and wide, doe eyes. Her ID badge read Karen Larsen.

"He's got a few minutes for you now," Karen said. Her tone was cool, not entirely unfriendly, but I knew this visit wasn't welcome. I had every suspicion the only reason Sydney even agreed to this meeting was because Jack LaForge told him to. Though he'd won the motion to suppress, he wouldn't want to give Judge Castor a reason for me to bitch that he was impeding discovery.

Karen led me into the inner sanctum of Kevin Sydney's office. The eight state championship basketball trophies took up one wall behind a glass case.

"Thanks for seeing me," I said, extending a hand to shake Sydney's. He rose from behind his desk. A former college basketball player himself, Sydney topped six foot five with broad hands and a grip that crushed mine. He had just a few wispy strands of hair combed above his forehead.

"I don't have a lot of time," he said. "I'm not sure what help I can give you. I didn't really know your client." He said the word client as if it burned in his mouth.

I took a breath, knowing my next statement would turn the meeting into something else. "Mr. Sydney, I appreciate your schedule. And I won't take up much of it. But I'm not actually here to talk about my client. I'm here to talk about Larry Drazdowski."

Sydney leaned back, keeping his face a mask. I reached into my bag and handed him a copy of the subpoena I knew his office had already received. I'd asked for a copy of Drazdowski's detailed personnel file. Sydney's eyes flickered, but he didn't look at the paper as he took it from me.

"What do you want to know?" he said, leaning back in his chair; he hooked his hands behind his head.

"I want to know about any complaints you might have received. Disciplinary action. That sort of thing."

Sydney's face betrayed nothing. "He was a basketball coach. A great one. Larry dedicated his entire life to kids. Saved a lot of them from wasting their lives at the bottom of a beer bottle."

His eyes narrowed and I recognized the dig for what it was, a veiled shot at my father and brothers. I was used to it. I kept my own mask of a smile on my face.

"I know this is a difficult time for everyone," I said. "And I also know I'm not the most popular citizen of Delphi right now. But I hope you can appreciate that I'm doing my job, Mr. Sydney."

Kevin Sydney's eyes sparked with rage and he leaned far forward, planting his palms on the top of his desk. "I don't appreciate anything about you, Miss Leary. I lost a good friend two months ago. A great man. No, he wasn't a perfect man. None of us are. But I know what you're trying to do. You think you can dig something up and smear Larry's name. It's what all you bottom-feeder defense lawyers do. I don't have to help you."

"No," I said. "But you do have to cooperate. I can promise you, I'm not trying to smear anyone. I'm just trying to get to the truth."

"The truth is that Eastlake-trash client of yours murdered a man I loved like a brother. She admitted it. And yet, here you sit, talking to me about truth and every second that goes by you rack up another billable hour that my tax dollars pay."

Eastlake trash. Well, there it was. And it took him less than five minutes to get to it. Sydney started to rise from his chair. As I sat across from him, he towered over me. I craned my neck up and up to meet his eyes. A cold chill went through me. I wasn't some teenage girl, unsure of herself. And I wasn't looking for this man's help. Others had.

"Be that as it may," I said, not looking away from him, "I work in a system that benefits all of us. You can call me any name you'd like. Believe me, I've faced far worse, Mr. Sydney. And you haven't answered my question. I asked you if Mr. Drazdowski ever had complaints filed against him or disciplinary action taken."

Sydney slowly sat down, but the look of contempt didn't leave his face. I tried to give him the benefit of the doubt. Whatever else he was, this man had lost someone he considered a friend. To murder. And Aubrey had done everything she could to make this town believe she was guilty. Still, I couldn't shake the vibe that anyone questioning Coach D to him may have met the same cold stare.

"A few helicopter parents here and there." Sydney flapped a dismissive hand. "Pissed their precious special son didn't get more playing time."

"That's all?" I asked. "And what kind of record keeping would have taken place? Do you make a note of anytime a student or parent has an issue? If so, how are those records maintained? Who has custody of them?"

"I'll answer your subpoena. But I can tell you, you're wasting your time with this."

Again, he hadn't answered my question.

"Mr. Sydney, I'm not trying to smear an innocent man." It was a true statement, but you could be damn sure I'd go after a guilty one. "I'm just trying to get a clear picture of who may have wanted to harm Mr. Drazdowski. You can believe me or not, but I want the person who killed him to get justice just as much as you do."

Sydney shook his head. "And you can sit there with a straight face and tell me you don't think that Ames girl did it."

He said "Ames girl" with such contempt it practically stung me. "Like I said, I'm trying to get a clear picture. A complete picture. That's all."

"I'll have Ms. Larsen copy the damn file. If I find one thing from it splashed over the local paper, I'll ..."

I snapped a little. "You'll what?" I asked. It was my turn to lean far forward and get in Kevin Sydney's face. I could have asked him about Lindsey or Danielle or Chelsea. Something made me hold back. The less he knew about where I was headed, the better. But I knew the next subpoena I would write.

Sydney set his jaw to the side, considering me. Then he settled back into his chair. "You're a piece of work, all right. Your client deserves you. If that's all you need, I've got other things to do. Your time is up."

"Thank you," I said, rising. I held out my hand to shake his. Sydney didn't stand and ignored the gesture. I smiled and turned on my heel.

As I opened the door, Karen Larsen rose from her desk. She gave me that same bright smile but there was something uncertain about the way she looked at her boss. I wondered how thick the walls were at Delphi High School.

"All set," I said, nodding to Karen. She stepped around her desk, tripping as she caught her heel in the plush carpet. I reached out a hand to help her.

"Oh," she said. "Thanks." She reached back and grabbed a ticket from her desk drawer. "You'll need this to get out of the parking lot."

I palmed the ticket and thanked her. Kevin Sydney had stepped around his desk and shut his office door hard. Karen gave it a nervous glance then went back to her own desk.

Grateful to be getting the hell out of there, I showed myself out. It wasn't until I got in my car and approached the parking gate that I really looked at the ticket Karen

Larsen had given me. On the back of it, there was a tiny square sticky note attached to it. In purple ink, it read, "Look in your own backyard."

My heart jumped as the red-and-white striped parking gate opened, beckoning me to leave.

Chapter 22

MY HEART THRUMMED with both excitement and dread as I drove down Kitchem Lane. My own backyard. Was that note even meant for me? I fumbled with my Bluetooth speaker and dialed Jeanie's number. She answered on the second ring.

"How did it go?" she asked by way of hello.

"Interesting," I said, then quickly filled her in on the highlights of my meeting with A.D. Sydney.

"Can't say I'm surprised. That's a good ole boys club if ever there was one. What about the principal?"

"She's still not returning my calls. Plus, this will only be her second year there. The last one, Rick Sullivan, he was there for over twenty years, but he passed away from colon cancer the summer before last. I did come away with one potential lead though."

"Oh?"

I told Jeanie about the mysterious sticky note. She didn't say anything for a long beat. Then she whistled low on the other end of the phone.

"You sure it wasn't just a mistake? Like a note she left for herself that just might have accidentally made it on to your parking ticket?"

"Sure. It could be. But I don't know. The woman seemed agitated. Like she kept looking over her shoulder. Maybe wondering whether Sydney was watching her. And I could also just be grasping for straws. Still, it's worth looking into. I'm going to subpoena Sydney's schedule for the last five years. I want to know who he met with and when. But my backyard? My literal backyard?"

"Who knows," Jeanie said. "I'll do some picking around on my end too. We'll figure it out between the two of us. We need a break on this, Cass. You know that, right?"

We. Such a little word, but it felt good to hear. I hadn't felt part of a "we" in a very long time.

"Thanks, Jeanie," I said. "I'm going to swing by Aubrey's house before I head home for the night. You feel like coming into the office tomorrow morning? Or, I could come to you."

Jeanie covered the fit of coughing that overtook her. "I'm fine," she said, before I could ask. "And yeah. It would do me some good to ..."

Headlights flashed in my rearview mirror, nearly blinding me as I looked back. Jeanie's voice trailed off as the car behind me sped up, kicking dirt behind it. I started to move over to the shoulder to let it pass. The thing was big and black, a pickup truck.

"Cass?" Jeanie's voice came to me like I was underwater as my body responded to the danger before my head had a chance to catch up. Then she was drowned out by the sickening crunch of metal on metal as the truck rammed me from behind. My wheels spun and locked. I got hit one more time and my car fishtailed wildly as I tried to regain control.

I don't remember screaming. I don't remember the pain as my airbag deployed and I went end over end, landing upside down in the ditch by the side of the road.

I may have lost consciousness for a moment. But I woke up surrounded by white plastic. I reached forward, trying to clear my vision. Pain shot through my arm and sticky wet blood ran down my cheek. My ears rang as the sickening bleat of my stuck horn filled the air.

Booted feet filled the window frame to my left. My car door opened and a pair of dark eyes peered down. He didn't ask me if I was okay. He didn't ask my name. He didn't tell me he'd called for help. Instead, he leaned down, getting close enough that his hot breath kissed my ear.

"Back the fuck off," he said. "You've been warned." He stood up and walked away. My vision blurred, but I could make out the green and gray of his jacket with white lettering across the back I couldn't read.

"Uhhhh." I tried to speak, but my breath wouldn't fully come. I heard shouts behind me, then the world went white and cold.

Chapter 23

THE TASTE of bile brought me back to earth. My insides churned and pulled at me. I tried to get out of the way of my own vomit. Pain seared my side as I tried to roll. Mercifully, nothing came out. A pink kidney-shaped bowl appeared in my field of vision.

"That's gonna hurt for a bit," a raspy female voice said. "Try not to strain too much."

The nurse helped me center myself back on the bed. I was in a hospital room. I had a blood pressure cuff around one arm, an oxygen sensor on my finger, and an IV line sticking out of my left arm. I brought my hands up. It hurt to do even that. It felt like I had an anvil pressing down on my chest. Gauze wrapped around my head. My heartbeat fluttered, sending the monitors beeping.

"Hang on," the nurse said. She was tall, formidable, probably in her fifties with snow-white hair and a strong, solid grip. Her name tag read Bertie Tully. Tully. I knew that family too. West siders. Great.

Bertie grabbed a hand mirror out of the cupboard behind me. She handed it to me. I was afraid to lift it.

"Probably nothing too permanent," she said. "Dr. Bass will be in soon."

My face was a mangled mess. My eyes were nearly swollen shut. I had a fat lip and the bandages covered my forehead. I vaguely remembered hitting my forehead on the steering wheel or something harder.

"Ten stitches," a young male voice sang out. Dr. Bass, I presumed. He looked younger than me but that couldn't be possible. He had a head of thick blond hair and green eyes that twinkled when he smiled. He held a tablet and tapped on the screen as he came in.

"The cut is right along your brow," he said. "At worst, it'll look like a frown line. You can consult with plastics in a few days but I think we did pretty good work down here. You've got some bruising around your ribs, but nothing's broken. Mild concussion. You're gonna have a hell of a headache for a day or two. And you'll be pretty sore. But all in all, today's your lucky day, Ms. Leary."

"How did I get here?" My voice cracked and my throat burned. Nurse Tully brought a straw to my lips and told me to take it slow. The water felt like fire at first, then it felt like heaven.

"Driver came up on your wreck, I guess," Bertie said. "Called 911. They had to cut you out, but like the doctor says, you're one lucky lady."

"Lucky," I muttered. I pressed my head back against the pillow. Had I dreamt it? The driver behind me had rammed into me. The memory of his brutal threat skittered down my spine like ice.

"He's been hanging around," Bertie said. "We can't get rid of him. Not until he's sure you're okay. You mind a quick visit?"

My heart slammed in my chest. Before I could protest, or get the word HIPPA out, Dr. Bass opened the door. An

elderly man shuffled in. He held a baseball cap in
both hands.

"Here's your good Samaritan." Bertie smiled. "Go
ahead, Richard. See for yourself."

Richard. Recognition jarred me. Richard Petersen. He'd
been the high school janitor since maybe my mother went to
Delphi. He was still wearing his blue overalls as he gave me a
gap-toothed smile. "You gave me a little scare there," he said.
"You, uh ... bled a lot."

"You?" I said, trying not to cough. "You found me?"

"Yeah. I tried to get you out of the car, but the operator
told me better not."

"Thank you," I said. Emotions flooded through me.
Richard Petersen's kind face lit up. He came to me and put
a weathered hand over mine. Long ago, he'd driven Joe
and me home from school when the call came about my
mother's fatal car accident. There had been no one else to
come for us that day. He remembered. Of course he did.
And today, he found me in a mangled car wreck just
the same.

"Thank you," I said again. "I'm glad ... I'm glad it
was you."

There was a soft knock on the door behind me. Richard
gave me a small smile and a heartfelt wink. He was a quiet
man. Kind. Dignified. And I realized I might owe him my
life. Had he seen the crash itself?

"Is this a private party or can anyone join?" Eric Wray
stood in the doorway looking grim. He wore a suit and tie
and his detective's badge hung around his neck. So this
wasn't a social call.

"Just a few minutes," Dr. Bass said. He came to me and
shined a penlight in my eyes, asking me to track it. He did a
quick assessment, making me squeeze his fingers and push
away from him. Satisfied that I wasn't in any immediate

neurological danger, he tapped on his tablet again and he
and Nurse Bertie left the room.

"Thanks for all your help, Mr. Pete," Eric said. Mr.
Petersen pointed a warning finger at Eric, but it was in jest.
Then he shot that same quick wink at me.

"Watch out for this one," he said. "He's a charmer but
he's full of bullshit."

I couldn't help but laugh and it made my sides ache. Mr.
Petersen and Eric shook hands, then Petersen quietly excused
himself. Eric shot me a hard look, then pulled up a chair
beside my bed.

"Look," he said. "I won't keep you. But I need to get
your statement. Do you feel up to that?"

"My statement? I would have figured they'd put a traffic
cop on this. I feel pretty special."

Eric had a little notepad he pulled out of his breast
pocket. His shoulders sagged as he exhaled, then he put the
notepad away.

"Trouble sure does seem to follow you, Cass. I talked to
Mr. Pete for a while after they brought you in. You gave him
a pretty big scare. He was pretty much in tears when I
walked in. Kept saying it's like Lynn all over again."

His words hit me like a brand-new blow to the gut.
Maybe it was the memory Richard Petersen conjured of that
horrible day twenty years ago. Maybe it was just the trauma
of what just happened and my adrenaline finally catching up
to me. Whatever it was, at the mention of my mother's
name, I lost my strength. I hiccupped into a great sob that
tore at the stitches in my forehead and pummeled my
sore ribs.

It shocked Eric a little. He scooted forward in his chair
and put a light hand on my arm. "Shit. I'm sorry. We don't
have to do this now. I can come back. It's just better if we ..."

I held up a hand. "No. It's okay." When Eric produced a

tissue, I accepted it gratefully and blew my nose. The act of it made my guts feel like they could spill out at any moment.

"I didn't see much," I said. "I think it was a pickup truck that hit me. Somebody got out of it and came up to me. I couldn't see his face. But ... I'm pretty sure he was wearing a Delphi High varsity jacket."

A ripple of fury went through Eric Wray's face. "Could you read the name on the front?"

I shook my head. It hurt to do even that. "No. I'm sorry. But he told me I should back off."

Eric's nostrils flared. He wrote in his notepad. "That's enough for now. You need to rest. When you're up to giving a full statement, I'll come back."

"Is my brother here?" I asked. "Did someone call him?"

"Not yet," Eric said. "I can do that for you."

"No. Please, don't. Not yet. I don't want him to know about Mr. Pete. He doesn't need the reminder."

"Reminder of what?" Eric asked. It finally occurred to me that he no idea what Richard Petersen had been talking about when he mentioned Lynn to him.

I was spent. Wrecked. Every ounce of bravado and wall-building I usually mustered just left me in that hospital bed. Damn him to hell. Eric Wray just looked so strong, confident, sure of himself. It must be nice not feeling like the world was falling apart on you every single second.

I sniffled. "He had a little bit of a part in what happened the day my mother died. That's what he meant by Lynn."

Eric's eyes lit with recognition. "Oh shit. I'm sorry. I forgot. Your mom died in a car accident. Aw hell." He produced another tissue and handed it to me. I dabbed at my eyes. As quickly as the tears came over me, laughter started to now. I was a complete mess of emotions.

"Almost lost your dad that day too, didn't you? Your mom was driving him to work or something," Eric asked. "I remember they pulled your brother out of class. He was a sophomore. I was a senior, I think. But we had a foods class together, I think it was."

"Yeah," I answered. "Sounds about right." I wanted to change the subject. If Eric pressed me, I didn't trust that I couldn't keep my mouth shut about the rest of it. The Leary walls started to go back up. Protect. Deflect. Survive.

"They were going to arrest him," Eric said. "Right? But your mom told the police she was the one driving."

Alarm bells clanged in my head along with the pounding that was already there.

"You have a good memory," I said.

"Right. And if you remember anything else ... we can talk ..."

"Eric ... it's all kind of a blur."

"You've made a lot of enemies," he said. "Quickly."

I shrugged. "Just doing my job. I figure you've got a few haters yourself."

Eric smiled. "More than a few. It's how I know I'm doing my job."

"Touché."

He raised a brow. "Right. It's just ... I'm sorry you have to deal with this."

I pressed my head back against the pillow. "I know. And I'm okay. I'm a lot tougher to get rid of than that." And I was starting to realize how true that really was.

Eric straightened. He regarded me with those cool, blue eyes. He paused for a second, maybe considering how hard to press the issue. In the span of a few seconds, he worked something out for himself. His hard stare melted into a kind smile and he put a hand on my arm.

"I'm just glad you're okay, Cass. And I'm glad there are still people in this town like Richard Petersen who are looking out for you."

"Me too," I said.

He pulled out his business card and scribbled something on the back. He handed it to me. "If you think of anything else. Or if you just … if you need something. That's my personal cell on the back. I'll work on getting to the bottom of this. Take care, Cass. I'll see you around."

I gave him a weak salute that had to look fairly pathetic with my new gauze headdress. Eric rose to his full, considerable height. I think he had something more to say, but a shadow fell over the doorway.

My heart skipped as Joe rushed in, his face white as bone. As I gave him a welcoming smile, color came back into it. I was okay. I was whole. And it was time for my mother's ghost to stop haunting us all today.

Chapter 24

TWO WEEKS AFTER THE ACCIDENT, the swelling on my face had gone down. The bruises under my eyes had faded to a sort of neon yellow and I could mostly cover them with concealer. There was just the bandage above my brow hiding the stitches, and the stiffness in my core when I tried to bend or reach for something. I was back to work and Aubrey Ames's trial date loomed.

Besides Aubrey, I was down to two other clients. Sandy York, though luckily, the outcome of our last custody hearing had sidelined her creep of an ex for now. Lucky for Mrs. York, not so lucky for my bank account. And I had one real estate closing lined up for an abandoned farm supply store on the east end of the lake. That would bring in just over a thousand dollars. I was running on financial fumes and two months behind in my rent. Miranda was covering for me with the landlord, but I knew there was a good chance I'd be doing trial preparation out of my house in another month.

The saving grace in all of this was Jeanie Mills. Finished with her last round of chemo, her initial blood tests were good. Her spirits were even better. And she was working with me on Aubrey's case free of charge for now. We'd set up camp in the middle of my living room for a Monday morning strategy session. It was Jeanie's turn to play nurse to me while my ribs healed. She stood in front of a giant white-board studying the murder timeline.

"Even if they buy her story about the phony confession, this block of time between ten thirty and midnight is the kicker," she said. "Where the hell was Aubrey?"

"I know," I said, sitting up. "She swears she was just driving around. It's weak as shit."

We had Kevin Sydney's scheduling records spread out on my coffee table. They were useless too. There was no mention of any meetings with any of the girls we suspected Coach D had assaulted.

"So that leaves the secretary," Jeanie said. "What does that sticky note say again?"

Jeanie knew it by heart as well as I did. "Look in your own backyard."

Every time she said it, every time I read it, a hollow pit formed in my stomach.

"What about Aubrey?" Jeanie asked. "Are you putting her on the stand or not?"

That was the million-dollar question. She couldn't recant her confession without testifying. But it meant exposing her to cross-examination. If I'd learned nothing else, it was that Aubrey Ames excelled at digging herself into ever-deepening holes. Jack LaForge could hand her the biggest shovel of all.

A car pulled up in my driveway. Jeanie looked out the window first. She grabbed an old bedsheet off the floor and covered the whiteboard. I gathered Sydney's records and stuffed them back into their file.

"It's quittin' time anyway," Jeanie said as Matty came up the walk. He and Joe had taken turns checking up on me since the accident. I didn't like the role reversal. It had

always been my job taking care of them. Today, he brought
Joe with him. As Matty came in the house, Joe waved a hand
from outside. He wanted to finish up the repairs to the shed
roof. It was good. It would give me a chance to talk to Matty
alone.

"Hey, Jeanie," Matty said, smiling. As a kid, he had been
scared shitless of her. I could still see some of that little boy
in his eyes as he gave her a sheepish grin.

Jeanie grabbed my brother's face and planted a kiss on
his forehead. She had to go way up on her tiptoes to reach
him. "Look at that face," she said. "So handsome. Such a
little shit you were."

"Still is," I said. Matty glared at me, but it was through a
smile. Jeanie swatted him on the back and took her leave.
Matty came to me and gave me a quick hug hello.

"You look less hideous today," Matty said. I flipped him
off. He smiled as he sat down, but I couldn't miss the
haunted look in his eyes. The first couple of days after the
accident, he wouldn't leave my side. They weren't talking
about it, not either of my brothers, but I knew they were
thinking of what happened to our mother. The police were
no closer to figuring out who hit me. Detective Wray
wouldn't come out and say it, but I had a feeling somebody
loyal to Coach D was protecting their own.

"So," I said. "What's the word on the street about
the case?"

Matty dropped his head. Of the two of them, he was
liable to hear the most gossip. I'd asked him to be my eyes
and ears. He worked in a machine shop on the east side of
town, though he was currently laid off. He survived there by
keeping his head down. I just hoped my role in Aubrey's case
wouldn't jeopardize his call back. Though I knew it probably
would. My bigger fear was that it would be enough to knock
Matty back off the wagon.

"I don't know, Cass," he said. "Everybody thinks that girl ... Aubrey ... they think the coach was balling her."

"Ugh. That's a horrible term for it," I said.

Matty put a hand up. "Yeah. Sorry. You asked what people were saying. That's it."

"She's nineteen," I said.

"Right," Matty continued. "People think she got into it with him. He was a single guy. No kids."

"And they're okay with a fifty-year-old man messing around with a nineteen-year-old former student?"

He shrugged. "I didn't say that. They think he was an idiot for it. But it's all kind of lost in the fact that it got him killed. You know?"

I wanted to tell him so much more. Aubrey's truth burned through me. I couldn't though. Even having this much of a conversation about her case was skirting a line.

"That's not all they're saying," Matty said. "Some people are starting to guess that she's gonna say he raped her. It's rumbling all through the town. People have come to blows over it. And with what happened to you ..."

"Shit," I said, leveling a hard stare at him. The words on that damn sticky note rang through me with the power of church bells. My breath left me. A question burned inside of me and I had to get it out. I turned to my brother.

Joe picked that exact moment to walk in the house. He took one look at me and knew something was up. I thought about asking him to step out again. If I did that, he'd never leave me alone. So I took a breath and asked.

"Matty, I need to ask you something about Vangie."

Matty cocked his head to the side. He'd done that since he was a baby, trying to work something out in his head. It reminded me of a puppy and I couldn't help but smile. Matty didn't like to talk about her much. He took Vangie's leaving the hardest of all of us.

"Did she ever talk about Coach D?" I asked. Joe's face went white. He ran a hand over his face and took a seat on the other couch.

I wanted to tell him everything I suspected. I wanted to tell them about the note. *My own backyard.* Never mind the ethical issues about discussing this case, there were parts of this I had to keep secret, even from him. If Matty went down to Mickey's and started drinking and talking ... it would be a disaster.

Matty shook his head. "That's the thing, Cass. Vang stopped talking to me that last year before she left. She stopped talking to everybody. She just ... tried to turn invisible. And the rest you know. She took off the day after she finished her last exam and that was it."

That was it. My baby sister ran away from home and never looked back. My heart churned. I saw the same thing happening to Joe across the room. *My own backyard.*

"She never talked about anything," I said. I'd had these conversations with my brother a thousand times. I knew the answers. No. Vangie never said why she left. Of the three of us, I was the last to actually spend any significant time with her. She came to Chicago that summer and stayed in my apartment. Until one day I came home from work and she was just gone.

"Nope," Matty said. "She ghosted us. She sends the occasional Christmas card. But it's been a couple of years since the last one."

"What about Dad?" I asked, hating bringing him up. In the five months I'd been home, I hadn't even seen him. I didn't think even Joe knew where he was.

Matty picked at his shoe. "Yeah," he said. "We all know Vangie was his favorite. She could do no wrong in Pop's eyes. Until she left just like Mom."

"Stop it," Joe said. "Mom didn't leave, Matt. She died. And I don't really feel like rehashing any of this."

I hadn't spoken to my father in years. Last I heard, he'd shacked up with some woman in Jackson. Matty kept in touch, though he'd never admit it. He had always needed Dad's approval the most. In a lot of ways, his own sobriety was wrapped up in my father's. If my father couldn't get it together, Matty thought he was doomed to failure too.

"Matty, what?" I pressed on. My brother's face fell.

"He talks to her, okay? I don't know how often. But he does. I'm pretty sure if there were some kind of emergency, Dad would be able to get a hold of Vangie."

Joe was on his feet and storming right out the front door. I dropped my head and let out a sigh. "Thanks for that," I said and meant it. "Don't worry about Joe. He's just ... I'll handle it."

Matty smiled. "You always do, Cass."

I squeezed Matty's shoulder as I moved past him and followed Joe out to the dock. He immediately started skipping stones again. A sure sign he was pissed and likely to brood for a good long while.

"Joe," I started.

He turned to me. "Don't say it. Don't even think it."

"I don't want to. God. I want to throw up. But you tell me. You were here that year. I wasn't."

His whole body contorted as if he'd just been socked in the gut. I realized he had. We both had. If it was true ... if there was even an inkling of a possibility ... *My own backyard.*

When Joe straightened and turned to me, his eyes were red and his whole body shook. "Cass ... she went out for track at the end of her junior year. She was good at it. She was trying to get a scholarship."

"I know," I whispered. "I remember."

"Her senior year, she wouldn't ... she wouldn't do

anything. Oh God. Did I miss it? Did that fucking animal touch her? Is that why she left?"

He reached for me—clawed at me, more like it. My heart shattered in a thousand pieces and it felt like my world fell apart. I saw my sweet little sister in my mind's eye. Blonde. Thin with fine features. So much like our mother. A carbon copy. And she also looked a hell of a lot like Aubrey Ames.

Chapter 25

WEEKS WENT BY. Summer loosened its humid grip on southern Michigan and gave way to fall. Mid-October and the centuries-old maple and oak trees lining the lake reflected brilliant golds, lusty reds, and shimmering auburn over the calm water. We were just over two weeks out from Aubrey Ames's November 1st trial date, and nothing but those leaves had changed.

Delphi existed in a state of suspended animation and hushed whispers. The death threats had mainly stopped and no one tried to run me off the road, but the people in town avoided me like I had leprosy. It was starting to carry over to the rest of my family. Matty hadn't been called back to the shop. His frantic calls to the union had gone unheeded. Emma's mother Josie had just filed for more child support and to change their custody order. One fire at a time.

The one bright spot in my life was Jeanie. The tumor in her lung had shrunk and there were no signs of it spreading. She was the one person the Aubrey Ames's case seemed to have a positive effect on. She'd finally taken me up on my offer to move into the spare office at the top of the stairs.

Though I begged her not to, she covered my rent for the remainder of the year.

Then there was Vangie. The last number she gave me was no longer in service.

Matty was now staying at my place a few nights a week. He was as worried about me as I was about him. The good news was Katy and Emma had mended fences and she and Joe moved back home.

I took a bite out of one of the donuts on the table and kissed my brother on the head. "You gonna be here when I get home from work today?" It was a passive-aggressive question, I knew. I'd been on Matty's ass for a couple of weeks about finding a temporary job. The plant couldn't stall him forever, but the more idle he was, the more likely he'd start drinking again.

"Maybe," Matty answered. "I'll let you know. Don't worry about me for dinner. I might go out."

I grabbed my messenger bag and pulled my keys off the hook. "Whatevs. Can you take a look at the pontoon though? It was running rough the other day. Joe said he thinks the spark plugs need switching out."

Matty shook his head in disgust. "They just need a good cleaning. He thinks the answer to everything is buying new."

I nearly choked on my donut. Matty sounded exactly like our dad just then. I gave him a weak thumbs up and headed out the door. I had a strategy session planned with Jeanie this morning on the Ames opening statement. I made it halfway to the office when she called.

"Change of plans," she said, barking her words out. "You need to head over to the jail."

Shit. My heart raced as I did my mental family roll call. Matty was at the house. Whatever trouble my father may have gotten into, he was far out of Woodbridge County. At least I thought. That just left Joe unaccounted for.

"Ah God, Jeanie."

"Relax," she said. "I mean, don't relax, but this is a new pile of shit. Not an old one. It's Dan Ames. He's been charged with assault."

My head spun. "What now?"

"He's asking for you. It's a mess. Word is he followed Kevin Sydney home last night and beat the shit out of him in front of his house. In front of witnesses."

I bounced my skull off the headrest. I put my blinker on and made a hard right. "Is he talking? Good lord. Maybe I don't want to know. I can't seem to keep the Ames family's mouths shut to save their lives."

"Right," Jeanie said. "That's why you need to be over there. You can sort out the ethics shit later. Just make sure he does a better job exercising his rights than his daughter did."

"Got it," I said, pulling into an empty spot right in front of the jail. A car screeched into a turn behind me. My heart flipped, but it was a black SUV, not an old pickup. I watched the driver parallel park along the curb behind me. The driver wasn't wearing a varsity jacket. Far from it. He had slicked-back blond hair, mirrored sunglasses, and wore a dark suit that straightened through his massive shoulders.

"Well, hello, asshole," I whispered. He didn't look my way as I got out of the car and headed for the jail. Whoever he was, I'd have to deal with him later. After getting through security, I headed up to the detective bureau where they were holding Dan Ames.

Sergeant Ramos was working the desk again. His face fell when he saw me.

"Don't tell me," he sighed.

"I know, I missed you too, Ramos. We can save the small talk though. You got my guy down there?"

"Your guy?" Ramos asked. "You're a real glutton for punishment, Leary."

Ramos gestured to one of the uniformed officers. She gave me a curt smile and led me down to the interrogation rooms. Dan Ames was in the third one on the left, cuffed and seated at a conference table. He'd sobered up, but barely. His shirt was torn at the collar and he had scratch marks over his neck and chest.

"Don't suppose that was a werewolf attack, huh?" I said. Dan looked up. His shoulders sagged with relief when he saw me and his eyes filled with tears. Shit. Whatever happened last night, the harsh light of morning had already filled him with remorse.

"Take your time," the officer said as she nodded to Dan and started to shut the door behind her.

I sat down opposite Dan and crossed my arms on the table. I had about thirty seconds to look over the charging document. Misdemeanor assault. He could do up to ninety days.

"Did you tell them anything?" I asked.

Dan shook his head. "Didn't have to. About ten of that asshole's neighbors saw the whole thing. I couldn't help it, Cass. That fucking smug fucker. He *knew.* I know he knew. How many girls did that monster get his hands on? He groomed them. Every year he had his pick. For how long?"

I let out a sigh. "Dan, this isn't helping Aubrey."

"I wanted to kill him. God. She knew I wanted to kill him. I should have. Do you know how many nights I lay awake fantasizing about it? Coach D. Saint. Hero."

I put my hand over Dan's. "Dan, this is sticky for me. You need a lawyer. You did a good thing asking for one. But it can't be me. Not as long as I'm representing Aubrey. Whatever happened between you and Kevin Sydney is wrapped up in what's going on with her. There's a conflict of interest. I can figure out whether they're going to release you or try to hold you over for bail. But you're going to need somebody else to appear on your behalf. I don't know how deep a pile of shit you've stepped in. A lot of it depends on your record. Do you have one?"

Dan shrugged. "I got into some trouble when I was a kid. Underage drinking. That sort of thing."

"Anything since you turned eighteen?"

"No. Speeding tickets, yeah. I got into a fender bender a couple of years ago and they cited me. I've done what I can. You know? I tried to live my life right. Diane and I weren't in love. Aubrey wasn't planned, but I did the right thing by her. I love her mother now. I've worked my ass off and put a roof over her head. We teach the kids how to work hard. Get good grades. They've done it all. They're smart. But none of it mattered. That fucking bastard. He *did* things to her. I should have known. Why didn't I see it? I left it to her mother. Teenage girls are moody. She used to laugh. She stopped doing that. Not even a smile. Then, her grades went to shit."

Dan tore at his hair. My heart cracked for him. At the core of it, I was sitting across from a man who was trying to do the very best for his family. The only similarity between him and my own father was our zip code and the side of the lake we lived on. And yet, here he was with the world crashing down around him.

"He *knew*," Dan said. "I know it in my heart. That fucking Sydney knew what was going on. Aubrey said that son of a bitch Drazdowski told her he'd bury her. He *knew* no one would ever believe her if she squealed on him. So he kept doing that shit to her over and over. I can't get it out of my head. I can't stop imagining his fucking hands all over her and everything else. She's my baby. And now she's going to rot in jail for the rest of her life because I couldn't protect her."

"Dan," I said. "This isn't your fault."

"The hell it's not! You want to know what one of the worst parts is? The thing that guts me?"

I braced for it.

"Of *course* she thought I killed that fucker. Any father would. Except I didn't. I'll take that to my grave. I could have done a thousand things differently. Why didn't I go to Eric? He's a cop. My friend. He would have known what to do, maybe. You have to let me confess to it. Let me undo this now."

"No. No more lies. That's the one thing you can't do."

He let out a bitter laugh. "I should have stayed home that night. I should have at *least* stayed home that night. But no, I had to go to fucking Mickey's where everybody in the goddamn town saw me, including Eric Wray and even one of your brothers, I think. Scotty had me on his damn security tapes. I was drunk while my little girl was out there trying to deal with her own monster."

That was the rub. Of everyone in town, Dan Ames had the most airtight alibi of anyone. I saw his heart as he sat across from me. If it weren't for the crowd at Mickey's, I had no doubt in my mind he would have taken the fall for Aubrey just like she tried to do for him. It was the worst irony of all.

"Dan, I'm sorry. I really am. I wish I had a magic wand I could wave and make this all go away. But you have to stop beating yourself up over this. No matter what happens, you *have* to be the strong one. For Aubrey. For Sean and Diane. You being in jail does them no good. With any luck, whoever you *do* get to represent you will keep that from happening. I promise, I'll try to hook you up with someone great."

"She's going to prison, isn't she?" Dan's eyes cut into me. He was a desperate father hanging on by a thread. It would have been easy to tell him pretty things. But it wouldn't do any of us any good.

"If the jury believes Aubrey's confession ..."

I didn't get to finish my sentence. Dan let out a choked sound, reminding me of a wounded animal. In many ways, that's what he was.

"She knows," he said. "God help her, she knows. She's been so fucking brave through all of this. She's been preparing herself for it. Withdrawing even more. Giving up. Cass, I'm worried she's going to kill herself."

My heart twisted. "One thing at a time, Dan. You keep your mouth shut in here. This is not over. Do you hear me? I plan to fight like hell for your daughter and every girl in her place. We're going to get the truth out."

Tears spilled down his cheeks. "Except it won't matter for my daughter."

"It'll matter to her," I said. "And you're right. She *is* brave. So you have to pull yourself together and be there for her. Can you do that?"

He gritted his teeth but nodded. "Okay," I said. "Now let me go do my job."

I just prayed it would be enough.

Chapter 26

NOVEMBER 1ˢᵀ FELL ON A MONDAY. A cold snap hit overnight and Delphi woke to a dusting of snow that covered everything. This was southern Michigan though. It could be eighty degrees by midweek.

As I pulled into a parking space a block from the court-house, my blood started to hum. My fingers tingled as I gripped the steering wheel. I knew my case law cold. I knew every nook and cranny of the case the state was about to put on. I knew my opponent's strengths and how to exploit his weaknesses. And I had never in my life tried a case I wasn't supposed to win. Until today.

That doesn't mean I haven't lost. I have just one thing to say to any lawyer who tells you he's never lost a case. Tell him he hasn't tried enough of them. Witnesses go south. Judges fixate on things you don't expect. And juries are unpredictable. No matter how strong your case or how prepared you are, any one of those things can flip a case against you. As I readied myself to walk into that courtroom and fight for Aubrey Ames's future, I felt like we were upside down from the get-go.

A crowd had formed on the sidewalk on the opposite corner of the courthouse. The sheriff's office sent a dozen deputies to keep them back. Still, I was greeted to catcalls, hate speech, and picket signs bearing Coach D's smiling face and a list of his state championships. Within the crowd was a sea of green varsity jackets worn by new graduates and those closer to my age. The Fighting Shamrocks had come out in force. There was a good chance one of them had tried to run me off the road last month.

They brought Aubrey and her family in through a service entrance. Two more deputies had been assigned to ensure her safety as she came through. I made myself a sort of decoy. Everyone expected my client to walk in with me.

I ignored the crowd as they booed and called me gutter trash, a whore, a bottom feeder, and a dozen things even worse. I saw that same shiny black SUV parked parallel to the courthouse again. Its driver talked into his cell phone and his eyes followed me as I made my way up the courthouse steps.

Jeanie was already there. She waited for me on the wooden bench just past the metal detectors. Her color was good and she dressed smartly in a navy-blue suit jacket and white linen pants. She looked hearty; her cheeks flushed with excitement and her eyes narrowed with determination as she saw me approach.

"Ready, boss?" She smiled.

I rolled my eyes. "Cut it, Jeanie. Like you'd ever take orders from me."

"Orders? No. Helpful suggestions? And you didn't answer my question. You ready for this?"

"Yeah," I said. "Have you seen Aubrey yet?"

"She's already in the courtroom," Jeanie answered. "Her dad's with her. Her mom is a no-show."

I frowned. "That's not great, Jeanie. I made it pretty

clear we need a united family front. The jury is going to be watching every second."

"I know. I've got a text into Miranda. She's going to go over there and see if she can drag Diane here after lunch. With any luck, we'll have her seated before we get to opening statements."

"I guess it'll have to do," I said. I didn't like this one bit. Optics mattered. The jury needed to see Aubrey's adoring parents and their anguish over her fate for every possible second.

We headed into courtroom number two. Aubrey had taken her seat at the defense table to the left of the courtroom as we faced the bench. Jack LaForge leaned casually over one of the gallery pews, talking to the bailiff from another courtroom. He had a team assembled. Two assistant prosecutors, a paralegal, a couple of interns. The county had put every available resource behind him.

At my table, it was just me with Jeanie at my back. A year ago, my team would have dwarfed Jack's. The Thorne Group would have hired a cadre of jury consultants alone. I smiled at the memory. Today, I wouldn't need them. I knew the people of this town. How they thought. What they liked. What they feared. Right now, every metric was stacked against my client. But if I could plant the seed of doubt. If I could get them to understand the biggest lie this town hid … then Aubrey had a fighting chance.

Castor took the bench promptly at nine. Aubrey shifted in her seat beside me. I put a hand on her knee beneath the table. She had to play her part starting right now as the gallery filled with dozens of potential jurors.

Voir dire went smoothly as those things go. We eliminated ten people who had played on one of Coach D's teams. I tried to stretch it and get rid of anyone who even went to Delphi High. Jack pushed me to use my freebie peremptory challenges. I pushed back. As we broke for lunch, we'd settled on a twelve-member jury with four alternates. Six men. Six women. Three mothers, one of them also a grandmother. Five of the men were fathers. I was as pleased with that as I could be.

"I think we're set," Judge Castor said.

I raised a finger. "Your Honor, I need to renew my motion for a transfer of venue in this case. We've completed voir dire. We have a tainted jury pool by their own admissions."

Judge Castor flapped a dismissive hand as Jack rose to speak. "Ms. Leary. The jurors have been extensively questioned. They have stated they believe they can render an impartial verdict in this case. I'm going to take their word for it. Your motion is denied. You've preserved your issue for appeal. Let's move on. I'd like to see if we can get through opening statements and have the state call its first witness before we end for the day. What are the chances, Mr. LaForge?"

"I'll do my level best, Your Honor," Jack answered.

The jury had already been dismissed for lunch with the standard admonishment not to discuss the case outside the jury room. For the rest of us, we would treat them like plutonium if we bumped into them in the hallway.

Judge Castor pounded his gavel and we rose as he left the bench. I patted Aubrey on the back.

"It's good," I said. "As good as we can hope for right now. You're doing great, Aubrey. It's going to get harder after lunch. I need you to be strong, okay?"

I turned back to her father. He'd come through the gate separating the gallery from the lawyers' tables. He went to his daughter and hugged her. I looked back at Jeanie. Diane Ames was still absent. Jeanie guided Aubrey to the back of the courtroom. Miranda had arranged to have some sandwiches delivered and we had access to a conference room one floor up. It would be private. It would keep Aubrey from having to face the angry crowd outside.

"Dan," I whispered as soon as Aubrey was out of earshot. "Where's your wife? She needs to be here."

Dan shrugged. "She's a wreck, Cass. Hysterical. Sean's no better. The second she gets going, she sets Aubrey off. I'm working on her for tomorrow. Today, it's no good."

I let out a hard breath. "It matters. The jury knows you're not a single parent. They need to *see* her. They need to start putting themselves in your shoes and your wife's. Figure out what Diane needs and get it for her. Are we clear?"

He shrugged. "I'll try."

"Good. As for you ... You wanna cry? Get red in the face from anger? You do that. No outbursts though. No matter what you hear. And you're going to hear plenty today. Jack LaForge is going to stand up there and paint your daughter as some kind of jilted lover, or lethal Lolita. Both. Keep your cool. Got it?"

"Got it," he said through gritted teeth.

Dan was the last one to leave the courtroom except for me. I was alone. I took a moment to breathe. I'd said all the things I needed to say to my client and her father. Now I just had to heed them for myself.

Jeanie poked her head back in. "You coming? Miranda ordered your favorite. Turkey on rye with a dill pickle spear on the side."

"I'm good. I'll just grab a bottled water." Jeanie came all the way into the courtroom.

"No good."

"No. Seriously. I don't eat during trial. I'll carbo-load tonight. Promise."

"Suit yourself. No luck on Diane Ames though. Miranda couldn't even get her to come to the door."

"Yeah. I put the fear of God into her husband about it. I'm pretty sure he'll drag her in tomorrow. For now, I can only fight one battle at a time."

Jeanie tried to bully me into eating something again, but finally gave up. I took the space and time to collect my thoughts. Center myself. Get ready.

Judge Castor took the bench again at half-past one.

"Mr. LaForge? Is the State ready to open?"

"We are, Your Honor."

Jack cleared his throat and stepped out from behind his table. He straightened his tie and faced the jury. For now, they were on the literal edges of their seats. That would wane of course, but at that moment, he had them.

"Ladies and gentlemen, this is a hard thing we are asking you to do. The hardest thing there is in the justice system. For that, I want to thank you for your time and attention in advance."

Jack took measured breaths and struck a casual posture at the end of the jury box. I knew he would play well with them. He was average-looking in an almost studied way. His suit was gray, not shiny, and he wore a maroon tie. In his early fifties, he had all his hair and just a slight pouch to his mid-section. Everything about him was neutral. Not too handsome. Not too homely. Just ... average. Non-threatening. Whatever impression the jury had of him, they would not be jealous, nor intimidated by this man. That of course is exactly what he was after.

"You may have heard of the victim in this case. Larry Drazdowski. Coach D as most of the people in this town knew him. He liked that. Loved it, actually. Coach D wasn't from around here. He was born near Traverse City. An outsider. Coming to Delphi was a risk for him. He had other offers. Better ones, actually. But Larry Drazdowski saw something about Delphi that stirred his heart. He saw this town *had* a heart. And it had kids he believed he could help.

"He came here when he was just thirty years old. Twenty-one years ago. In fact, at the end of this last school year, the school administrators arranged a party for him, celebrating his twentieth anniversary at Delphi High. There was a lot to celebrate. Coach D wasn't your ordinary basketball coach. Or track coach. We've all seen the signs on the outskirts of town. Eight state championships. We take pride in it. It's a badge of honor. If you're ever outside the city limits and you tell somebody where you're from, I'll bet you hear it. Oh, you're the school with the basketball team, right? I know I've heard that plenty. Yes. That's my town. That's my school. *We* did that.

"But if you talk to any of the kids who played for Coach D. And a whole lot of the ones who didn't. If you ask them about the coach, they won't mention those state championships. They'll mention the man. The coach. Coach D. Sure, he cared about those trophies. I'm sure he was proud of that record. He knew what it took to get there.

"If you asked Coach D what he was most proud of, he'd tell you it was the kids. He wouldn't take credit for those trophies. Not one of them. Even all these years later, he'd be able to tell you the names of each and every kid he ever coached. Not just the starters. The benchwarmers. The managers. And plenty who were just fans who came to all of the games.

"Coach D had no kids of his own. No wife. No immediate family. His students were his family. He brought them into his home. He had a knack for seeking out kids in need. Not necessarily those starters. The ones from broken homes. The ones who needed just a little bit of extra help in the classroom.

"He was a mentor. A friend. He wasn't just a tough

taskmaster on the basketball court. Though he was that too. You can't win those trophies without putting the work in behind them. But the boys on those teams would do anything for Coach D. He meant that much to them. They were a family. The only family Coach D ever needed."

Aubrey bristled beside me. Her posture went rigid. I touched her knee beneath the table again, bringing her back to the present. She cast her eyes downward and I watched her exhale. Jack pivoted on his heel and walked to the center of the courtroom. I gave Aubrey an encouraging squeeze again. Here came the hard part.

"Ladies and gentleman, on the night of June 22nd when another troubled student reached out to him, he was there. You'll see just how much. How he went against his own instincts, put aside obvious reservations, maybe did something against his better judgment. But when this student asked for help, Coach D couldn't turn her away. It was the last thing he ever did.

"Now, I don't have to dazzle you with fancy legal theories. I don't have to make you hate the defendant. You shouldn't hate her. In fact, I beg you not to. The only thing I will beg you to do is listen to her. Her very own words. You might go home debating the whys, the what ifs. I sure have. But, in the end, this case is simple.

"Aubrey Ames reached out to Coach D. She knew he'd listen. She knew he would answer her call for help just like he did for hundreds of other students. Only this time, it cost him his life. This time, Coach D made the fatal flaw of meeting the defendant alone in Shamrock Park. He thought it was safe there. Neutral. Private. Because whatever the defendant wanted to talk to him about, he'd give her that dignity.

"Coach D went to the park that night. Was it wise? Was it appropriate? Probably not. But it's who Larry Drazdowski was. He didn't leave the park alive that night. Instead, the end of the world happened. In Coach D's reality, the end of the world was a cold blade slicing through his body, driving straight into his kidney. He died alone, ladies and gentlemen. Bleeding to death. When it was his time to ask for help, none would ever come.

"So, I want you to listen to the evidence presented in this case. All of it. I'll admit, some of the things you'll hear about the coach might not be flattering. He was a flawed human being, just like the rest of us. He made bad choices. But, once you've heard everything, I believe your job will be simple. Not easy. But simple. All you have to do is take the defendant, Aubrey Ames, at her word. Thank you."

Aubrey turned a soft shade of purple. I put a hand on her back and she started breathing again. I'd prepared her for this moment as much as I could. She needed a champion. The thing she never had before now. But I had a giant elephant on my back. I could not tell the jury about facts that weren't yet in evidence. If things went how we planned, this jury would hear every sordid detail of Coach D's life and what he'd done. I just couldn't tell them that right now.

"Ms. Leary?" Judge Castor said.

I gave him a nod and rose from my seat. "Thank you, Your Honor. Members of the jury. I too would like to thank you for your time here today. My name is Cass Leary and I represent the defendant who you see sitting over at that table. Her name is Aubrey Ames.

"Ladies and gentleman, Larry Drazdowski was the victim of a horrible crime. The manner in which he died is gut-wrenching. He *did* die alone. He did bleed to death. And he didn't deserve it. None of us do. Those are facts. We may wish they weren't true, but they are.

"In this case, I will tell you. Things aren't always what they seem.

"Larry Drazdowski wasn't the only victim in the park that night. Throughout the course of this trial, you're going to hear some things that will probably shock you. They'll make you angry. They should. And my colleague, Mr. LaForge, he got something right just now. Aubrey Ames *was* a troubled former student. She's never denied that. She's made some pretty big mistakes. And she *did* go to the park that night. She did have a relationship with the coach that you'll hear about over the next few days. Again, I offer you this. Things aren't always what they seem.

"When Aubrey Ames left Shamrock Park, Larry Drazdowski was still very much alive. Right now, we don't know who killed Mr. Drazdowski. So, when you listen to the lead detective on this case, you might get frustrated. There are a lot of unanswered questions. Larry Drazdowski was a former college athlete. A basketball player. He was six foot six and over two hundred pounds. Physically fit. He worked out with those boys on the court all the way up until the week he died. Boys who were half his age. Strong. At the peak of their physical prowess. He hung with them. You might even hear a few of them say how he 'kicked their you-know-whats on a regular basis.'

"And then there's my client." I turned to Aubrey, leaving the question in the air. From the looks on the jury's faces, I knew they were thinking it. She was tiny. Almost frail looking.

"We'll ask those questions," I continued. "And we'll answer many more. Mr. LaForge is right. This is a hard case. But the law is clear. You've been asked to judge whether my client is guilty or not guilty. You must presume she is innocent. And it's the prosecution's responsibility to prove to you that she committed this crime beyond a reasonable doubt. That means there can be no other reasonable alternative explanation for what happened that night. That's a very heavy burden. It's the highest burden we have in the criminal justice system. It should be. The defendant's life, her future, is at stake. And it's in your hands.

"I know you'll take the responsibility seriously. It's why you're still here. But I want you to keep something very important in mind over the next few days in this case. Things aren't always what they seem."

I left it at that. It was all I could do for now.

The judge shifted in his seat. "Mr. LaForge, you may call your first witness."

Chapter 27

JACK CALLED Marian Emmett to the stand. At sixty-seven she was fit, trim, and wore a deep-green designer suit. Her hair was perfectly coiffed and dyed jet black. I had the immediate impression that Marian had spent weeks figuring out what to wear today. It mattered to her. But the moment she was sworn in, the woman fell completely apart.

Jack took his foundational testimony and Marian got through that reasonably well. She lived in the neighborhood abutting Shamrock Park. She and her husband Frank walked there together every single day. At the beginning of June, she'd finally convinced her husband to buy her a puppy. They'd gone for a Shepherd mix and on the night of the 22nd, they went out for a late-night walk with him so he could do his business before they all went to bed. They'd named him Thumper and it turned out he was too much dog for Marian Emmett to handle.

"Mrs. Emmett," Jack wound up. "Can you tell me what you saw the night of the 22nd when you took that walk in the park?"

Marian folded. Silent tears rolled down her eyes. "We'd

just gone past the jungle gym. You know, the new one they put up that's supposed to be A.D.A. compliant. There was something on the ground up by the park bench. Someone. I thought he was sleeping. That happens sometimes. The cops patrol, but not enough, if you ask me. We get drunks in there. Pretty soon it'll be kids doing drugs if they don't do something about it. Anyway, I told my husband he should call the police. That's even before we came up on him. I mean, I would have just turned the other way. But we didn't. We kept on walking. I wish to God Frank had listened to me."

"The man wasn't sleeping, was he, Mrs. Emmett?"

She shook her head and openly wept. "No. He was dead. All white. Staring right at me. He looked terrified. All that blood. Dead. Just dead. Who would do that?"

"Can you tell me what time this was, approximately?"

"Right around midnight."

After that, Marian became incoherent. She turned purple and asked for a glass of water. Jack tried a few more questions but her answers were unintelligible sobs. The court recorder kept asking her to repeat them. Judge Castor called for a five-minute recess. After which, Jack turned the witness over to me.

There was very little help I could get from Marian Emmett. She was in the wrong place at the wrong time and I knew every member of that jury sympathized with her. Other than Thumper, she literally had no dog in this fight.

"Mrs. Emmett, thank you for taking the time to be here today. I know how hard this must be for you," I said.

"Thank you, honey," she said. "That's such a nice suit you have on." God bless this woman. It was time to get her off the stand as quickly as possible.

"Thank you. I just have one question. You said you came

upon the victim at around midnight. Is there any chance you could be more precise with the time?"

"Oh," she sniffed. "Right. We left my house at midnight exactly. He stays up way later than I do. That's something that happens when you get a little older like we are. You don't need as much sleep. Anyway, he takes his last pill right before bed. He's got an application thing on his phone that tells him when to take it. It goes off at twelve fifteen. It hadn't gone off yet when we found … that poor man. It did though. When I was on the phone with 911. It scared the heck out of me."

"And you called 911 as soon as you found the victim?" I asked.

She nodded. "Oh yes. I already had my phone in my hand. I don't think I'd been on the phone a minute before Frank's alarm went off. So that means we must have found that man probably at ten after midnight. It takes us that long to get to that side of the park and Thumper hadn't done his business yet so we were walking sort of fast."

"Thank you," I said. "That's very helpful. I have nothing further."

Jack waived his redirect and Marian Emmett left the witness stand.

Jack called Detective Tim Bowman to the stand next. Bowman strode in tall, confident. He said a polite hello to the judge and stood straight, speaking in a clear, booming voice as he was sworn in.

"Can you state your name for the record?" Jack started.

Bowman leaned forward, speaking directly into the microphone. "Timothy Randall Bowman."

"And what's your profession, Detective Bowman?"

"I'm a senior detective with the Delphi Police Department. Personal crimes division."

"Personal crimes," Jack said, his tone easy, conversational.

"Right. That's crimes to persons. Assaults, homicides. As opposed to the property crimes division where they handle theft."

"Thank you," Jack said. "And can you tell me how long you've held that position?"

Bowman settled in. "I was hired in just out of college. I've been with D.P.D. for twenty-six years. I made detective sixteen years ago. Worked in property crimes for about three years and I've been over in personal crimes for going on thirteen years now."

"Okay. And within the personal crimes division, is there a particular type of case you specialize in?"

Bowman shifted in his chair. "Well, I do the majority of the homicides that take place within the city of Delphi. It's not *all* homicides. Thankfully, our homicide rate is fairly low for a city this size. But when there is one, I'm most likely going to catch it. Either myself or one of the three other senior detectives in our division. Megan Lewis, George Knapp, and Eric Wray. But of that group, I've been in the bureau the longest."

Bowman went through the rest of his credentials methodically. He served on a human trafficking task force with the F.B.I. and received a series of accolades from the department. The jury listened with rapt attention for about the first five minutes, then their eyes started to glaze over. Perfect, it was what I was after. This was part of the dance.

Finally, Jack steered him to the night in question.

"Detective Bowman, can you explain your role on the night of June 22nd?"

"Sure." Bowman had been getting bored with himself too up until that point. He put his shoulders back again and spoke into the microphone.

"I caught the call from a uniformed unit at five minutes past one in the morning on the 23rd"

I made a quick note to circle back to that with him.

"Can you tell me what happened when you came on the scene?"

"It's in my report, but I arrived at Shamrock Park at one twenty-one. I worked with our crime scene unit, they arrived at the same time, and we finished efforts to secure the scene. But as I arrived, I immediately saw a white male victim, approximately fifty years old, lying face up in a pool of blood with what looked like a knife wound in his side. He was already dead."

"Who else was there at the scene?" Jack asked.

"Four uniformed officers, their names are in my report. I can refer to it. Myself. Officers Wyler and Forste from crime scene. The M.E., uh, medical examiner had already been called and was en route. There were two witnesses there as well. The uniformed officers had taken them some distance away and they were sitting in the back of one of the patrol cars. That would be Frank and Marian Emmett. I later learned they were the ones who found the body."

Jack established Bowman's credentials and experience. Bowman was folksy, looking straight at the jury for most of his testimony. He was good. But the gut punch came as Jack moved to introduce the first of the crime scene photographs.

As they went in one by one, I'd already told Aubrey to brace herself. She'd seen them in my office, of course, but not in the giant display Jack LaForge had prepared. Once the photos had been admitted, Jack turned the easel he set up with the collage of Larry Drazdowski's dead body toward the jury. I objected and succeeded in getting some of the more gruesome and gratuitous photos left out, but the ones they saw were disturbing enough.

Jack played it just how I would have. He said nothing for

a few seconds and let the jury absorb it. Larry Drazdowski was dead, his lips blue and curled. The worst was his eyes. Frozen. Staring directly at the camera and therefore directly at the jury. And there was that damn Fighting Shamrock t-shirt he wore. Two of the male jurors looked like they might be sick. Two of the women had tears in their eyes.

It would only get worse from here.

"Detective Bowman," Jack said. "What evidence did you find at the scene?"

"Objection to use of the word evidence," I said. "It's for the court to determine what is or isn't admissible evidence." It was a nitpick of an objection, but I used it to break up Jack's flow a little.

"I'll rephrase," Jack said. Castor nodded.

Bowman described the knife, the contents of Larry Drazdowski's pocket, and the cell phone. Later, Jack would call a forensics expert to establish that the phone was Aubrey's and enter the transcript of her text messages. But the introduction of the phone now captured the jury's attention. I debated objecting to the crime scene photos just being left out during the remainder of Bowman's testimony. It was a catch-22. On the one hand, they were jarring. Horrifying. LaForge wanted to keep the severity of the crime in the forefront of their minds at all times. On the other hand, the longer the jury stared at those photos, they would become desensitized to them. I would let it go until it was my turn to cross.

"Detective, were you able to make an arrest in this case?"

"I was," Bowman said. "Later on the morning of the 23rd."

"On what basis?"

"On the basis of further witness testimony and after receiving the preliminary phone forensics."

Careful, I thought. The forensics report wasn't in

evidence yet. But Bowman was cool. He never mentioned the results of those reports.

"And who did you arrest?"

"We arrested the defendant, Aubrey Ames, for the murder of Coach Drazdowski."

"Did you read the defendant her rights when you arrested her?"

"I did. And she exercised them. She asked for an attorney straight off."

"Did you question her after that?"

"After her initial arrest? No, sir, I did not."

"Did you have occasion to speak with the defendant anytime after that?"

Bowman cleared his throat. "Yes. I did."

"All right. So if you would, explain to the jury the circumstances of that communication."

"Well, it was July 10th of this year. I was working at my desk. Mark Ramos was working as my desk sergeant that day. He called me up and told me that the defendant had come into the station and wanted to talk to me."

"What did you do?"

"Well, I'll admit, it shocked me. I had Detective Lewis, that's Megan Lewis, show the defendant to an interrogation room. I met them there. I asked the defendant if she wanted me to contact her attorney."

"Objection," I said. "Hearsay."

"Sustained," Judge Castor said. "Let's just stick to what she said to you, all right?"

"Fine. The defendant said she didn't want her lawyer. She said she wanted to talk to us. She said she wanted to confess."

"Detective, did you make a recording of this conversation?"

"Of course. Yes. Immediately. But first, the defendant wrote out her confession."

"Detective, I'd like to direct your attention to what's been marked for identification as exhibit fourteen. Can you tell me what that is?"

"This is the statement that was handwritten by the defendant. It's got her signature."

"Objection, foundation," I said.

"Sustained. Jack, let's try for a little finesse here," Castor said.

"I watched her write it out and sign it," Bowman interjected. Castor narrowed his eyes, but let him proceed. Jack moved to admit the written confession.

"I would like to renew my objection to the admission of this exhibit and any videotaped statement by my client."

The judge called us over for a sidebar. He covered his microphone with his hand. "You got anything new for me other than what you argued in your motion to suppress Ms. Leary?"

"Your officer just admitted that the defendant was in custody before she gave her statement. He took her to an interrogation room."

"Nice try," Castor said. "That's not new. I told you before, I hate the shit out of the way this was handled, but I don't see anything other than a voluntary waiver, counselor. I'm admitting the witness's written statement. I'm admitting the videotape of that statement if Jack authenticates it."

"Fine by me," Jack said.

"And for the umpteenth time, I need to renew my objection on the record to the admission of it."

"You do what you gotta do," Castor said. "Let's get this going."

He sat up and we went back on the record. "Counselor?" he looked at me.

"Thank you, Your Honor. The defense would like to renew its objection to this testimony and the proposed exhibits fourteen and fifteen as marked for identification on the grounds that they were improperly obtained in contravention of my client's Sixth Amendment rights."

"I appreciate that," Judge Castor said. "And for the reasons set forth in my written opinion, your motion is denied. We're moving on."

Ten minutes later, the jury got to watch Aubrey's so-called confession to killing Larry Drazdowski.

On the big screen in the courtroom, Aubrey looked even more pale and frail. She trembled and stumbled over her words.

"Tell us what happened." Megan Lewis's voice was hard to hear on the tape, but subtitles ran beneath it.

"I did it," Aubrey said. "Okay. I just … I did it. I killed Coach D. I just want this to be over."

Over and over, Lewis and Bowman tried to get Aubrey to elaborate on what happened that night. Over and over, she simply said she'd just "done it."

"Walk me through it," Lewis said. "Just tell us exactly what happened."

"I wanted to meet with him. With Coach D. You read my texts. You already know this."

"Your words, Aubrey. We need to hear your words."

She buried her face in her hands. "You say all this like you want to help me. You don't want to help me. You want to help you. I just want it all to be over. I don't want anybody else getting hurt by this. It's enough."

"Who's going to get hurt?"

"Me. My dad. My friends. You don't have any idea and if you did, you wouldn't care. I killed him. I just killed him. I took a knife and I killed him. I didn't mean it. I didn't plan it.

It was in the heat of the moment. It just happened. I got angry. The next thing I knew, he was dead."

"How did you kill him?"

"With that knife. You know how he died."

Lewis was good. I thought it the first time I saw this tape. And the hundred and first time. She kept Bowman on a short leash. But Aubrey would never say more than that she "just killed him" and that she hadn't planned it. Her written statement was identical.

I couldn't read the jury. They looked from the screen to Aubrey then back again. I knew what they wanted though. It was the same thing I wanted. Details. I could only pray they'd come away from watching that tape with more questions than answers. If that happened, Aubrey still had a chance.

There were muffled voices on the tape. Chair legs scraping the ground. It was at this point I arrived at the station and the interview ended. The screen went black.

"Is that the last time you spoke to the defendant?" Jack asked Bowman. One of the jurors snapped her head back, as if she'd just been pulled back to reality.

"I believe so, yes," Bowman answered.

LaForge spent some time cleaning up a few things, but he finished with Bowman's testimony at ten minutes to four. Castor looked at his watch. I was ready to throw a fit if he recessed for the day. It would put us at an extreme disadvantage if the jury were allowed to go home after Jack's direct and before my cross.

"Your witness," Castor said to me, edging my respect for him another notch.

"Thank you, Your Honor," I said and rose from my seat. "Detective Bowman, you indicated you've been a police officer for twenty-six years, correct? And a detective for sixteen of those?"

"Yes."

"And you've been trained to remember the specific details of any case, correct?"

"I have."

"So, you're observant. You have to be. Thorough."

"Yes."

"You'd never come to court without being thoroughly prepared."

"That's correct."

"So, you reviewed your reports, your notes, your case file on the Drazdowski matter before coming here today, right?"

"Of course."

"Have you been thorough and complete in your testimony today?"

"I have."

"Haven't left anything out?"

"No, ma'am."

"Would you add anything to the answers you gave the prosecutor if given a chance?"

He considered it for a moment. "I don't believe so, no."

"Thank you," I said. I had to tie Bowman to the statements he made today and his report. If he tried to change or elaborate on anything, the jury would notice. It was a thin straw, but an important one.

"Detective Bowman, were you in the courtroom when Mrs. Emmett testified?"

"I was," he said.

"And you interviewed her in the early morning of June 23rd, correct?"

"I did."

"And you testified and wrote in your report that you arrived at the crime scene just past one in the morning on the night in question, isn't that right?"

"That's right. Yes."

"And you also heard Mrs. Emmett testify that she called 911 after discovering the victim's body a minute or two before twelve fifteen, correct?"

"Uh, yes. That's what she said."

"So it was a full hour from the time the crime was reported before you arrived, right?"

"Apparently," he said, not liking where I was going.

"And you testified that when you arrived at one twenty-two or thereabouts, you assisted in securing the crime scene. Is that right?"

"I did. Yes."

"How did you secure the scene?"

He took a breath. "Well, we cordoned off an area around the victim's body. Put up tape. I had patrols looking for other potential witnesses. We took pictures of the body and such."

"Before you arrived … or rather, when you arrived, did you observe the uniformed officers walking around the scene?"

"Did I what? Yes."

"Thank you." I left the rest of it alone. For now, it was enough to let the jurors wonder what, if anything, may have happened at the scene in the hour before it was fully secured.

"Now, Detective, did you know who the victim was when you arrived on scene?"

He shifted in his chair. Tim Bowman had been around the block plenty. He knew exactly what I was teeing up. "I suspected," he said. "When I got the call, one of the uniformed officers on scene already knew who it was."

"How did he know?"

"Officer Marrin. He played basketball for the victim about ten years ago."

"Got it. But what about you? Did you know Larry Draz-dowski personally?"

Bowman paused for a second. Of course he knew this was coming. "I did. Yes."

"By reputation? Or did you know him to speak to him?"

"I knew him to speak to him. He was hired at Delphi after I graduated, but I have a nephew he coached."

"Who was that, your nephew?"

"Luke Bowman. He graduated, I think, six years ago."

"So he was on one of the state championship teams the victim coached?"

"He was," Bowman answered. "He was the captain."

"Thank you. So, how well did you know the coach? Did you go to your nephew's basketball games?"

"Every single one," Bowman answered; his lips got tight.

"Did you socialize with the victim outside of those basketball games?"

"My brother, Luke's father. He invited Drazdowski over for dinner a few times during Luke's years. I attended some of those dinners."

"Okay. So you knew him well enough to sit across a dinner table from him."

"Objection," Jack finally popped up. "This is irrelevant."

He knew damn well it wasn't. His objection was more to put that thought in the jury's mind than any real legal basis.

"Establishing a witness's relationship with a victim is relevant, Your Honor," I said.

"Overruled," Castor said. "But I believe you've made your point, counselor."

I moved closer to the witness stand. "Detective Bowman, you said you questioned the defendant in the early morning hours of June 23rd. Did you also examine her?"

"Excuse me?"

"Well, this was a violent crime, was it not?"

Bowman let out a sigh. "I'd say anytime a man is stabbed in the gut and left bleeding to death, I'd call that violent."

I gritted my teeth. I'd walked into that, but not in the way Bowman thought. "Detective, did you notice any marks on the defendant?"

"What? No."

"No defensive wounds?"

"Not a scratch on her, as far as I could tell," Bowman said. Perfect.

"Detective, how many other suspects did you focus on in this investigation?"

Bowman shifted again. "None."

"In your sixteen-plus years as a detective, have you ever had a suspect confess to a crime he or she didn't commit?"

"What? Yes. A few times."

"Generally speaking, what's the reason for that? Why would a suspect confess to a crime she didn't commit?"

"Objection, calls for speculation."

"Your Honor, this witness is trained to act on his powers of observation. I'd like to explore that. He just testified he's worked on cases where suspects confess to crimes they haven't committed."

Castor checked his watch. "Short leash. You may answer."

"Can you repeat the question?"

"Why would a suspect confess to a crime she hadn't committed? In your experience, from the other cases where that happened."

"Usually it's because they're trying to cover for some-body. They're scared. They were threatened. That sort of thing."

"Thank you," I said. "I have nothing further."

"How long are you going to need for redirect?" Castor asked Jack.

"Just a couple of questions, Your Honor," Jack answered.

"Let's go then," the judge said. "Then we'll break for the day."

"Detective Bowman, do you have any reason to believe the defendant in this case confessed to protect someone else?"

Bowman leaned into the microphone again. "I do not. No."

"And going back to the night of the murder. Do you have any concerns that the crime scene was not properly secured? At any point?"

My pulse jumped, stunned that Jack had left that open for me.

"Not a one," Bowman answered.

"Thank you, I'm finished."

"Your Honor." I rose. "I just have one question for recross, if it pleases the court."

"Go ahead."

"Detective, the victim's body was found at approximately twelve fifteen. You yourself didn't arrive on scene for almost an hour later. You can't really directly testify about the security or even the condition of the scene for a full hour after the body was discovered, let alone when the actual murder took place, isn't that right?"

Bowman squeezed his eyes shut and let out a sigh. He realized the dog doo he'd just stepped in. It was minor, probably. But the goal post was reasonable doubt.

"Yeah, that's right."

"Thank you, I have nothing further."

It was a small victory, but it ended Detective Bowman's testimony and the first day of trial on a sour note for the prosecution.

Except the jury would have Aubrey's confession in their minds forever.

Chapter 28

FIRST THING THE NEXT MORNING, Jack dealt with the cell phone forensics. He called Detective Marjorie Miller to the stand.

"Detective Miller, can you please tell the jury how you became involved in this case?"

Marjorie Miller was in her mid-thirties like I was, but looked far younger. She wore her platinum blonde hair in a sleek ponytail, the kind I could never in a million years achieve. She looked like she could be their daughter. Their sister. The younger male jurors might fantasize about asking her out. If I went after her too hard, they'd turn on me.

"I'm a detective with the Detroit Police Department. I work on computer forensics. Smaller counties like Woodbridge often contract out their cell phone dumps to me as we have more state-of-the-art equipment."

"Dumps?"

"Oh. Sorry. I was asked to retrieve cell phone data on both the victim in this case and a phone found at the scene."

Jack then spent the next thirty minutes on the science behind Detective Miller's job. It's mind-numbing stuff to any jury, but in the end, Jack cued the detective up to talk about the location of both Larry Drazdowski's cell phone and Aubrey's in the time leading up to the murder.

In Aubrey's case, it was a straight path from the end of her shift at Dewar's to Shamrock Park. In Drazdowski's case, there were no surprises either. He was home when he received the first texts from Aubrey. He then left home and stopped at a gas station at approximately ten p.m. Then he went to the park. Later, I knew Jack would call the witness who saw Coach D talking to Aubrey from his car just inside the park at ten thirty.

The damning testimony came from the context of Aubrey's texts. Jack methodically laid his foundation, then moved to admit the cell phone report including the transcripts of the texts. I had no solid legal basis to object to the entry so I saved my battles for later. Jack put the excerpt of the report containing the transcript up on the screen for the jury to see. He had Detective Miller read them into the record.

7:52 p.m.

Aubrey to Coach D: I'm ready to talk.

7:53 p.m.

Coach D: Glad to hear it. You can stop by my planning period on Monday.

7:57 p.m.

Aubrey: No. Now. Tonight.

8:03 p.m.

Coach D: I have a life, Aubrey. Anything school-related can wait for school hours.

8:03 p.m.

Aubrey: Stop it. I can't take another second of this. You know what I told you. I wasn't kidding around.

8:04 p.m.

Coach D: You need help, Aubrey. I'm not the person qualified to give it. Have you talked to your parents?

8:07 p.m.

Aubrey: Are you serious with me right now?

8:07 p.m.

Coach D: Absolutely. I'd be more than willing to meet with them too. I just don't want you to do anything you can't undo.

8:07 p.m.

Aubrey: You're unbelievable. Pick up your damn phone the next time I call. I hate texting.

8:07 p.m.

Coach D: Under the circumstances, so do I.

8:09 p.m.

Aubrey: I get off work at 10. Meet me then.

8:11 p.m.

Coach D: I'm not sure I'm comfortable with that. Let's set something up on Monday.

8:11 p.m.

Aubrey: You know exactly why this can't wait until Monday. Come to Dewar's. We'll go to the diner across the street. Bernadette's.

8:20 p.m.

Aubrey: ??

8:25 p.m.

Coach D: I'm not coming to Bernadette's.

8:27 p.m.

Aubrey: Then where?

8:28 p.m.

Coach D: Why don't you swing by my house on your way home?

8:28 p.m.

Aubrey: No way.

8:31 p.m.

Aubrey: Fine. Shamrock Park. The entrance to the bike trails by that stupid shamrock statue.

8:41 p.m.

Aubrey: I need an answer.

8:45 p.m.

Coach D: Fine.

There was stony silence in the courtroom as the jury listened and read along. When she finished, Jack turned the witness over to me.

"Thank you, Detective Miller," I said. "In your report, you haven't indicated whether there was any DNA found on Miss Ames's phone. There wasn't, was there?"

"Um, no," she said. "We did not test for that in my office."

"Thank you. So there was no blood on the phone?"

"Objection," Jack popped up. "The witness just indicated she's not qualified to answer that."

"I think the witness is capable of speaking to her own qualifications, Your Honor," I said.

"Agreed," Judge Castor ruled.

Detective Miller leaned forward. "No. I didn't test for blood on either the victim or defendant's phone."

"Did you see anything on the phones that looked like it might have been blood?"

She gave me a quizzical look. "Um … no. I don't recall that."

"Thank you. One more question, Detective Miller: you can't offer an opinion here today on whether the defendant committed this crime, can you?"

"No, I cannot," said Detective Miller.

"Thank you. I have nothing further."

Jack stepped forward for redirect and did something that surprised me a little. "Detective, on this issue of blood on the phones. You just said you don't recall there being blood on either of them. That means there could have been blood, correct? You just don't remember?"

"Objection, counsel is leading the witness," I said. This was so sloppy on Jack's part. The blood or absence of it was major straw grasping on my part. I knew it. Jack knew it. The witness knew it. I was pretty sure the judge even knew it. Jack's question was bound to lead the jury to think this was a more important point than it really was. I just sat back and let it happen.

"Rephrase, counsel."

"Okay." Jack cleared his throat, realizing his error. "I'll, uh … I'll just withdraw the question. I have nothing further."

The witness stepped down. "Call your next witness," the judge commanded.

Jack called Amelia Trainor, Medical Examiner for the County of Woodbridge. This case was the first time I'd had dealings with Amelia but I already liked her. I just wished she weren't about to deliver some of the most damning testimony in the case.

Chapter 29

IN HER LATE SIXTIES, Amelia Trainor was cool, confident, and fit every stereotype anyone ever had about a coroner. She was pale-skinned with light blue eyes. Tall, reed-thin, and she sat with her back so straight you'd think she had an actual stick up her ass.

Jack laid his foundation with Amelia's credentials. She'd been the Chief Medical Examiner for Woodbridge County for fifteen years. Before that, she worked in Wayne County. Before that, she'd spent almost a dozen years as an E.R. doc. The woman knew her way around gunshot and stab wounds.

Jack entered the autopsy report and pulled up the crime scene photos again. He could have used the autopsy photos, but didn't. It's exactly the call I would have made in his shoes. It's easier for a person to detach themselves from autopsy photos. In many ways, the bodies don't look real, more like wax figures. But that picture of Larry Drazdowski's dead eyes pleading with the camera had seared its way into the minds of the jurors.

"Dr. Trainor, what was Larry Drazdowski's cause of death?"

"Cardiac arrest," she answered.

"Brought on by what?"

"The victim suffered a fatal stab wound to the left side of his abdomen. The blade punctured his kidney and severed the left renal artery. Massive blood loss caused his heart to stop, Mr. LaForge."

One of the jurors gasped.

"Doctor, can you estimate how long it took for Coach D to die?"

"It's hard to say exactly."

"Was death instantaneous?"

"I wouldn't think so, no."

"So, Coach D felt every inch of that blade going in."

"Objection …"

Judge Castor put his hand up before I could even finish. "Let's stick to the facts, Mr. LaForge."

"I'll rephrase. In your expert medical opinion, Dr. Trainor, would the victim have lost consciousness immediately?"

"Probably not, no. His heart would have still been beating after the initial stab wound. In layman's terms, the victim bled out. As I indicated, his renal artery was severed. Without prompt medical attention, a wound like that is very often fatal, as it was in this case."

"Thank you," Jack said. "And just to be clear, in your opinion, the victim was most likely awake while he bled out?"

"I can't say for sure how long he was conscious. But I would think for a period of time, yes."

"How long, in your educated guess?"

She sighed. "This victim eventually lost over ninety percent of his blood volume. He most likely passed out before the point of medical death. He would have gone into shock. But, if you're asking me if he would have remained conscious for a time after he was stabbed, the answer is yes. I can't give you a precise countdown. Not hours. Seconds. Probably in the neighborhood of thirty seconds."

Jack let that answer simmer for the jury. Thirty seconds. In closing, he would of course have the jury imagine what those thirty seconds must have felt like for Coach D.

"Was he in pain?" Jack asked. "Do you know that?"

"No," she answered. "Pain is subjective. You can ask a hundred stabbing or gunshot victims whether they felt their wound. Some will tell you they felt every second of it. Some will tell you they never felt a thing until much later. Shock and adrenaline are unpredictable things. But yes, I would imagine a wound like this victim's would have caused a great deal of pain."

"Thank you. I have nothing further."

"Your witness, Ms. Leary," the judge said.

I straightened my skirt and rose. "Thank you. Good afternoon, Dr. Trainor. I just have a few questions. Were you able to determine what type of knife was used to stab the victim?"

"Actually, yes," she said. "The wound was consistent with a smooth-edged blade. No serration. About two inches wide and four inches long. It was a single, sharpened edge with a slight curve to it. This was a hunting knife, probably."

I hadn't asked her that last bit, but she'd just given me a gift and Jack knew it.

"Thank you. And you testified earlier, it's in your report, there was just one stab wound?"

"That's correct."

"How tall was the victim? You may refer to your report if you need to."

"He was taller than average. Six foot five and a quarter. One hundred and one point six kilograms. That's roughly two hundred and twenty-four pounds."

"Was he fit?" I asked.

"Excuse me?"

"Was the victim physically fit, in your opinion?"

"Oh. I would say so, yes. He would have rated as over-weight if we're talking straight body mass index. But the victim had good, well-developed muscle tone consistent with someone who worked out regularly. I did appreciate some minor plaque build-up in one of the main arteries that feeds the heart, but he was remarkably fit for someone his age, in my opinion."

"Just so I'm clear again, you only found one wound. One stab wound."

"That's correct."

"Would you agree that a kill shot, or stab wound like that would have taken some strength to pull off?"

She considered my question. Jack leaned in to whisper to his co-counsel.

"Not necessarily," Dr. Trainor answered. "The path of the wound went through all soft tissue. The knife went in up under the ribs without hitting any of them."

"Remarkable," I said. "Can you estimate how close the victim was to the person who stabbed him when the knife went in?"

"Objection, as to form."

"Let me rephrase. Doctor; in light of the trajectory and character of the wound, do you have an opinion on the position of the victim and the perpetrator?"

"The blade went just past vertical." Dr. Trainor gestured with her hand, holding it at about a twenty-five-degree angle. "The killer was close. This isn't the kind of wound that would have been made by a lucky throw."

"Thank you," I asked. "Nothing further."

"Just one question, Your Honor," Jack said, straightening his tie. "Doctor, the stab wound you've described, could it have been made by someone who was in an embrace with the victim? Are we talking that close?"

"Objection."

Castor made that now trademark stopping gesture with his hand.

"You opened the door, counselor."

"Yes," Dr. Trainor answered. "I suppose it's possible that the killer was close enough to be in an embrace with the victim when the stabbing took place. But that's just a guess. This was a quick, deadly jab, Mr. LaForge."

"Thank you, I have nothing further."

We broke for the day. As soon as the last juror left the courtroom, Aubrey broke down. Her face became a mass of purple blotches and she started to hyperventilate.

To his credit, to all of their credit, the judge gave us the courtroom and Jack quickly took his team and left.

"They think I did it. They won't believe me. They think I … that I … hugged … that I …"

"Aubrey, calm down. That's your chief job right now. To hang in there. You're doing great so far. You knew this would be a hard day. It's over. You got through it."

There was so much harder to come. Dan Ames came to his daughter's side. His face told me he already understood what I had to say next. Diane Ames had yet to show up in court. With everything else swirling around, that looked terrible. I made a mental note to have Jeanie try with her again.

"Tell her," Dan said to me. With just one look, I knew we were on the same page.

"Aubrey," I said. "You know we've debated this for weeks. Months. I think after today, there can be no more debate."

She surprised me by nodding. "I know. I know. Oh God. I can't though."

"You have to," I said. "The jury heard that confession. We've made a few dents today. Dr. Trainor actually helped us. I can feel it. The jury is already trying to work out how someone your size could pull off a stab wound like that on someone of Larry's size at close range."

"Because they think I was … that I'd let him touch me."

"Aubrey, you know I wouldn't ask this if we had any other choice. But it's time. Jack is getting close to wrapping up. I told you I've done damage, but I don't know if it's going to be enough. The jury has to hear from you. They have to know why you confessed. They have to know it all."

She squeezed her eyes shut and let out a hard breath.

"And Diane *must* be here for it all. Get her a Xanax, I don't care. But the jury needs to see Aubrey's mother just as much as they see the two of you."

Dan nodded and started to lead her away. Aubrey's testimony might come as soon as tomorrow if Jack called no further witnesses. But I trusted Dan to manage his daughter. I needed her as fresh as possible. I gave him a grim-faced nod and let them leave the courtroom ahead of me. Three sheriff's deputies would escort them to Dan's car through the service entrance again.

I gathered my messenger bag and looked back at the empty jury box. I hadn't been to church in years, but I found myself praying now.

Jeanie had gone on ahead. I pulled out my phone intending to call her. I'd parked two blocks over in front of the post office. On the third day of trial, the angry spectators had thinned out. I almost felt normal again as I waited for Jeanie to pick up.

As I pulled out my keys, two of Coach D's former players emerged from the side of the building wearing their letterman jackets. Jeanie had taken to calling his supporters the Lettermen. If she didn't watch it, that would stick and end up in the newspaper.

These particular Lettermen were pretty young. The

numbers on their jackets indicated they were just two years past their graduating class. Aubrey's classmates. I couldn't breathe. I was back in my upturned car in that ditch by the side of the road. I was on the deck of the Crown of Thorne, the icy blue water coming up at me.

"You're a real bitch, you know that?" the taller of the two said. He had thinning blond hair that would likely disappear by the time he hit thirty. He stared at me with cold, blue eyes as his companion puffed his chest out and stood at his shoulder.

I held my keys between my fingers, forming a fist. Surely they wouldn't be bold enough to try anything. The post office was closed now, but there were still a smattering of people walking one block down.

"It's been a long day for everyone," I said. They moved, blocking my path to my driver's side door.

"Really?" I asked.

"Really," the ringleader said. He wore a state championship ring and flashed it.

"What's your plan here? Huh? You gonna knock me out?"

"That little bitch is a liar and a whore. You should rethink who you side with."

"Did you ever talk to her? Huh? In the halls? At the games? Do you even know her?"

"We know enough. She's a slut."

"Great. Whatever. I'm done debating this. Now get out of my way."

They closed in. My heart jackhammered. I took a ready stance, not really believing these two would be dumb enough to actually assault me in the middle of the street.

Tires screeched behind me. That familiar black SUV pulled up and its driver got out. He was huge. Even taller than these two Lettermen. He wore a dark suit and a shiny blue tie. His jacket bulged at the side from the weapon I knew he carried there. He unbuttoned that jacket and flashed the weapon he carried. The boys turned white and backed up.

"Listen …"

"No, you listen," my suited protector said. "You're done here. You come near this woman again, you're not going home again. Got it?"

He didn't draw his gun. He didn't have to. The message was clear and the two Lettermen tripped over each other scattering in different directions. For my part, I concentrated on remembering how to breathe.

The suited man turned to me. I didn't recognize him. Not personally, anyway. But even before he spoke, I knew with cold dread who had sent him.

"Miss Leary," he said, reaching back into his jacket. He pulled out a business card and held it out to me. I didn't even want to touch it, but my body went on autopilot and I took it from him.

"Are you okay?" he asked.

I swallowed hard. "Yes," I said. "Tell your boss I'm fine. And tell him no thank you."

He raised a brow. "No thank you? I don't know if you were paying attention, but those two idiots back there weren't really looking to make small talk with you."

I fingered the raised lettering on the business card. I had another one identical to it underneath my mattress. I'd sworn to myself I'd never use it. I swore it again now.

"Mr. Thorne just wants to make sure you're settling in all right," the man said. "He's concerned about your well-being. Is there anything you'd like me to tell him for you?"

There were a million things I'd like to say to Killian Thorne. And there was nothing at all.

"No," I said, brushing past his bodyguard. Then I stopped and turned.

"What's your name?" I asked.

He looked left and right. No one else was nearby. "Corwin."

I nodded. "Okay, Mr. Corwin. I think I can guess what your orders are."

"I'm just here to make sure nothing happens to you. Mr. Thorne understands there are people in this town who want to do you harm at the moment. He's apparently right."

"Fine," I said. "So you do your job. You just make sure you do it from somewhere I don't have to see you. Can you do that?"

Corwin was a man built for taking orders. He rebuttoned his jacket and gave me a curt nod. Then he got back into his SUV and pulled up to the curb. He would let me go. He might even keep his distance. But I knew he wasn't going away.

Chapter 30

THE NEXT MORNING, Jack LaForge called Kevin Sydney to the stand. Jeanie leaned in; grabbing me by the shoulder, she whispered, "What the hell's he doing?"

I answered through the side of my mouth. "I have no idea."

"He's not on Jack's witness list," Jeanie said.

"No," I answered. "But he's on ours." Except I hadn't yet decided whether I would call him. Every bone in my body told me Sydney would do whatever he could to hang Aubrey Ames.

"Ms. Leary?" Judge Castor said.

I straightened in my chair. "Sorry, Your Honor."

There was a murmur through the gallery. I looked over my shoulder at Judge Castor's bailiff. He gave a curt nod and went out through the double doors. A few seconds later, he brought Sydney in. The man was wearing the same dark-blue suit he'd worn when I met him a few weeks ago. He also chose a black tie with tiny green shamrocks on it. If that weren't enough of a clue as to where his loyalties lay, Kevin

Sydney wore a shiny green button on his lapel that read #neverstopfighting. It was an homage to Coach D that had sprung up just after the start of the new school year. I'd heard through the grapevine that it was a phrase the coach used with his players all the time. There was even a banner hanging in the locker room with it on it.

Kevin Sydney adjusted his tie and smiled after the bailiff swore him in. He gave a wide smile to the jury and crossed his legs. I'd suspected it before, but with this little display, the idea cemented in my mind that Kevin Sydney, high school athletic director, was an idiot. Except I knew he wasn't stupid. I held my breath, sensing this little roller coaster ride was about to drop down the first hill hard.

"Go ahead, Mr. LaForge," the judge directed.

"Thank you. Mr. Sydney. Can you state your full name into the record and tell me what it is you do for a living." Jack practically strutted to the podium.

"Kevin Thomas Sydney. I am the athletic director for Delphi High School."

"How long have you held that position?"

"I was hired by the district twenty-two years ago."

"Thank you. Were you the person responsible for hiring Larry Drazdowski as head basketball coach then?"

"I was." Sydney actually puffed out his chest. "Best thing I ever did."

"How long ago was that, if you recall?"

"I do. I was hired just before the start of the school year in August. At the conclusion of that basketball season, so early spring the following year, we started a search for a new coach. We hired Larry in, I think it was April of that year. It was an easy choice. So I guess that's twenty-one and a half years ago Larry came into our family."

"Your family?"

"Yes. The Delphi High team, we're a family."

"You mean the basketball team?"

"No. I mean the faculty, staff, administrators, coaches. We are a team. We are a family, in my mind."

Lord, Jack was doing my work for me. "So, you'd consider yourself close to Mr. Drazdowski."

"I was. Very. Yes." Sydney swiped a finger beneath his eye. Jeanie squeezed my shoulder again. I knew her spidey senses were tingling as hard as mine were.

"Did your relationship with Mr. Drazdowski go beyond professional then? In other words, did you socialize outside of the workplace?" Jack asked.

"Absolutely. Larry Drazdowski was as solid a man as there ever was. He lived, breathed, and apparently died in service of those students."

"Your Honor, I'd ask that the last part of this witness's answer be stricken," I said.

"Sustained, stick to facts, Mr. Sydney, not speculation," Castor said.

Sydney's gaze fell to me. He had a glint in his eye I didn't like one bit.

"Mr. Sydney, when was the last time you spoke to the victim?" Jack asked.

"We spoke all the time. Weekly. Larry was a single guy. My wife and I looked out for him. His parents are getting on in years and they live up near Traverse City. There were lots of times Larry was alone on certain holidays. When that happened, he'd come to our place. I loved that man."

Kevin Sydney teared up. He fidgeted with his tie.

"Mr. Sydney, I know this is hard. I can't even imagine the loss of a friend like that. But I have to ask you to answer my question. When was the last time you spoke to Larry Drazdowski?"

ROBIN JAMES

"The night before he was murdered. He was going through some stuff. He got depressed sometimes. He was tough on himself. You have to understand. Those kids were everything to him. When one of them was going through something, it was like it was happening to him too. He had a hard time letting go."

"Did Mr. Drazdowski ever talk to you about the defendant, Miss Ames?"

"Yes," Sydney answered. My blood began to boil.

"When was the last time you had a conversation with the victim about Miss Ames?"

"I can't say for sure. Maybe a few weeks before he … before all this. I wish I'd done something. I should have seen it. I'll never forgive myself for that."

"What won't you forgive yourself for?"

My heart thundered. Jeanie whispered to me again. "You have to stop this, now!"

Aubrey started to hyperventilate. Every juror shifted in their seat. The roller coaster glided down the next hill. I gripped a pen in my right hand. But I said nothing. Instinct fueled me.

"I didn't understand it at the time for what it was," Kevin said. "Larry was as codependent as they come with those kids. It's what made him so great. It's also what tortured him the most. But in this case. With Ms. Ames. I don't know what was going on. But Larry said to me, I'll never forget it. Kev, I think this girl is going to try to kill me."

The gallery behind me erupted in murmurs.

"That's a lie!" Aubrey whispered.

I knew Jack expected me to make a hearsay objection. It was. Oh. It was. But I had to bite my lip past a smile. This was a dangerous gamble, but Kevin Sydney may have just opened a door Jack LaForge could never close.

234

"I have nothing further," Jack said, still smirking as he turned toward me. He didn't realize it.

Jeanie did. "Hot damn," she whispered.

He was lying. The bastard was making this shit up as he went. And it was going to be my supreme pleasure to expose him for the snake he was.

Chapter 31

Jack asked for a twenty-minute recess. I objected. Just a slight change in Jack's color told me he was starting to realize what he'd done.

"I just have a few questions for this witness on cross, Your Honor," I said. "I'd really like to proceed now."

"Okay," Judge Castor said.

"And may I have permission to treat this witness as hostile, Your Honor?"

"Granted," Castor said.

I dove right in.

"Mr. Sydney. You considered Mr. Drazdowski like family, right?"

"Of course. And I want justice for Coach D."

"Right. Justice. Of course. And yet, you never bothered to go to the police with this little gem you now want us to believe, did you?"

"Objection ..." Jack said.

"Ms. Leary, thin ice here," Castor replied.

"You've never told the police about this conversation you claim to have had with Larry Drazdowski, have you?"

"No ma'am, I didn't. I regret that now."

"Mr. Sydney," I continued. "At any point in Mr. Draz-dowski's tenure with Delphi High, were you aware of complaints made against him by students?"

"Complaints? What kind of complaints? I mean, sure. And I told you this when we met. It wasn't unusual to get a parent or two calling and complaining that their precious Johnny wasn't getting enough playing time. But I took the position that it was up to my coaching staff to make judgment calls. There was never anything about what Larry was doing that I had issue with."

I gave the judge side-eye. He was already on top of it though.

"Mr. Sydney," he said. "I'm going to have to again admonish you to stick to the facts when you're asked a question. Counselor?"

"Mr. Sydney, I'm not asking about parents right now. I'm asking you if any students ever came to you to complain about Mr. Drazdowski's behavior with them?"

He took a great pause, chewed the side of his mouth, looked skyward, then leveled a hard stare back at me. "I don't think I know what you mean."

"It's pretty simple. Did any students ever come to you to lodge a complaint about Larry Drazdowski?"

"Objection, Your Honor," Jack said. "I've let this go longer than I should. To the extent counsel is asking about complaints about inappropriate behavior, that's asking for hearsay."

"Sustained."

I knew this was the roadblock I'd face. But I was banking on the fact that Jack and Sydney had just given me the hook I needed to hang Aubrey's defense on. "I'm not asking for the substance of any complaints. I'm asking whether they were lodged by students in the first place. This goes to the witness's credibility."

"I'll allow the question on that limited basis. Mr. Sydney, you may answer."

He leaned far forward into the microphone. "No. I didn't take student complaints on Larry Drazdowski."

"You didn't take them, or they were never made?"

"They were never made," he said. "Not by students. Not once."

My heartbeat skipped. I had to remind myself to breathe. He couldn't have just said that. I had to be hearing things. I wanted to repeat the question to convince myself I'd heard his answer correctly. Luckily, I knew better than to give him the chance to clean it up.

"So you never took a meeting with a student by the name of Danielle Ford?"

Sydney's eyes narrowed. "No. Not that I recall."

"You never took a meeting with a student by the name of Lindsey Claussen?"

"No. Not that I recall."

"And you never took a meeting with a student by the name of Chelsea Holbrook?"

"No. Definitely not. And if there had been a problem, I would have counseled those students to address their concerns with Mr. Drazdowski first."

"Even if Mr. Drazdowski was the source of the problem? You'd have counseled those students to meet with him first? Alone?"

I was pushing it with the last bit. Sydney's face changed color. "I would ... I suppose it would depend on the nature of the complaint."

"Well, assume the nature of the complaint was that Mr. Drazdowski was acting inappropriately with them. You're telling me it was your policy to counsel that student to meet with Mr. Drazdowski alone first?"

"Well, no. Not in that case. But I never received complaints that Mr. Drazdowski was behaving inappropriately toward a student so it's a moot point."

Maybe, but I'd just gotten him to answer the question.

"Mr. Sydney, who keeps your schedule of meetings?"

"In my office? That would be my secretary, Karen Larsen."

"How long has Ms. Larsen worked for you in that capacity?"

"I'm not sure. I had a few different secretaries. She's been with me the longest though. You'd have to ask her yourself, but I'd say it's fifteen or more years."

"Okay. Just so I'm clear. If you have a meeting scheduled in the course of your workday, Ms. Larsen is the one who keeps track of that."

"For sure. I'd be lost without her. She puts everything in an electronic calendar for me. And she keeps a book on her desk."

"I just want to go back to something you said earlier. This question of family. What does that mean to you? In the workplace, I mean."

I expected Jack to pop up with a relevancy objection. Miraculously, he didn't. When I stole a glance over my shoulder, he was deep in hushed conversation with his paralegal.

"It means we look out for each other. We're a team. We have each other's backs."

"Are the students part of that family in your mind?"

"Are they what?"

"Thank you," I said. "I have nothing further."

Jack finished his whispering and rose. He shook his head, in an almost pantomime of confusion. He saw. He heard. He knew. Kevin Sydney had just opened the floodgates on Larry Drazdowski.

Chapter 32

Two things happened on Friday, the fifth of November and the fifth day of trial. First, the prosecution rested its case against Aubrey Ames. The second thing came much later and was the thing I swore I'd never do again.

As the jury filed back in, I scanned the gallery behind me. Praise the lord, Dan Ames sat in the row directly behind the defense table. Diane Ames sat beside him, sinking into her husband. Even Aubrey looked surprised as she turned back. Tears quickly sprang to her eyes and she turned back to face the bench. Good girl, I thought. She could cry later. I needed her focused and in control today.

A few members of the press took up the back benches, including a sketch artist. The *Detroit Free Press* had picked up this story and was featuring it in their second news section this week. I had my own version of a cheering section here today too. Joe had shown up and Katy was with him. In the far corner of the courtroom, the mysterious Corwin had found a bench all to himself. Terrific. A few curious members of the Woodbridge County Sheriff's department rounded out the spectators along with some D.P.D., including Detective Wray. He gave me a tight-lipped nod as I made eye contact. I'd seen him talking to Dan Ames in the hallway before court began. I was grateful for any moral support the Ames family could muster and realized the risk it was for him to associate with them.

"You ready to call your first witness?" the judge asked me.

"Yes, Your Honor," I said, taking a breath. Here we go. "The defense calls Aubrey Ames to the stand."

There was a collective gasp through the courtroom. Aubrey rose beside me. She wore a pair of black dress pants and a royal blue blazer I'd pulled from my own closet over a simple white blouse. She had her hair pulled back into a bun. Just a touch of make-up. A little blush in her cheeks and mascara. Aubrey looked small, serious, very young, but most of all scared.

The bailiff towered over her as she raised her right hand to be sworn in. I hadn't planned it, but Judge Castor's bailiff stood just over six feet tall. A full five inches shorter than Larry Drazdowski. Still, he dwarfed Aubrey. I hoped it resonated with the jury.

Aubrey stepped up to the box and took a seat. The microphone pointed at her forehead and she moved it into place.

"Good morning," I said, giving her the kindest smile I could muster as Aubrey walked into the lion's den. "Can you state your full name for the record?"

"Aubrey Ann Ames."

"Aubrey, how old are you?"

"I'm nineteen. Er ... I'll be twenty tomorrow."

"Okay. Aubrey, why don't you tell the jury a little about your background. Have you lived in Delphi all your life?"

"Yes. I was born here. My dad, um ... Dan Ames. He's a

general contractor. Builds houses. Ames Construction. My mom, Diane. She stays at home. She does bookkeeping for my dad's business. I have a brother, Sean. He's seventeen. We live in Delphi. Um … east side. We all went to Delphi High School. My brother still goes there. Or, I mean he did. He's … he's going to finish his senior year at home."

"When did you graduate?"

"Um … a year ago June."

"What were your future plans?"

Aubrey fidgeted in her seat, playing with the end of her ponytail. It's a habit I'd tried to break her of when we did our role-playing in the office. I moved to the center of the courtroom and folded my hands in front of me. She mirrored my movements and brought her hands into her own lap. I saw her exhale and her answers came a little easier.

"We don't … my dad does okay. We have a nice house. But I have to pay my own way for college. I don't … I don't want to take student loans. I got a job at the bakery. Dewar's. I started working there after my sophomore year. I like baking. They needed somebody to make the donuts in the morning."

"You're speaking of Dewar's Country Store?" I asked.

She nodded. I gestured and Aubrey leaned into the microphone. "Yes. Dewar's Country Store. I started out there baking the donuts. It worked out because even when school started, I'd go in at five in the morning, work for two hours then get to school. I did that for about a year and then they put me in the main store. Mostly as a cashier. But I stocked some too."

"Do you still work there?"

"Um … no … after … after all this started, I lost my job."

"What kind of hours were you working?"

"Toward the end … I mean, through this past June, I was working an afternoon shift. It was good because I took morning classes at the community college then I'd go into Dewar's around two or three in the afternoon, depending. Usually I got off at ten p.m."

"What are you studying at college, Aubrey?"

"Well, I'm just trying to finish up my gen ed classes. General education. The basics. But had wanted to get an accounting degree. I was always good at math. My mom doesn't want to do the bookkeeping forever. I was going to maybe start working for my dad but …"

Her voice caught. I heard Dan heave a sigh behind me.

"But what, Aubrey?"

"He's … he's lost a lot of business since all this started."

"Objection," Jack said. "This entire line of questioning is irrelevant."

Judge Castor gave Jack a withering stare. Technically speaking, he was right as it related to Dan's business. But this was pretty standard background testimony. Jack's strategy was more to rattle Aubrey than anything else.

"I'll move on," I said, not wanting to disrupt the flow of Aubrey's narrative on Jack's trivial bullshit.

"Aubrey, were you familiar with Larry Drazdowski, the victim in this case?"

She closed her eyes. Aubrey's entire demeanor shifted and two red spots formed on her cheeks. She wasn't breathing. Shit. I couldn't have her falling apart this quickly. Finally, it was as if a switch turned on and Aubrey snapped her eyes open.

"Yes," she answered in a loud, clear voice.

"How did you know Mr. Drazdowski?"

"As I said, I went to Delphi High. Coach … Mr. Drazdowski was a teacher, a gym teacher. Also the boys' basketball coach and the girls' track coach. I ran track my freshman and sophomore years. I knew *of* him before all of that. Everyone did."

"So he was your track coach?"

"Yes," she answered. "And during my freshman year, he was the gym teacher. Well, not specifically mine. Mrs. Powell was the girls' gym teacher. I took it second hour. But they ran the boys' class and girls' class at the same time. So it was kind of like they co-taught it. He knew me by name after that."

"Okay. And did you say you ran track for him?"

"Uh ... yeah. My freshman and sophomore years."

"So you didn't run track after your sophomore year?"

Aubrey quickly shook her head. Those red spots came back into her cheeks. "Aubrey, you have to answer verbally. The court reporter can't pick up gestures."

"Sorry. No. I decided not to run track the spring of my junior year."

"Why was that?"

"It got ... I didn't ... I wasn't all that great at it. And I tried ..."

She started to cry. Silent tears that ran down her cheeks. "Aubrey," I said. "I need you to answer the question."

"Okay. I thought it would help. I thought it would make things better if I didn't have to see Coach D every single day after school."

"Help what?"

She trembled. I came up to the witness box. I wanted to take her aside. It was now or never. I was fighting for Aubrey's future. Come hell or high water, I needed her to join that fight right now.

"I want to know what you thought would get better if you didn't see the coach after school every day."

"It's hard," she said. "My dad runs his own business and

sometimes it's not great. He works his butt off … but sometimes … We thought we were going to have to sell our house in the middle of my sophomore year. And I had a boyfriend, Mike Vaughan. He went to another school. We broke up and I wasn't really handling it all that well. I was sad. Coach D … he seemed like he cared. He listened. It felt like nothing shocked him and everyone felt more comfortable talking to him than to our parents sometimes. You know?"

"Are you saying you went to Coach D for advice?"

Aubrey continued. "It was after Christmas my sophomore year. I was really upset. I skipped gym class and somehow he found me. I was on a bench in the parking lot. He came out there and we went to his office. He listened. I told him the things I'd been keeping from my parents. How I didn't feel like anybody was ever going to like me. I was worried about having to move. Just all of it. But he listened. It helped."

"Was that the only time you ever met with Larry Drazdowski?"

She shook her head. "No. He said I could … we started meeting on Tuesdays, I think it was. During homeroom. He had an office across from the gym. Sometimes he wasn't even in it but he told me I could go in there to just clear my head whenever I wanted. So I did."

"What happened next, Aubrey?"

"It started out as back rubs. And I mean … I'm talking way later. I'd already started junior year. In the fall of that. He said he knew some techniques that would help me relax."

"Objection," Jack said. "We're getting into hearsay territory here."

"Counsel?"

I looked at the judge then to Aubrey. "Let's stick with what happened, not what the coach said or didn't say."

"Okay," Aubrey said. "He gave me back rubs. Shoulder rubs. I was ... I didn't ... the first time or two, it didn't seem that big of a deal. But I don't know. It changed. Went on longer. Then one night, I stayed after school to help paint the locker signs for the football team. A friend of mine, Kaitlyn. She was a cheerleader and she asked me. We got done late. I mean, it was dark out. Kaitlyn left and I was waiting for a ride. My dad was late on a job. Coach D came out and offered to take me home. I said okay."

She went deadly silent.

"Aubrey? What happened? Did the coach drive you home?"

The red spots in her cheeks turned purple. "He ... he got aggressive."

"Aggressive how?"

"He didn't drive me straight home. He took me to Shamrock Park. I was really upset that day. Homecoming was coming up and I didn't have a date. It was a whole stupid drama. He stopped and gave me a back rub. But then ... it changed. He pinned me down and started rubbing me in ... other places. My back, then in front."

"What did you do, Aubrey?"

"I told him no. God, I was so scared. I couldn't really believe it was happening. If I'm being honest, I went kind of outside myself. He was ... I mean, he was who he was. But ... he didn't stop. He ... kept going. All the way."

"Aubrey, I need you to be specific. I know this is hard. What do you mean, he went all the way?"

She buried her face in her hands. "He raped me. Okay? God, he'd been telling me for months how special I am. No one understands me the way he does. He could see me. I was different. I was too big for this school. I was such an idiot. I needed to hear that. It was like he knew. But he raped me. In that car in Shamrock Park. All those things he said over the past few months. He used them. Twisted them. And I didn't know what to do."

I waited a beat. Jack didn't object. It wouldn't have mattered anyway. Her words were out there forever.

Something happened to Aubrey Ames in those few minutes it took for her to get the hardest part of her story out. Her color slowly returned to normal and her voice got stronger. It was as if some dam had burst. With each word she spoke, I understood what was happening. She was taking back her power.

"Aubrey," I said. "Tell me what happened next."

"He drove me home. I asked him to let me out about three houses down from mine."

"Why?"

"I didn't … I didn't know what to do about any of it. I think maybe I was in shock. I didn't want anyone … my family … I didn't want them to think anything was wrong."

"Did you tell anyone what happened?"

She dropped her head. "No. Not then. I think I wanted to pretend it hadn't happened. I felt like maybe I did something, gave off some wrong impression. Coach D said that. He said he knew it's what I wanted and things would be so much better for me now."

I paused, walking to the end of the jury box. I couldn't say for sure how they took Aubrey's story, but every single one of them kept their eyes on Aubrey.

"So what happened at school after that? Did you have further contact with Mr. Drazdowski?"

She nodded. "He acted like everything was normal. I tried to pretend it was too. This was just before basketball season started. It was early October. For a few weeks, I saw him less and less. He was busy with the team. Then, just before Christmas, he started calling me back to his office."

"And you went?"

Aubrey's shoulders dropped and a little of that defeated look came into her eyes. I needed her to be strong. I needed the jury to understand how predators work and it could only happen from Aubrey's story.

"I was ashamed. But I was trying to act like everything was normal."

"What happened?"

"I told the coach I wanted him to stay away from me. He started to get angry. Maybe I wasn't as special as he thought. Maybe I was just the Eastlake trash everyone thought I was. And he got physical again."

She nodded. "You have to understand. He was just so strong. When you're in the room with him … it's like he *is* the room. He started hugging me and rubbing my back. He used his fingers on me … Then he sent me back to class."

"Did you tell anyone what happened? Your parents, friends, another teacher?"

She lifted a shoulder. "Things were pretty messed up for me then. Our house was in foreclosure. There was no work coming in for my dad. I didn't know how to tell anyone. I thought … I knew … I knew no one would believe me."

"Why did you think that?"

"Because he was the coach! No one ever said anything bad about him. Everyone loved him. And I believed him."

"Believed what?"

"That I was trash. I mean, I believed that about myself before. He was the first person who I felt ever really listened to me. Then he changed. I was so confused."

"Aubrey," I asked. "Remind me again how old you were when you started meeting with Mr. Drazdowski?"

"I was sixteen. Then I turned seventeen."

"Did these meetings with him continue after the incident at the park, and then in his office?"

She nodded. "For a long time. Yes. He drove me home from school a few more times. Every time, he'd pull off and take me to Shamrock Park. The ... um ... incidents would usually happen there."

"Incidents. Can you be specific?"

"Rape. Okay. He would take me to the park and have sex with me."

"Did you tell him no? Or that you didn't want to go there?"

"I tried. I'd say please, just take me home. After a while, I just kind of shut down, you know. I was on auto-pilot. But he knew things. I mean, I had told him just about everything about me and my family. He knew my father's business was failing. I'm sorry, Dad. I have to tell these things. So Coach D got him a job."

"The coach got your father a job?"

"Yes. He got him a job working at Spirit Sporting Goods over on Fletcher Highway. Coach D was friends with the owner and he put in a good word for my dad. He did all these things for us. He started coaching Sean, my brother. He was just in junior high at the time, but Coach D would come over sometimes and work with him out in the driveway. They put up a basketball hoop."

"So it's fair to say that Coach D had become a family friend?"

"Yes."

From my periphery, I watched Dan Ames. He clasped his hands in his lap but his whole body quaked.

"Did you think what the coach was doing with you was wrong?"

"Yes! Every second of it. But I was scared. He could make real trouble for my family. He got my dad that job. He could get him fired. And he *told* me no one would believe me. I knew he was right."

"Aubrey, how long did this go on?"

"Years," she said, crying again. "That's why I decided not to run track. I thought if I could keep myself out of his sight, he'd forget about me. It got better through the summer. Out of school, he didn't have as many reasons to see me. But once my senior year started again, so did he."

"Can you estimate how many times these incidents happened between the coach and you?"

She looked skyward and shook her head. "I don't know. I did keep count for a while. I quit after twenty. I thought it would maybe stop after I graduated. I thought if I could just keep quiet it would go away. I'd be gone."

"Did it?"

"No," she said. "He started coming into Dewar's when I was working. I was saving money for school and he knew that. He offered to help me."

"Did you take his help?"

"No."

"Just so I'm clear, you're saying that Mr. Drazdowski sexually assaulted you multiple times over the course of how long?"

"Two and a half years. This past January is when things changed."

"How did they change?"

"I … I heard a rumor. There was a girl a few years older than me in school. I heard a rumor that Coach D used to spend time with her. So I decided to ask her about it."

"Who was the girl?"

"Danielle Ford," Aubrey answered, her voice barely more than a whisper.

"Danielle Ford?" I repeated.

"Yes."

"And did you ever talk to her about Coach D?"

Aubrey dropped her eyes. "No. I couldn't."

"Why is that?"

"I found out that Danielle Ford had passed away."

"Do you know how she passed away or when?"

"I found her obituary in the paper after somebody told me she'd died. It was about a year ago. Right before Christmas. It said in the paper that she took her own life. I don't know how. I mean … I don't know how she did it."

"Okay. So who did you talk to about what was going on with the coach?"

"I was shocked. I mean, I worried about whether Danielle was having the same trouble as I was. And whether that's why she did what she did. And I felt so awful. Like, maybe if I'd said something, she wouldn't have felt alone if that's what happened. And I thought … I mean … it was the first time it even occurred to me that maybe I wasn't the only one. I told my friend. Kaitlyn."

"What exactly did you tell her and when?"

"It was, I think, this past February. I didn't tell her everything, but I told her Coach D had been inappropriate."

"What was her reaction?"

"Objection to the extent her answer calls for hearsay," Jack said.

"I haven't asked what Kaitlyn said."

"Try again, counselor," Judge Castor directed.

"So then what happened?"

"Kaitlyn wanted me to tell my parents. She rode me about it all the time. It got to a point where I knew if I didn't say something, she would. So in May of last year … I remember it was Memorial Day weekend. I … I finally told my dad."

"What did you tell him?"

"It was really hard. Things had gotten a lot better for him. His business had picked back up and he was able to quit

the sporting goods store job Coach D got him. I told him …
I mean … I didn't give him many details … he's hearing that
for the first time today. But I told him Coach D raped me."

"How did he take it?"

Aubrey let out a bitter laugh. "Not well. He's my dad."

Dan Ames was doing a fairly good job stoking the jury's
imagination. He sat white-knuckled behind the defense table.
Diane had an arm around his shoulders. Silent tears poured
down Dan's face.

"Did he confront Coach D? Do you know?"

"No," she said. "I don't know. I begged him not to. But I
think maybe he did. Things had kind of died down with the
coach going into the beginning of this year. It was like, he'd
moved on. I pray to God it wasn't to some other girl. But …"

"Objection, this is improper speculation."

"Sustained," Judge Castor said before I could even
respond. "The witness is advised to stick to facts she has
direct knowledge of."

"I don't know," Aubrey said. "But … he stopped coming
into Dewar's."

"Okay, Aubrey, let's move to the night of Coach D's
death. We've seen and read the texts between the two of you.
Why did you contact him?"

"Telling my dad and telling Kaitlyn. It was like I woke up
from this nightmare all of a sudden. If he *was* messing with
anyone else, I wanted it to stop. He was so angry with me
that I'd told my father. He knew that by then. I thought …
when we talked, he never even covered anything up. He
would routinely talk openly about what happened between
us and the things he wanted to do to me the next time he saw
me. I thought if I could get him to do that … I was going to
record it. I was going to get him to admit to what he'd done
on tape. I know now how stupid that was."

"What happened when you met with Coach D at Shamrock Park on the night of the 22nd?"

"He wanted me to sit and talk in his car. I wouldn't. So he had his car parked by that stupid shamrock statue. I got out of mine. I went up to him and asked him to come to the middle of the park. There were lights on in all the houses that are around the park."

"Aubrey, did anyone know you were there with the coach that night?"

"No," she said. "I knew my dad would never let me try it. We'd gotten in a pretty big fight just before I left for work that day. He wanted me to go to the cops. He has a friend who is a detective. He grounded me, actually. I was supposed to come home straight from work."

"But you didn't. You defied him?"

"Yeah. I … I'm nineteen years old. It was stupid. I know he was trying to protect me. But … once I'd decided to try getting the coach to admit what he'd done, I don't know. It was like I was obsessed."

"So what happened when you met with the coach?"

"He did get out of the car. He walked with me until we were by the swings. He kissed me. And he hugged me and went on about how much he missed me. I got scared. I confronted him. I told him I knew what he did was wrong. I knew he was trying to do it to other people. And I was going to make sure he paid. But it was all me talking. He acted different. Pretending like he didn't know what I was talking about."

"What happened then?"

"I got scared. I should have kept trying. But, like I said, he started hugging me. I was afraid he was going to go too far again. So I chickened out. I told him I had to leave. He let me go."

"Did you record the conversation?"

"I tried. But I found out later it didn't work. I don't know. I had my phone in my back pocket. I must have forgot to hit the record button or shut it off without realizing it. I don't know what happened. I must have dropped my phone though. A little later, after I left the park, I realized I didn't have it anymore. I'd been driving around for a while, trying to get my head together. I knew I was going to be in huge trouble for breaking curfew anyway. And it was all for nothing."

"What time did you leave the park?"

"I don't know exactly. It was before eleven. Probably around ten thirty. I got there at ten fifteen, straight from work. We didn't talk for very long. Ten minutes, tops. Then I left."

"Where was Coach D when you left?"

"He was still standing by the swings. I watched him sit on one and start swinging as I drove off."

"Where did you go next?"

"I don't know. I know what it sounds like, but I was numb. I drove around for a while, I guess. I got home really late. It was after one in the morning. I was trying to wait my parents out. Make sure they were asleep before I got in."

"Aubrey, did you kill Larry Drazdowski?"

She went still as stone and leaned into the microphone. "No. I did *not* kill him. He was alive when I left that park."

"Aubrey, you have to help me out here. You have to help the jury out here. A week later, you went into the police department and you told them that you *did* kill Coach D. Now you're saying you didn't?"

She looked at her father then back at me. "I lied to the police. I'm ashamed of it now. But when I found out the coach was dead, that he'd been stabbed, I thought for sure I knew who did it."

"Who did you think stabbed this man?"

She fidgeted. From the corner of my eye, I saw Dan Ames give her just the slightest nod.

Aubrey's voice broke as she got her words out. "I thought it had to be my dad. I know he *wanted* to kill Coach D. I just wanted all of this to go away. I wanted my family to be normal. We can't be normal if my dad goes to prison. He's already ruined my life, Coach D. It was my fault. I should have said something so much sooner. I should have never let that man touch me in the first place. Maybe if I'd worn different clothes. Or been stronger. But I wasn't. I couldn't. And now they were going to take my dad away next. It wouldn't just be from me. My mom wouldn't survive that. My brother wouldn't have a father. And I knew if he did it, he did it for me. So I told the cops I killed Coach D. It's such a mess. I take it back. I did *not* kill him. My father didn't either. I just didn't know it at the time. He told me, but I didn't believe him. I thought he was lying to me to protect me. Oh God. I can't fix it. I tried to fix it, but I can't."

Aubrey collapsed in tears, leaning over the edge of the witness box. She'd testified about the abuse she'd suffered and its impact on her. She denied killing the coach. She recanted her confession and she'd given a reason for it I hoped the jury would believe. There was nothing more I could ask of her. So I didn't. Even though I knew in my heart it might not be enough.

"I have nothing further for Miss Ames, Your Honor," I said.

"Okay," Judge Castor said. It was eleven a.m. Aubrey had been on the stand for over two hours. "Let's take a fifteen-minute break. Mr. LaForge can have his cross before we break for lunch."

Aubrey stepped down and went into her parents' arms. Jeanie shouted questions to me, but I had to get a moment to myself.

I slipped out of the courtroom and made my way to a corner of the building just off the law library. Squeezing my eyes shut to steel myself for what I was about to do, I pulled out my phone and did the second hardest thing I would do that day.

Chapter 33

THE PHONE RANG TWICE, then Killian Thorne's Irish brogue cut through me as he answered simply, "Thorne."

I took a breath. Then another. It was all posturing on his part. He knew damn well it was me on the other end. The number on the card Corwin had given me probably went to a burner phone he'd saved just for me.

"Killian, it's Cass," I said.

In my mind's eye I could see him. Those cold, pale-blue eyes, anvil-sharp jaw, the deep cleft in his chin.

"Are you all right?" he asked. Of course, he knew I was. Corwin had likely reported every second of my day to him since he got here.

"I need ... Look. I didn't want to call. And you can call your dog back home. You know you don't have anything to worry about with me. It's done. Everything you do is still protected by attorney-client privilege."

"Attorney-client, ay?" he said. His voice had a lilt to it that I knew meant he was smiling. Smirking, more like. My heart jackhammered in my ears.

"Killian ... listen ..."

"How's championing the downtrodden going? I've heard some rumors."

I let out a sigh. "It's going. And I'm fine. Send Corwin home."

"Not likely. And he's not there for me, *a rúnsearc*. He's there for you. Like always, you don't know when to ask for help when you need it. It's a serious character flaw."

We'd had this conversation so many times before. I bit my bottom lip. "You win. Okay. You always win. I'm done even trying with you. This time, I *am* asking for help. And you know damn well you're the last person I want to need it from."

Silence hung between us. I imagined Killian standing on the pier watching his cargo ships leaving port. It was his meditation. His solace.

"Cass, I'm sorry. I'll keep saying it. Things didn't go down how I wanted. If I'd known sooner what my brother and the senior partners had planned, you never would have been on that ship. He never would have gotten close enough to touch you."

"Stop," I said. If we went down this road, it would break me. For the rest of my life, I'd hear Killian's lilting ringtone as his brother's men held me on the deck of that ship. If he'd called just a few seconds too late …

"What is it?" he said.

"Killian, I need you to help me find someone who doesn't want to be found. I've … I can't do it by myself. I know you can."

He let out a soft chuckle. It was the kind I'd heard so many times before. The kind that made his eyes dance just before he moved in for the kill.

"You only needed to ask." He paused. "I've missed you."

I squeezed my eyes shut and pressed my forehead to the wall. "Killian …"

"I'll do this for you. You knew that. But you'll owe me something, Cass. You knew that too."

"Yes," I said, swallowing past the word. "And I know you always collect."

Sure enough, I heard the foghorn of one of Killian's massive freighters in the distance.

"Good," he said, going all business again. "Give me a name."

I did, sealing my pact with the devil all over again.

Chapter 34

JACK'S CROSS-EXAMINATION of Aubrey was short, simple, and devastating. He did exactly what I would have done. He did the only thing that mattered.

"Miss Ames," he began. "I need to understand a few things. You're claiming that the victim in this case made unwanted advances toward you beginning three years ago. Is that correct?"

Aubrey started to blink rapidly. She stayed remarkably composed other than that. "I'm telling you that he raped me. Yes. It started three years ago."

"You didn't tell anyone about it at the time, yes or no?"

"No."

"And you're saying you continued to meet with the victim. In fact, you testified that you let him drive you home from school on more than one occasion."

"Yes. I was scared of him. I don't know how else to explain that."

"Okay. Let's move on. On the night of June 22nd, it was you who reached out to the victim, isn't that right? You started texting him from work. Correct?"

"Yes."

"He didn't call you. He didn't come to your place of work."

"No. I told you … I was trying …"

"A simple yes or no," Jack said. I shot Aubrey a look. We talked about this. I didn't want her to try arguing with Jack. If there was anything I felt it necessary for her to clean up after cross, I'd ask her on redirect.

"No," she said.

"And he came to Shamrock Park, the place he was later murdered, because *you* asked him to meet you. Correct?"

"Yes."

"And you've testified that Shamrock Park was one of the most frequent locations where the victim allegedly abused you. Correct?"

"He raped me there, yes," she answered. Good girl. This was rape, nothing less.

"When the police initially arrested you for Coach D's murder, did you tell them you were innocent?"

"Did I … I didn't … I didn't say that. No. I asked for a lawyer."

"And you went to the police station on July 10th of your own volition, didn't you?"

"Yes."

"You admitted to murdering Coach D, didn't you?"

"Yes … but …"

"You said, and I quote, 'I did this, I stabbed Coach D. I was angry, it was the heat of the moment. But I did it.' Correct?"

"Y-yes."

"You said it over and over."

"Yes."

"Today, you testified that you didn't kill Coach D. So, were you lying then or are you lying now?"

"I didn't kill him."

"That's not what I asked you. Were you lying to the police then or now?"

"But I didn't …"

"Did you lie, Miss Ames?"

"Yes. Yes. I lied to the police on July 10th."

"How did you feel about Coach D, Aubrey?"

"How did I feel?" She looked at me. I tried to will strength to her with the force of my gaze. The jury was watching everything.

"I hated him. That man stole who I was. He stole my dignity. My confidence. My virginity. I trusted him. I looked up to him. And he twisted all of it and used it. For years, I blamed myself for what happened. Maybe I dressed too revealing. Did I give off some signal? I didn't though. And even if I did, it doesn't matter. I know that now. I was sixteen years old. And he hurt me. He hurt me physically. He hurt me in my head. And he ruined my family."

"So you're glad Coach D is dead then?"

"Objection," I said.

"I'll withdraw. I have nothing further."

Aubrey trembled. I wanted to get her the hell off the witness stand. But I had one last thing, one last chance to leave an impression in the jury's mind.

"Aubrey," I said. "Did you kill Larry Drazdowski?"

"No!" She said it loud and clear. "He was alive when I left that park. He was sitting on the swings when I left that park. And I left that park running. I dropped my phone … running."

"Thank you."

Jack didn't look up from his notes as he waived his redirect.

"You may step down, Miss Ames," the judge said. "But I'd like to admonish you that you will remain under oath."

Aubrey stood, straight-backed as she walked past the jury, and took her seat again at the defense table. I wanted to wrap my arm around her and tell her how strong she was. All I could do was touch her wrist with my finger. It was enough. I felt her exhale.

Chapter 35

I CALLED one more witness on Friday. Karen Larsen dressed in a simple, conservative navy-blue skirt with a cream-colored cardigan. She had a shiny flower brooch above her left breast and brown hair hung in a neat bob that swayed when she walked toward me. She had a thin manila file folder tucked under her arm.

We had just a few moments before the bailiff would call us in.

"Are you ready for this?" I said, putting a hand on her shoulder.

Karen's eyes flickered. "I'd rather be anywhere else." She'd come under my subpoena. Damning as it was, Kevin Sydney's testimony had given me a gift, an opening. Now I needed Karen Larsen to help me exploit it.

She blinked back tears. "I should have done more. You have to get those girls to believe me. I didn't know. I wasn't sure."

Those girls. As Karen collected herself, I finally realized something I should have weeks ago.

"It was you, wasn't it?" I said. "The yearbook at my office. The circled names. You left that for me, didn't you?"

Karen bit her lip. She took a breath to answer but didn't get the chance. The bailiff poked his head out and called us back to the courtroom. I gave Karen a tight-lipped nod, then made my way in. The bailiff guided her past the jury and swore her in as I took my place at the podium.

"Can you state your full name for the record?" I began as soon as Karen adjusted herself in the witness box.

"Karen Culpepper Larsen," she answered.

"And where do you work, Ms. Larsen?"

"I'm a secretary at Delphi High School. I'm assigned to the athletic department. I manage the A.D.'s office for Mr. Sydney."

"How long have you worked there?"

"This is my seventeenth school year starting this past September. I got hired just out of community college. I have an associate's degree in office administration."

"Thank you. Have you always worked for Mr. Sydney?"

"No. I was in the main office for the first year and a half, then got switched over. So it's been about fifteen years since they put me in the A.D.'s office."

"What do you do for Mr. Sydney?"

"Well, I handle all his correspondence. He's very traditional in that sense. He still dictates letters to me. All of his calls come through me first. His scheduling. I coordinate with payroll and the union when it's time for new hires. Basically, whatever paperwork is involved it goes through me."

"Can you tell me more about keeping his schedule?"

"If anyone wants an appointment with Mr. Sydney, I schedule it in the system. I enter all appointments, meetings, whatever requires Mr. Sydney's presence into the school's electronic calendar. It also goes to his phone. And I keep a traditional paper day planner for myself."

"So, is it fair to say Mr. Sydney doesn't take meetings unless you know about them?"

"That's pretty much true, yes."

"Pretty much?"

"Well, yes. It's entirely true. Mr. Sydney has a lot of balls in the air, so to speak. If something isn't on his schedule, it doesn't happen."

"Ms. Larsen, you are here under a subpoena, are you not?"

"Um … yes. The school liaison officer served me with the paperwork at the office last week."

"Okay. As part of that subpoena, you were asked to bring copies of certain records you keep in the course of your employment. Did you do that?"

"I did. You asked for scheduling records for the last seven years."

"And I'm sure you're aware, but Mr. Sydney testified about these office procedures the other day. If he said that you keep track of every meeting he has, is that true?"

Her eyes darted back and forth. "Yes," she said. "That's true."

"Okay. Do you recall ever scheduling a meeting between Mr. Sydney and a student by the name of Danielle Ford?"

Ms. Larsen cast a nervous glance toward the jury box then out at the gallery. "No," she answered.

"No, you don't recall scheduling it, or no, the meeting didn't happen?"

It was such a small thing. A tremor in her hand. Then Karen Larsen's upper lip started to sweat. The roller coaster crested one more hill.

"I didn't schedule it," she said.

"Did a meeting happen between Danielle Ford and Mr. Sydney in his office?"

She dropped her head. "Yes."

"I'm sorry, can you speak up?"

"Yes. Danielle Ford met with Mr. Sydney in the spring of 2012. And I didn't schedule it."

My heart pounded so loud I could barely hear myself think. "Ms. Larsen, if it was your normal practice to schedule all of Mr. Sydney's meetings, and you recall one taking place, why didn't it make it into your records?"

She pursed her lips. "Because I was asked not to put it there."

"By whom?"

"By Mr. Sydney."

"Okay. Do you know what the substance of that meeting was?"

"Objection. Calls for hearsay?" Jack called out.

"Your Honor, I've asked if she knew the substance of it. So far, that's all."

"Overruled, the witness may answer."

Karen adjusted the microphone. "No."

"Moving on. Do you recall whether Mr. Sydney ever took a meeting with students Lindsey Claussen or Chelsea Holbrook?"

"Yes," she answered. "He took meetings with both of those girls. The Claussen meeting took place four years ago on September 24th. He met with Chelsea Holbrook the following January on the 14th."

"Were those meetings recorded in his electronic calendar?"

She leaned forward. "They were not."

"Why is that?"

"Because Mr. Sydney asked me not to."

"And how is it you're so specific about the dates of these meetings seeing as how they weren't officially recorded?"

"Because he'd never asked me to do that before. I thought it was strange. And because I *did* record them in my

day planners. I brought them with me if you'd like to
see them."

My heart lifted. I wanted to kiss this woman. "I would
very much. But first, did you ask Mr. Sydney why he didn't
want them recorded?"

She looked on the verge of tears. "You have to understand. You don't ... you don't ... I didn't know for sure. I still
don't. I didn't want to get fired. If I had any inkling ..."

"Objection," Jack said. "Could we have some guidelines
here? This witness is not responding to questions."

"Ms. Larsen, please answer my question. Do you know
why Mr. Sydney instructed you *not* to record those meetings
with Danielle Ford, Lindsay Claussen, and Chelsea
Holbrook?"

"No."

"Were you aware of the substance of those meetings?"

"No," she said. "The girls wouldn't tell me."

"Did you ever become aware of the substance of those
meetings later?"

She hesitated. Karen Larsen's face changed color, going
to a pale gray. "I heard rumors. I understood it had to do
with Coach Drazdowski."

"Objection. This entire line of questioning calls for
hearsay and innuendo. But more than that, none of this is
relevant."

"Your Honor, Kevin Sydney has made some shocking
allegations about conversations he had with the victim about
the defendant. His credibility is absolutely at issue."

"Sustained in part," Judge Castor said. "The jury will
disregard the witness's last testimony about what she heard
about the substance of those meetings. As far as whether
those meetings took place? I'll allow it."

I knew I was pushing the envelope. But the jury had
heard the most important part. To the extent Sydney claimed

he'd never met with these students, he was toast. Karen
Larsen had no reason to lie.

"Your Honor, I'd like to move for the admission of Ms.
Larsen's scheduling records and day planners into evidence."

Jack was seething, but I had him.

"They're admitted as exhibits thirty through thirty-six.
Let's move on," Castor said.

"I have nothing further for this witness except to thank
her for her time," I said, quitting while I was ahead.

"Your witness, Mr. LaForge."

Jack rifled through his notes. He made a noise that made
me think he was merely going to dismiss Karen. At the last
second, he changed his mind.

"Ms. Larsen, do you personally have any knowledge
about the circumstances surrounding Larry Drazdowski's
murder?"

"I ... no. I'm afraid I don't."

"Do you even know the defendant, Ms. Ames?"

"Not well. No. I was acquainted with her prior to this
trial when she was a student at the high school. I made it a
point to try and get to know all of the students, at least to say
hi in the hallway."

"Thank you. You're free to go as far as I'm concerned."

Karen Larsen stepped down and Judge Castor adjourned
trial for the weekend.

Chapter 36

DAN AMES PACED like a caged tiger. Aubrey looked as exhausted as I felt. I'd asked them to meet me in my office conference room to talk about our plans for Monday morning. It was getting late. Joe waited for me downstairs. He wanted answers about my new shadow, Corwin.

"It's good, right?" Dan asked, tearing a hand through his hair. "That secretary, she pretty much proved that fucking Sydney is a liar. Those girls. He *knew*! The bastard knew this whole time. And he did nothing. He covered for that piece-of-shit Drazdowski."

"Yes," I said, striking as calm a tone as I could. Jeanie sat beside Aubrey. She put a maternal arm around her.

"So, we're good. This is good."

I met Jeanie's eyes. Her grim expression matched my own.

"It's good in this sense," I said. "People are starting to question whether Larry Drazdowski was the hero they thought he was."

"But those girls, Lindsey Claussen. You can subpoena

her. You can make her tell the truth about what happened with that monster," Dan said. His words came out rapid fire.

"I could try," I said. "But there's still the issue of relevance. Whether we like it or not, Larry Drazdowski isn't the one on trial. Aubrey is."

"Do you think they believe me?" she said, her voice thin.

I let out a hard breath. Jeanie rubbed her back. There was no easy way to say any of this. "Aubrey, I don't know. Like I said, I think they are starting to question Larry's character. They are certainly starting to question Kevin Sydney's. That crack about Coach D telling him he was afraid of you was a total lie."

"But … that still doesn't mean they'll believe I didn't kill Coach D."

"I'm sorry, honey," Jeanie chimed in. "But you've got it."

Dan threw a chair across the room. It bashed into the wall, making the whole building shake. There was some commotion downstairs as my brother heard it all. Miranda once again earned her salary ten-fold by keeping him down there.

"It comes down to one thing," I said. "If the jury believes Aubrey's story, they'll acquit her. If they don't, they'll convict."

"They already know I lied once."

That was the grim truth. Aubrey, for her part, seemed willing to accept it. Her father wasn't.

"I can't believe this. I can't stomach it. That asshole ruined my little girl. Ruined her life. And he's going to get away with it?"

I bit my lip past the obvious answer. Larry Drazdowski was done getting away with anything. But I knew what he meant.

"Dad," Aubrey said, her voice soft. "I'm sorry. I know I've only made things worse. I shouldn't have tried to get

Coach D to admit to it on tape. I shouldn't have gone to the park that night. And I shouldn't have gone to the police to try and protect you. This is all my fault."

Dan crumpled into the seat opposite her. "Baby, don't ever say that. You've been so brave. You've been trying to protect me when I'm the one who should have been protecting you."

"But you didn't know. How could you?" She looked back at me. "Cass … if I go … if they find me guilty. Can you promise me something?"

It was in me to blurt out "anything," but I couldn't. I sat down at the end of the conference table and waited for her to finish.

"Promise me that you won't stop trying to get the truth out about Coach D. If they send me to jail … if people find out the truth. I mean … all of it … then at least this won't feel like it was for nothing."

I reached across the table and took her hand. "That I can promise you, Aubrey. No matter what happens, I'll do my best to try and get the truth out. You've already opened the door. Kevin Sydney is lying. He covered it all up. I'll try and track down the Holbrooks. Danielle Ford's family. Others will come forward. I feel it."

Aubrey gave me the first genuine smile I'd seen since I first met her. Tears rolled down her father's cheeks, but it wasn't just sorrow. I knew he felt pride.

"So that's it," he asked. "Monday morning, you rest your case?"

"Maybe," I said. "I need a night to sleep on it. I may yet have a trick or two up my sleeve."

"Put me on the stand," he said. "Let me tell the jury what Aubrey told me."

"I could," I said. "But the trouble is, you're a biased witness."

"I don't care! Let me say what I have to say so the whole damn town can hear it."

I gave him a grim nod. "We'll all have fresher heads in the morning. Okay?"

With that, I left Dan and Aubrey the room. Jeanie and I walked down the stairs together.

"Well," I whispered to her. "What do you think?"

She shrugged. "I think if Jack offers a deal, she's got to think long and hard. They give her second degree, it's twenty to life. She could be out in less. She's twenty years old. She could still have a life."

I let out a hard sigh. Twenty years in prison and Aubrey Ames would never be the same. But Jeanie had a point. Still, I wasn't kidding about needing a fresher head come morning. We rounded the corner and nearly ran headlong into Miranda. She was carrying a huge bouquet of white roses.

My throat ran dry. There was only one person on the planet who sent me white roses. These were Killian Thorne's calling card. Joe stood in the doorway of the office, fuming.

"These just came for you," Miranda said. She pulled a card out of the massive bouquet and handed it to me. The envelope had already been torn open and my eyes shot to Joe. Of course he'd bullied Miranda and already read it.

"I'm sorry," she whispered. "Your man in the big black car came up with the delivery guy. Your brother answered the door before I could."

"It's all right," I said, taking the card from her.

Ask and you shall receive. There's a present waiting for you back at your house. K.T.

God. He worked fast. Too fast. It had been a mere eight hours since I called him. I shuddered, realizing he'd had the means to grant me this favor all along. What had I done?

"Come on," Joe said, reading the card over my shoulder. "No way in hell I'm letting you go back there alone."

Resigned, I handed the flowers back to Miranda. "Well, let's get going then," I said. I felt terrible for leaving Jeanie in the dark, but this was now a family matter.

As I left with my brother, I hoped to God I was wrong about what I'd find back at the house.

Chapter 37

JOE PEPPERED me with questions I wouldn't answer. "I'm so sick and tired of this," he said. "How long are you going to keep me in the dark? I see that guy following you. He's been on you for days."

He pulled up my gravel driveway, unsettling one of the sand cranes that fished on this side of the lake. It took off in a graceful arc, its gray wings flapping as it looked for a more hospitable resting place.

Corwin had beat us to the house. A second, identical black SUV was parallel parked in front of my neighbors. The living room light was on and my pulse jackhammered. This was either going to go poorly or disastrously.

"What the actual fuck is going on?" Joe got out just ahead of me. He reached beneath his front seat. He had a concealed carry license and he was going for his Nine.

"Joe, don't!" I shouted. Corwin stood beside his vehicle, his eyes stone cold. My brother was a skilled hunter and one hell of a shot. But he was no match for one of Killian Thorne's trained bodyguards.

"It's okay," I said. "He's not here to hurt me."

"It's the opposite," Corwin said, slightly amused.

I grabbed my brother's arm. His muscles tensed into granite. But he let me pull him toward the house. He was ready to launch into another tirade. But the moment we stepped inside, his words died on his lips and my heart dropped to the floor.

My sister Vangie sat cross-legged on the couch, staring out at the lake. She was like a statue, an apparition. She was exactly the same and yet completely different. I hadn't seen her in over six years. Then, she'd been a skinny eighteen-year-old girl with hair down to her waist that she'd dyed pitch black with a homemade rinse. Now, she was thin, not skinny, her hair back to its normal blonde. She stared straight through me with those luminous green eyes. She was beautiful. Stunning, even. And she looked exactly like the mother she could barely remember.

Joe let out a choked sound beside me. He took a faltering step. I knew what he felt. We were both scared to take a breath or blink. Would Vangie vanish into thin air again if we did?

She was real. She was here.

"I hate you for this," she said.

"Vangie," Joe gushed. He went to her. He dove to the cushion beside her, throwing his arms around our little sister. Vangie's eyes flickered. Just as quickly, she put her mask back in place as she let Joe hug her. She kept her cold gaze fixed on me.

"When did you ... where ... how?" Joe was dumbstruck. "Jesus. Vangie. Do you have any idea how worried I've been?" He sat back, giving her space again.

"I'm sorry about that," she said. Her cold façade slipped a bit and her eyes glistened with tears she was trying so hard not to shed.

Vangie ran a finger beneath her eye, fixing the black

eyeliner that threatened to smudge. She rose from the couch and came to the big bay window, looking out at the water. The sand crane was back, swooping low to catch a tiny bluegill with expert precision.

"Place looks nice," she said. "Quite the coup getting Gramps to leave it to you, Cass. But I'm guessing Matty threw a fit."

"He got over it," I said. "He knows he's welcome here whenever he wants. So are you."

"Right. But it's a pretty big step down for you, huh? She ever invite you to her fancy penthouse on Lakeshore Drive, Joe? You could get a nosebleed just stepping off the elevator in that place."

"Vangie," I started. She turned to me, whipping her hair behind her shoulders.

"You didn't really get out from under that life though, did you?" she asked. "Still got his thugs at your beck and call. They sure rattled my cage this morning. What's the price for dragging me back here? I hope it was worth it."

Joe stepped between us. "What the hell are you talking about? Cass? Who dragged you? Did they hurt you? Was it that asshole outside? You did this?" He turned to me, his eyes accusatory.

"Joe ..."

"No," he said. "Enough secrets. This is me you're talking to. What are you involved in? And what the hell did you do to get Vangie in the middle of it?"

"Nothing," I said. "I just need to have a conversation. That's all. I was worried about her. Vangie ... I'm not the only one with secrets, am I?"

Her armor was cracking and I hated that I was causing it. But Joe had one thing absolutely right. We'd kept our secrets long enough.

"Tell him," Vangie said. "Tell Joe what you did."

"Vangie …"

"They found me at work. Two men. The one out there parked in front of the Fletcher's drove me all the way here. Four hours. All the way from Indianapolis. At work. Did I say that? Do you know how hard it's been for me to rebuild my life? After everything I've tried to push behind me. And you want me to what?"

Joe looked dumbstruck from me to Vangie. "Everything that happened. Vangie, you took off. Disappeared. I've been trying for years to get a hold of you. You cut yourself off from Dad. From Matty even. It gutted him. He needs you. He's been drinking."

"That's not on me!" she snapped.

"What men, Cass?" Joe asked. "Who the hell are those guys?"

I dropped my chin. If I was going to ask my sister to tell me her secrets, I had to tell her some of mine.

"They work for Killian Thorne," I said. "He was … he was a client of the firm I worked for."

"The Thorne Group," Joe said. "Killian Thorne. Sounds like more than just a client."

"It's his brother Liam's firm. Killian runs the family business," I said. "We parted ways. It's complicated, okay? And most of it I can't talk about anyway. Attorney-client privilege and all that. But … let's just say we ended up at crossed purposes."

"How does he make his money, Cass?" Joe asked.

"He's … he's an exporter. Like I said, it's complicated, Joe. But it's over. I'm out."

"But you asked him to find me," Vangie said.

"Did they hurt you?" Joe asked, his eyes wild. "Jesus. What kind of people are these?"

"They didn't hurt me," Vangie said. "And they told me I didn't have to come with them but …"

"But what?" I said. My sister was like a coiled snake ready to strike. She was angry with me. But there was something else brewing.

"Why?" Vangie squared off, meeting my stare. She was tiny, my sister. Barely topping five feet. She was fine-boned but had a natural tone to her arms. She'd been a gifted athlete at one time. Swimming. Gymnastics. Track. I could see her pulse racing from the little tremor near her temple.

"Vangie, I know you know what's happening in this town. And you could have said no. You didn't have to come, but here you are."

"You can be such a bitch," Vangie said, her voice trembling. I wanted so badly to take her in my arms until she cried herself out. She'd done that so many times when she was little after Mom died. She'd been both lost and strong at the same time. I felt that from her now.

"I know. Which is why I had to do this. I had to know."

Joe stood like a mountain between us. He had his fist curled around the doorknob on the French doors leading to the back porch. He squeezed it so hard he might have crushed it to powder.

"Know what? Vangie?" But he knew. He could do the math in his own head. My sister had run track. She was ours of course, the spitting image of Mom. But she looked enough like Aubrey Ames too.

"Oh God," Joe cried out, sounding like a wounded animal.

"Joe," I said calmly. "I need to talk to Vangie. Alone. Corwin, the guy in the driveway, won't leave. The other one, parked across the street. Tell him he can go. Tell him your sister has what she needs."

"I am not leaving," he said.

Vangie turned to him. Her face softened and she put a

light hand on his arm. "It's okay. I want to talk to Cass. I missed you, big brother. I'm sorry I made you worry."

She melted him, just like only she could. It was the same with our father. He parented her so much differently than the rest of us. Vangie could do no wrong in his eyes. And they were both right. She had been sweet and smart and better than all of us. And then she was gone.

Joe hugged Vangie, his eyes squeezed tightly shut. "Don't you dare disappear on me."

"I won't," she smiled.

Joe kissed the top of her head and saved one more glare for me. But he did what we asked and walked outside. I waited for the door to shut behind him before turning to her.

"Let's sit," I said.

"I don't want to."

"Vangie, I'm sorry. But I'm not sorry. And I need to know the truth. You know what's happening in this town. Coach D is dead."

"And you're defending his killer."

"No. Aubrey Ames didn't kill him. But she was his victim. And as hard as it is for me to hear it, as hard as it is for you to say it, I need to know. Is he the reason you left?"

She hugged her arms around herself. Her eyelids fluttered but she kept my gaze. "Cass, don't do this. They'll never let you get away with it."

"Who's they?"

"Everyone! Don't you get it? This is us we're talking about. Learys. Eastlake trash. You know, I read they're taking up a collection to erect a statue to that … that …"

"That what? That monster? He hurt Aubrey. Raped her. Over and over. He made her think she was nothing. Lindsey Claussen. Chelsea Holbrook. Danielle Ford."

At the mention of Danielle, Vangie had a physical reaction. She took a staggering step back as if she'd been gut-punched. I realized with cold clarity that she had. Danielle Ford was in the same grade as Vangie.

You of all people should know ... Lindsey's words haunted me. *Look in your own backyard.* I pulled a punch with Karen Larsen. I never asked her if Kevin Sydney took a meeting with my sister.

"Why didn't you tell me?" I cried. "That summer after your senior year when you came to live with me in Chicago. You could have told me then?"

Vangie shook her head. "No. I couldn't. I was so ashamed. I thought ... he made me think ..."

Just that one word. He. There could be no other person she meant. It was my turn to feel gut-punched. I'd suspected this for weeks. But I hadn't been able to bring myself to say it.

"You," I said. "Larry Drazdowski hurt you. He raped you. He did to you all the things he did to Aubrey?"

Tears flowed down my little sister's cheeks as she stepped away from the doors and went back to the couch. She drew her knees up and rested her chin on them.

"She really didn't do it?" Vangie asked. "Your client?"

I went to her and sank slowly on the couch beside her. "No," I whispered.

"But he's dead? You're sure he's really dead?"

I put a hand on her knee. She flinched but didn't draw away. "Yes. Baby, he's dead forever. He can't hurt you. He can't hurt anyone ever again."

"Yes, he can," she whispered. "Will you get her out of this?"

I pursed my lips together. "I don't know. But I *will* do one thing. I will make sure this town knows what he really was. And I'll be damn sure to bring down anyone who ever helped him hide it."

She nodded slowly and wiped her eyes. "But you need my help to do that."

"Not if you don't want to. God. I'm so sorry. I never should have …"

"Yes," she cut me off. "I'm not going to lie and say I don't hate you for it. But yeah, you should have. It's been a long time. And I think I'm finally ready to fight back."

My heart shattered in a thousand pieces as I watched my sister's eyes flicker with the steel she was made of. Then she straightened her back and began to tell me her story.

Chapter 38

"THE DEFENSE CALLS EVANGELINE LEARY."

Whispers went through the gallery. I couldn't look back. My brothers were there, lining the back wall. I welcomed their support and their strength. I hoped Vangie felt it too.

"Your Honor," Jack said, breathless. "I object to this witness being called."

I'll just bet you do. I bit my lip.

"Approach," Judge Castor said.

"This witness was not expected," Jack said.

"She's a rebuttal witness to Mr. Sydney's testimony," I said. "The man claims the victim warned him about my client. He's lying. I have the right to explore that."

Castor glared at Jack over his reading glasses. "She's right, Jack. What's your beef?"

"This witness is biased. She's defense counsel's sister."

"Your Honor," I said. "She is my sister, yes. The prosecution is free to make that case to the jury. Her testimony will speak for itself and the jury can weigh it however they choose. That is within their purview, after all."

"The substance of her testimony is irrelevant and highly prejudicial," Jack said.

Jack suspected what Vangie had to say. Quiet rage simmered within me. It meant Jack had been talking to Kevin Sydney. I'd sent a courtesy email to Jack last night telling him I was calling Vangie today.

"Your Honor," I said. Here was the real battle. Vangie didn't have anything to say about the murder itself. She didn't even know Aubrey. Allowing the most shocking bits of her testimony *was* the kind of thing Jack should object to on relevancy. But it was worth this fight. "My client's credibility is at issue. It was an issue the moment she took the stand. Mr. LaForge fell just short of calling her a liar. We all know he's going to do just that in his closing. Ms. Leary's testimony goes to the veracity of Ms. Ames's claims."

Judge Castor let out a great sigh. "I'm going to allow the witness to take the stand. This better not be a litany of hearsay though, Ms. Leary. My patience for that is wearing very thin."

"Thank you, Your Honor."

"Ms. Leary," Judge Castor said, straightening his robes. "I mean, the other Ms. Leary, you may take the stand."

The bailiff swore Vangie in. She wore one of my cream-colored suits. Her blonde hair hung just past her shoulders and she'd blown it out until it shimmered. My sister was beautiful and she'd grown into a strong, determined woman. My heart twisted with love, but also anger for everything I was about to put her through.

"State your name for the record, please," I said.

"Evangeline May Leary."

"Ms. Leary, let's get this out of the way. Can you tell the jury how we know each other?"

"You're my older sister. We're ten years apart."

"Thank you. Did you come here today willingly?"

"No," she said, her voice rising. "I most certainly did not. I'd rather be anywhere else in the world. Sorry. You had some guy serve me with a subpoena yesterday morning at the bar where I work in Indianapolis."

"Vangie, how long has it been since you and I have spoken?"

Her eyes went up and I knew she was looking at our brothers. "Almost six years," she answered. "I spent a summer with you right after I graduated from high school. But I haven't talked to you or the rest of our family in almost six years other than a few texts with my brother, Matt."

"You ran away," I said.

"Yes."

"Okay. Let's go back to that high school graduation. You knew the victim in this case, Larry Drazdowski?"

Vangie paused. "Yes." She said it with venom.

"How did you know him?"

"He was the basketball coach. And the girls' track coach. I ran track. I also tried out to be a basketball cheerleader my senior year. But they don't pick girls from the east side. I'd taken a few years of gymnastics when it was still free at the Y. They always put me in the advanced classes. I could tumble. I could jump. But they didn't pick me for the squad."

"How did that make you feel?" I asked.

"Angry. Sad. Just … defeated. Coach D was one of the judges for that set of tryouts. The day they posted the results, he came up to me and asked me to meet with him in his office."

"Did you?"

Vangie dropped her head. I hated myself for making her go there. I hated myself for not protecting her.

"Yes. I went. It was like he knew what I was feeling. He didn't want me to be discouraged and kept telling me how special I was. I feel like such an idiot now for not cluing into what was happening."

"What was happening, Vangie?"

She looked up and shook her hair behind her shoulders. "He was grooming me."

"Grooming you for what, Vangie?"

"Can I say it? Can I just get it out and get it over with?"

The courtroom fell deadly silent. My heart thundered in my chest and sweat broke out between my shoulder blades. I kept my back straight and my eyes laser-focused on my sister. If there was any way I could transmit strength to her, I was trying my damndest.

"He raped me. It happened after about the third time I met with him in his office. I needed a ride home. In those days, I hated riding the bus. I hated people knowing where I lived. The rest of you had all moved out and Dad lost the house. We were living in this crappy trailer that wasn't even his. He had a girlfriend that wasn't so nice to me. I told Coach D all of this. He listened. So he drove me home one afternoon. It was late. I stayed after school to get some tutoring help with calculus. But he didn't take me home right away. He took me to Shamrock Park. We sat and talked for a while. But then he started rubbing my shoulders. I went kind of numb because in my mind I knew it wasn't … appropriate. But then he got aggressive. I told him no. He didn't stop. He pinned me down on the floor of the front seat and he raped me."

I squeezed the sides of the podium. I let Vangie's words hang in the air then sink in for the jury.

"What happened next?" I asked.

"He took me home. I was scared. I thought it was maybe my fault somehow. He was … he was Coach D. Maybe I really just was Eastlake trash. It hurt. I mean physically, yes. But inside. I couldn't rely on anyone else at that time. Everyone had their own problems. That's when my brother Joe was having issues with his ex and trying to get custody of his kid back. Matty was drinking. And Dad ... well ... he just wasn't present. I had no one. I had Coach D. He's the one who arranged for the tutoring. Did you know he actually signed some of my permission slips? Forged Dad's name so I wouldn't be left behind on field trips and stuff. He did all these things for me. I felt like I owed him."

"Was that the end of it, Vangie?"

"No." She whispered it. "That was October my senior year. Just before Thanksgiving, Dad got thrown out of the trailer we were staying in. So I was pretty much homeless. Somebody told Coach D and he came and got me. He brought me to his house. His parents were in town and they were so nice. They seemed so normal. His mom cooked this amazing Thanksgiving dinner and I could just pretend. You know? I wanted so badly to *be* normal and have good things happen to me. But then ... he did it again. Thanksgiving night. He came to the room I was staying in. I woke up and he was on top of me."

"He raped you a second time?"

She nodded. "Yes."

"Did you tell anyone?"

"Not then. I was just so ... so panicked. And I didn't have anywhere else to go. I lied about where I was staying. I told my brothers I was staying with one of my friends."

"Which friend, Vangie?" I asked.

"Danielle Ford."

"Did anyone else know you were staying with Mr. Drazdowski?"

"Just his parents. It was just for that weekend. When school started up again, I left his house. My brother ... Matty was crashing over at a friend's house. They let me stay there for a couple of weeks until school let out for the holiday break."

"Did you tell Matt or anyone else what was happening with Coach D?"

She shook her head. I motioned to the microphone. "I didn't, no."

"Why not?"

"It's just … you know this. You all know this. This man. It was Coach D. He was idolized in this town. He still is. I was just barely seventeen. If I could go back in time and talk to my younger self …"

"What would you say?"

"I'd tell myself he was wrong. He told me I was special and worth something. He was the only person … the only adult who said that to me. I know you tried to protect me. Joe too. All of you. But it's different when it's coming from people who love you. It's just so much easier to believe the bad things people say behind your back. And it was like Coach D fed into that. He knew I was vulnerable. I needed to believe him. Even though deep down I knew he was just using me and what he was doing was wrong. It's just … I didn't know how to fight back. I went numb. He used that too."

There is a reason they use the term predator. I wanted to knock over that podium and throw my arms around my strong, brave, beautiful sister and take all of her pain away from her and into myself. Joe made a primal noise behind me. A guttural gasp. Vangie hid it all away, but we should have known. We should have seen.

Jack LaForge sat at the prosecution table with his head down. There were about a hundred different things he could have objected to at that moment. I could say a lot of things about him, but the man knew how to read the room. And he knew as damaging as my sister's testimony was to Larry

Drazdowski, he still wasn't the one on trial. It wasn't his job to save the man's reputation. It was his job to put his killer behind bars.

"Vangie, after Thanksgiving, were there any other incidents with Coach D?"

She shrugged. "Yes. After we came back from break, in January. He was busy with basketball. I didn't see him very much. But that season ended, I think, in March. Track season started. It was my senior year. I wanted to quit. But if there was a chance I could get a scholarship. I was a pretty good pole-vaulter."

"I remember," I smiled.

"He cornered me a few times after practice. Offered to take me home."

"Why didn't you say no?"

"People saw him ask. And it wasn't just me. He'd take a group of us in his car and drop them off first. I didn't want to draw attention to myself. Believe me, there are so many things I wish I could go back and change. The more distance I have from the kid I used to be. But you have to understand. People looked at you … treated you differently if they thought you were one of Coach's favorites. They didn't mess with you. It made you more popular. It was like … if Coach D thinks you're worth the time, even if you're just Eastlake trash, then they were more willing to give you a chance. It was so hard to reject that. Then later … I *did* try to say something."

"Tell me about that."

"It was at the end of April my senior year. I started to suspect that the coach had been messing with my friend, Danielle. I heard that he'd been giving her rides home too. So I confronted her about it. She didn't admit it, but she didn't deny it. I was so angry. I felt like it was my fault. Like maybe if I'd spoken up or at least tried to. So I convinced her to go with me to see Mr. Sydney."

"What happened at that meeting?"

"He told us we were trash. He said he'd make it hard for us if we kept saying things about Coach D. He scared me. I mean ... really scared me."

"Objection," Jack said, weary. "This is hearsay."

"Sustained."

"Vangie," I said. "Did anything else happen between you and Coach D after that?"

"Track season was over. I was just so ... so angry. I didn't want to let him get away with any more, you know? When I thought it was just me, it was one thing. When I realized this was something he did to other girls, I knew I had to try to do something about it."

"What did you do?"

"I confronted him. I told him I was going to figure out a way to make him pay."

"Vangie, what was your plan?"

She ground her teeth and gripped the neck of the microphone. "I recorded it."

"You recorded what?"

"All of it. I recorded our conversation. Or actually, I videotaped it. I hit the record button on my phone and put it on the floor of his car, just under my seat."

"He didn't see you do that?"

"No. I was careful. Then he got aggressive. I knew there was a chance it might happen but I was so angry, I was ready to fight back the only way I could. I got him on tape."

"Vangie," I asked. "Do you still have a copy of that tape?"

"Yes."

The courtroom erupted. Judge Castor banged his gavel and the shouts from the gallery nearly drowned out Jack's objection. When the dust settled, I reminded the judge and Jack that I hadn't moved to enter the tape into evidence. Yet.

"Vangie, did you ever play that tape for anyone?"

She dropped her head again. Tears rolled down her eyes. "No. Some stuff happened."

"What happened, Vangie?"

"Coach didn't know I had that recording. But I think he finally understood it wasn't safe for him to mess with me anymore. About a week before graduation, I got followed home."

"Followed home?"

"I had my own car by then. Joe rebuilt one from scratch and gave it to me as a present. I was driving home from work. I worked at Coney's as an ice cream scooper. Anyway, some kids ran me off the road. When I tried to get out of the car, they blocked my door and threatened me. They said if I didn't stop saying things about Coach …"

"Objection, Your Honor," Jack said. "This is hearsay."

"Sustained," Judge Castor ruled.

"Did you recognize these kids?" I asked. I could barely breathe. They ran her off the road, just like me.

"Yes," Vangie answered. "It was Luke Bowman and Bryce Mitchell. They weren't even trying to hide it. They were wearing their letterman jackets even though it was like eighty degrees and right after Memorial Day."

Luke Bowman. If the jury didn't remember that name, I'd make a point of reminding them in closing. Captain of the basketball team. Nephew to the lead investigator of this case. Bile rose in my throat.

"You said *some* things happened. Was this roadside incident the only thing?"

"No." Vangie's tears dried up. Her face was covered in red blotches and her breathing became erratic. She got through it though.

"No," she started again. "Danielle died."

"She died?"

"She killed herself. Swallowed a bottle of pills."

It got hard to breathe. She still blamed herself. I could see it in her face. Danielle was not her fault. She was failed by every person in her life that was supposed to protect her. Maybe me, most of all. Kevin Sydney. Our absent father. I walked around the podium, intending to end my questioning and give her over to Jack after moving to admit her recording. God help him if he tried to badger her. From the sickened look on his face, I didn't believe he would.

"And there was one final thing," Vangie said, her voice small, almost unrecognizable to me.

I turned to her. There was nothing else. This was where her story ended last night. But my sister's face changed, growing hard. Some deep part of me wanted to stop her. I wasn't a lawyer anymore. I wasn't there for Aubrey. I was my little sister's big sister and I would take any bullets meant for her.

"I found out I was pregnant," she said and it felt like that bullet ripped through my own heart.

My brothers rose to their feet in unison. She stared straight at them, willing them to be still with her eyes.

"Vangie," I said.

"I found out I was pregnant and before you ask, yes. It was Coach D's. Despite all the rumors people like to spread, it could be no one else's. I've seen the way people look at me. I know what they think. I can prove it if I have to. I have the tape I made. It's hard to see what's happening, but you'll know what it is. And then there's my daughter. She'll be six years old in January. I gave her up for adoption but I'm still close to her parents. Take a DNA test if you want."

I was floored. Gutted. Shattered. But I *was* still a lawyer and Vangie wasn't the only young woman in this room I was trying to protect.

"Your Honor," I said. "At this time, I'd like to move for admission of the video recorded by Ms. Leary." It was a long shot.

"Objection," Jack said. "It's not relevant. No one is accusing Evangeline Leary of murdering Larry Drazdowski. Once again, as much as defense counsel would like the jury to believe otherwise, Mr. Drazdowski is not on trial. I'd also like to move that this witness's entire testimony be stricken for the same reasons."

"Counsel, I'd like to meet in chambers. Bring the tape. Ms. Leary, Ms. Evangline Leary, you may step down for the moment. But you're still under oath and under subpoena."

Vangie nodded. I gave her a quick, supportive wink. I wanted to wrap my arms around her. I wanted to get her the hell out of there.

Jeanie whispered to me from her seat directly behind me. "Go get 'em."

I turned to her, whispering back so she was the only one to hear. "Do you have any brilliant ideas? Other than bolstering Aubrey's credibility?"

Jeanie shrugged. "Afraid not, kid. You were lucky as hell Jack and the judge let your sister say the things she *did* say. I know Castor. He's pissed. He's disgusted. And I'm pretty sure no matter what else happens, he's damn glad that fucker Drazdowski is dead."

Jeanie was just telling me the things I already knew. I squeezed Aubrey's shoulder and followed Jack into Judge Castor's chambers along with my laptop and the flash drive containing my sister's video.

Jack was pacing in the corner when I shut the door behind me. Castor flipped his robe up as he took a seat behind his desk.

"Play it," Castor said.

My pulse pounding, I did. The video itself was grainy, dark. The phone was on the floor of Larry's front seat. You couldn't see much more than the back of Vangie's left shoulder and the interior roof of the car. But, for a few brief seconds, she moved enough so Larry Drazdowski's face was visible. His cheeks were flushed, making the old acne scars on his cheeks stand out. His blond hair was combed back and his blue eyes flashed.

"It's over," Vangie said. "I don't want this. You've twisted everything all up."

Coach D laughed. "Right. Sweetheart, you've wanted this since the minute you came into my office that first time. Don't tell me you don't love it. Because I *do* love you. I'm the only one who's ever appreciated how special you are. How smart. The rest of the world thinks you're just some Eastlake slut. You wouldn't have anything if it weren't for me. Do you realize what things would be like for you if I didn't treat you so well?"

"Get off me," Vangie said. "You're hurting me."

I couldn't breathe. In some ways, I felt like I was right there in that car with her. My fists curled and I dug my nails into the flesh of my palms, drawing blood.

"You love every second of it. People think you're special. One look, one word from me and your life turns to shit again. Never forget who I am."

The sound was muffled. When I'd watched this video with Vangie last night, she told me she'd changed her mind, gotten scared, and tried to get out of the car. Drazdowski threw himself on top of her then. She screamed "No!" and it tore through me. Judge Castor dropped his head and pounded his fist on his desk. Jack went still and cold.

There were no words on the tape then. Just the unmistakable sounds of a struggle. Larry's heated breath. My sister's cry. Then Larry Drazdowski's guttural, rhythmic grunt as he hurt my sister.

"Enough," Castor said. I stopped the tape. He was shaking with rage and snapped a pencil in half.

"Your Honor," Jack started. Castor glared at him and he fell silent.

"I can't put this monster on trial," Castor said looking at me. "Hell, I've probably already done enough to get this whole thing … I've got no choice. I'm going to deny your motion to admit this into evidence. As much as this town needs to know the full truth about what they were harboring, I can't do it."

I looked at the floor.

"What else have you got?" Castor asked.

"Vangie's my final witness," I said.

"Okay," Castor said. "Goddammit all to hell. Okay."

Jack gave me a grim nod and let himself out the door. I started to follow him. Castor rose, came around his desk and gripped my arm.

"What are your plans after this is all over?" he asked.

"I … my what?"

"I don't know how this is all going to play out. Juries are wild. And this town'll rip you apart for this."

"They've already tried," I said. "Other than my client, I'm probably the most hated woman in Delphi."

"Not by me," he said. "And are you the type of person who gives two shits about what people think of you?"

I lifted my chin. "No, I'm not. I used to be. But not anymore."

"Good," he said, smiling. "Because as a citizen of this town, I'm going to count on you to go get that son of a bitch."

"I will, Judge. Consider that a promise."

Chapter 39

"Ms. Leary?" Judge Castor regarded me with a furrowed brow, his hands folded neatly in front of him. His court reporter held her fingers poised over her keyboard waiting. She too sat stone-faced, the muscles of her jaw clenching. Vangie had just left. Our brothers rose to follow her out. Beside me, Aubrey Ames fell apart. She made no sound as tears fell down her face.

"The defense rests, Your Honor," I said. Several members of the jury twisted in their seats. To my right, Jack LaForge rose to his feet.

"Mr. LaForge, are you ready to proceed with your closing argument?"

"I've been ready, Your Honor."

Castor threw him a steely glare. "Then proceed."

Jack straightened his tie and stepped around the prosecutor's table. He took a position in the center of the courtroom, right next to the podium facing the jury. He shook his head and threw his hands up, pantomiming confusion. I wanted to throw my shoe at him, but I understood the strategy.

"Ladies and gentlemen of the jury. You've taken time

away from your jobs, your families, your lives and from the bottom of my heart, I appreciate it. The work that you do here is the greatest responsibility we have as citizens. I honor your sacrifice.

"Over the course of the last week and a half, we've learned some shocking things. It's up to you to choose which ones to believe. But let me offer you this. Maybe Larry Drazdowski really was the monster the defense has made him out to be. If so, well, I'm a father too. I have a daughter. If someone had done to her what Coach D's been accused of, I'll be honest. I'd want him dead. You might too. It's human. We might think of it as justice.

"But the law does not allow us to take matters into our own hands. So I'd like you to take the defendant, Aubrey Ames, at her word. Even if you believe Coach D did all the unspeakable, horrifying things she said he did. He raped her. He threatened her. He groomed her. Used her. Brutalized her. But then, you must also take her at her word that she killed him.

"As a prosecutor, I don't have to prove motive to you. Even so, Aubrey Ames had every reason to want Larry Drazdowski dead. And she just told you that's exactly what happened. You heard her words both on the stand and in that police video. By that alone, there can be no other verdict in this case, as much as we might think the defendant deserved what he got.

"We know that she herself lured the defendant to the place of his murder. You saw the texts she sent. We have witness testimony that Aubrey Ames was seen talking to Larry Drazdowski in his car near the shamrock statue. And we know that her cell phone was found near Larry's body in the park. She admitted she dropped it there. She's admitted to all of it.

"You might even secretly cheer Aubrey Ames for what

she did. That's between you and your own conscience and no one would judge you for that. But, according to the law, that just doesn't matter. The defendant admitted to carrying out the premeditated killing of Larry Drazdowski. Premeditation does not require hours of planning. It can be made in almost a split second. And that, ladies and gentlemen, is exactly what happened on the night of June 22nd. Aubrey Ames is guilty of murder. There is *no* doubt that's exactly what happened in this case. Aubrey Ames may be brave. She may be a victim herself. But, under the law, she is also a murderer and you cannot let that stand. This is not a case of reasonable doubt. The defendant has removed *all* doubt. I ask you to find her guilty of first-degree murder. Justice demands it. Your conscience demands it. And, like it or not, even Aubrey Ames demands it."

Jack dropped his shoulders, nodded one more time toward the jury, then took his seat. I held Aubrey Ames's hand in a death grip beneath the table.

Judge Castor eyed me. "Is the defense ready to proceed?" he asked.

"We are, Your Honor," I said. I straightened my skirt and rose to face Aubrey's jury.

"Ladies and gentlemen of the jury," I started. "I too would like to thank you for your time. This has been a difficult, emotional case for all of us. My client, Aubrey Ames, did not kill Larry Drazdowski. But yes, she had every reason to. She told you the truth on the stand. Believe what she said. The prosecution wants you to believe she's a liar. But she isn't. She is a victim. And she is a champion. Has she made mistakes? Yes. Could she have handled things differently? She is the first one to admit that.

"The prosecution has told you they don't have to prove motive. They're right. But the simple fact is, motive is the only thing they *have* proven to you beyond a reasonable doubt. Nothing else.

"There is no witness to this crime. No murder weapon. No defensive wounds on the accused. Larry Drazdowski towered over Miss Ames by over a foot and more than a hundred pounds. And yet, the prosecution wants you to believe she was physically capable of carrying out this crime. That she is some jilted Lolita when you now know nothing could be further from the truth.

"Aubrey Ames lied about one thing and we can't escape that. But she told you herself, she did it because she thought she had to protect her family one last time. She didn't want Larry Drazdowski, even in death, to strip one last thing away from her. He had already stolen so much.

"Aubrey is no killer. There's *no* doubt of that. She is a victim. She was failed by Coach Drazdowski in the most unspeakable ways. But she spoke them. Here. In this courtroom. She spoke them to you. She was failed by the administrators at Delphi High School. She was failed by me because maybe I should have known about the kind of man the coach was all those years ago. I will be forever sorry for that. And finally, she was failed by law enforcement in this case. You *heard* the lead investigator in this case testify about how much he admired Larry Drazdowski. You heard how his own star-player nephew was part of the cult of worship of Coach D. How he threatened another of Coach D's victims into silence. I put to you that Detective Bowman wanted to bask in that hero worship for himself. So that he could be the man who took down Coach D's killer. Except he's done the exact opposite, hasn't he? He's made it so that the killer may actually go free.

"When you review the evidence in this case, you must return the only just verdict. You must conclude there is reasonable doubt. Aubrey Ames was not the killer. Don't fail her now, ladies and gentlemen. I beg you. Be the champions of justice she has sorely deserved. Thank you."

"All right," Judge Castor said. "We'll adjourn for the day and start at nine tomorrow for the jury instructions. Let's see if we can't get this case to the jury by tomorrow afternoon." He banged his gavel. It went through me like the echo of a gunshot.

Chapter 40

As THE JUDGE dismissed the jury, I turned to Aubrey. She let out a sigh as her father's arms went around her. He was crying. Diane Ames slumped in her seat, her face buried in her hands.

"Time to take her home," I said to Dan. There was nothing else for him to do. There was nothing left for Aubrey to do.

"It doesn't matter, does it?" Dan said to me. "All of it. What that LaForge guy said. He's right."

I touched Dan's arm. "We're not out of this yet, Dan. I'm still fighting. So for now, you just keep your chin up and take care of your daughter."

He pulled me into a hug I wasn't expecting. It touched me, stirring my emotions to the point I felt I might lose control. I hugged him back but kept my cool. I couldn't afford to fall apart now.

"See you in the morning," I said. "We all need to try and get some sleep."

I was far too keyed up for sleep or anything else. Joe would take Vangie and Matty to the lake house. They would wait for me there. I gathered my things as Jeanie came back into the courtroom.

"You're all right, kid," she said, her eyes misted with tears. I knew Vangie's testimony would affect her almost as much as it did me.

"Hey, Jeanie." She let out a garbled sob and threw herself at me, embracing me in a hug that threatened to unravel me.

"I should have done something. How the hell did I miss it?"

"Jeanie, this isn't on you. If it weren't for you, my brothers and sister would have been scattered to the four winds in foster care."

She let go of me. "Maybe that would have been better! Maybe it would have put Vangie in some other school district and that fucking monster never would have learned her name."

"I love you, Jeanie. I'm going to have the rest of my life to second guess all the choices I made. At least you were here. When that kid needed me the most I was in Chicago. She *came* to me the summer after graduation. God. She was already pregnant."

My knees buckled. I took a deep breath to steady myself.

"Honey, you're right. It's no good trying to take the hit for this one. You just go on home and be with your family."

"For all the good it will do," I muttered. The cold hard truth was, Jack LaForge had delivered the closing argument I would have if I were on his side. I'd thrown up all kinds of smoke. I half expected Jack to move for a mistrial. Instead, he'd rolled the dice that the jury would see straight through that smoke. My only hope was they believed Aubrey's retraction of her confession and took the bait that she'd suffered enough.

Jeanie and I walked to the parking lot together then went

our separate ways. She made no comment about Corwin's steady presence in his SUV parked beside my car. I tossed my messenger bag on the passenger seat and started to pull out of the parking lot. I looked around; there were no more Lettermen lining the sidewalk across the courthouse. I had to take it as some small victory as I drove through the gate and headed toward Finn Lake.

Chapter 41

VANGIE WAITED for me at the end of the dock. I wrapped my arm around her and my heart burst as she tilted her head and rested it on my shoulder.

"I love you," I said. "What you did today …"

"Don't," she said. "Don't tell me I was brave. I should have been braver. I shouldn't have cut bait and just left this mess. Aubrey Ames paid for it. Those other girls you mentioned. Chelsea Holbrook. Lindsey Claussen. They paid for it. I should have posted that video online six years ago and exposed that asshole for what he was. If I'd done that … maybe."

"Stop it!" I shouted. "You were a kid, Vangie. And goddammit, you were failed by every adult in your life. Including me. Oh, Vang, why didn't you tell me? I *knew* something was wrong when you came to stay with me that summer. I just assumed so many things. I know what it's like dealing with Dad and all the Delphi bullshit. At least, I thought I knew what the real Delphi bullshit was. I had no clue. But you did."

She peeled herself away from me. "I swear to God, that

was why I came to Chicago that summer. I was going to tell you. I was ... I was going to get rid of the baby. I was going to ask you to help me pay for it."

I swallowed hard. My poor, strong baby sister. She'd faced it all alone.

"I couldn't do it," she said. "I kept thinking how it wasn't her fault. My daughter. I knew she would be a girl from the very beginning. It just felt like I'd be letting one more person pay for what Larry did. And you had this big life. You got *out*. I saw how people looked at you, how they treated you. You changed your fate. I was so proud of you. And jealous too. I was afraid ... I just didn't want to drag you back into this crap. I knew you'd drop everything."

I shook. Anger and guilt thundered through me. "Vangie ..."

"You don't have to be sorry. I just ... I wanted to be like you. And I wanted to do it all by myself. I had to prove to myself that I could. So I left. It just got easier to leave it all behind. Even you. Even Matty and the others. I'm sorry for that now. I'm still mad at you. But I think ... I think maybe I'm also glad that you found me and brought me here. What happened in court today, it was the missing piece, you know?"

I reached for her, running my hand along Vangie's arm. "Yeah. I do know. I've never been more proud of you in my life. I wish I could tell you it would matter for Aubrey. But it mattered in every other way. I'm going to take them all down. I swear to you. It's Kevin Sydney and every other asshole in this town and beyond who protected him. I don't care what it costs."

"Do you promise?" Vangie asked.

I gripped her tight as I faced her. "I swear it. I think it's why I'm here. You talked about me changing my fate. I think this *is* my fate. I couldn't protect you back then. I'm damn sure going to make the people responsible pay."

"Good," she said, smiling. "But Cass, I have to know. Those men who came for me. Who were they? What happened? Why *did* you come back here?"

My sweet, brave sister. She'd been brave enough to face her demons for me. I had to do the same for her.

"The firm I worked for ... they had some ... powerful clients. They did things for those clients I wasn't comfortable with. One of them got caught and gave my name to some federal investigators. They came to talk to me and the firm got wind of it. I didn't tell them anything for the same reasons I can't tell you everything. But somebody decided I was a weak link."

"They tried to hurt you," Vangie said. I hadn't said as much, but she must have read something in my eyes.

"Yeah," I said. "They were going to kill me, Vangie."

She put her arms around me and hugged me. "Are they done trying to kill you?"

"I hope so," I smiled. "The men who came to get you. I called in a favor so they'd help me try and find you. I still have one ... friend back there."

"Killian Thorne," she said. "Cass, I know who he is. That's a dangerous friend to have."

I couldn't tell her the rest. I couldn't tell her it was Killian who called off the men his brother paid to send me to the bottom of Lake Michigan just eight months ago.

"As soon as the trial ends, I'm pretty sure that guy in the SUV will go back to Chicago. He was sort of my bodyguard for the last few weeks. There were some people in Delphi who were willing to do anything to protect Coach D. I don't think we have to worry about that as much anymore."

"I'm glad."

"Vangie, your daughter." My eyes began to fill with tears. My sister's bright smile warmed me.

"Yeah," she said. She pulled her phone out of her back pocket and pulled up a picture. My heart shattered all over again as she turned it toward me. It was a picture of Vangie sitting on a park bench holding an ice cream cone for a skinny little girl with a toothless smile, scraped knees, and the most beautiful green eyes I'd ever seen. No. That wasn't true. She looked exactly like Vangie at the age of four or so except for one thing. This little girl had her father's white-blonde hair. She looked so happy though, giggling for the camera.

"She lives about fifty miles from here," Vangie said. "It was an open adoption. Her mom, Sarah, is amazing. She's a special ed teacher at a charter school. Her husband is an accountant with a big firm. They live in a big two-story house and have horses. Jessica. They named her Jessica, but everyone calls her Jessa. She's happy, Cass. And she's smart. A little spoiled, but I don't mind. I see her once or twice a year and get to send her birthday presents. I did a good thing, didn't I?"

My heart full, I smiled at my sister. "Yeah. Vangie, you did an amazing thing. I said I was never more proud of you. Turns out, I'm prouder still. I love you."

She finally let her tears fall, but my sister seemed happy, relieved. I wrapped my arms around her and promised to never let her go.

Later, Vangie climbed into the big canopy bed in the guestroom. Matty wouldn't leave her side and he wouldn't stop crying. The two of them had always been closest and he'd been completely blindsided by Vangie's story. I got an air mattress out of the closet and set it up in the hallway right outside Vangie's room. Weary-eyed, Matty gave me a hug and grabbed a pillow and blanket from my room. I worried today would drive him to the bottom of a beer bottle. So far, he was as sober as I'd seen him in months.

I left them in peace and headed downstairs. I found Joe standing by the back door, keys in hand. I shot him a smile, knowing he could read my mind.

"Mickey's?" he asked.

"Oh my God, yes." Then we climbed into his truck and drove to our favorite eastside bar.

Chapter 42

ARM IN ARM, my brother and I made our way to the front door of Mickey's. Two figures stood in shadow at the side of the building. One staggered forward. The other man put a hand out, pinning his companion's shoulder to the wall. It was no great shock to see a couple of drunks have a go at each other in Mickey's parking lot. It was part of the ambiance.

"Son of a bitch," Joe muttered as we drew closer and recognized one of the voices.

"I didn't fucking know, man. I swear to God!" Detective Tim Bowman slurred his words.

"That's the asshole whose nephew came at Vangie," Joe said.

"Yeah," I said, putting a hard hand on his arm.

"Do the right thing, Tim. For once in your life." The other man stepped out of the shadows. It was Eric Wray. Bowman might be drunk, but Wray was sober.

Tim answered, "It won't fucking matter."

"It matters to me!" Eric said. "And it should matter to you!"

"Yeah, what are you going to do about it?"

Eric Wray straightened. Bowman swayed on his feet. He was clumsy, dropping his right shoulder in a dead giveaway as he tried to take the first swing. Joe took it as an invitation. Leave it to Joe to use a stupid bar fight to blow off steam.

Eric Wray neatly dodged Bowman's blow and body slammed him against the wall. "You piece of shit," Joe yelled. He stepped in between the two men and grabbed Bowman. He held him up, twisting his shirt between two fists.

"Did you know? You motherfucker. Did you know this whole time? How many girls did your piece-of-shit nephew threaten besides my sister, huh?"

"The fuck you talking about," Bowman said, but his eyes told a different story. He was scared.

"Joe!" I yelled. My brother's rage clouded his judgment and he took a swing, landing a punch right across Tim Bowman's face. Blood gushed from his nose and he went straight down.

Eric grabbed Joe and threw him against the wall, holding him there with his forearm. "Cool your shit!" Eric shouted. "This isn't your fight."

This could get ugly, fast. Joe was carrying. He had a permit, but tensions were too damn high. Sure enough, Wray's eyes went wide as he pushed my brother back. No doubt he felt the outline of Joe's weapon.

"Are we going to have a bigger problem than we need?" In one swift movement, Eric disarmed my brother. He opened his jacket and shoved Joe's gun into his back pocket. I caught a glimpse of Wray's own off-duty gun and the small knife he carried in his belt loop. A shudder went through me and I found myself grateful that Eric Wray, for now, had the cooler head.

"I've got a permit for that," Joe said, his voice not much more than a hiss.

"Then you'll get it back, after you've cooled down a bit. You know where to find me," Wray said.

Bowman stirred beside them, but dropped his head back to the ground.

"Joe, enough," I said. "Let's just go inside and get the beers we came for."

Nostrils flaring, Joe squared off with Eric Wray. They would be evenly matched. Joe's last name got him in plenty of street fights. I knew Eric had been a beat cop before earning his detective's badge. But I was in no mood to watch them kick the shit out of each other.

"Listen to your sister," Wray said. "Go inside. First round's on me, okay?"

My brother mercifully relaxed his posture.

"Come on," he said to me.

"I'll be right in," I said. "Find us a booth."

Joe passed a look from me to Eric, his silent threat unmistakable. Eric lifted his hands, holding them palms out in a gesture of surrender.

"Thanks," I said, as Joe disappeared in the bar. "It's just … it's been a long day."

Eric turned and helped Bowman to his feet. Bowman swore at his fellow detective then staggered off into the night. Eric showed me a set of keys he'd just pulled off Tim Bowman. I nodded, impressed.

"You did good today," he said. "In court."

"Oh, you saw all that?" I asked as we started toward the bar's entrance.

"I saw enough," he answered. He held the door out for me. I hesitated before going in. Eric had a somber expression on his face that matched my insides.

"Then you know it's not going to make a damn bit of difference. That girl is going to prison for this."

Eric met my eyes and his shoulders dropped, almost as if I'd been the one to deliver a gut punch. He grimaced. "Maybe …"

"Maybe nothing," I said. "You've been at this as long as I have, Detective. I was sunk the second that girl went in and confessed. If we're lucky, she gets second-degree and maybe she's out in eighteen years."

"Yeah," he said. "Yeah."

"Come on," I said. "Let's make the first round a pitcher."

He froze. Something went through his eyes. "Tell Mickey to put it on my tab. Watch out your brother doesn't go overboard. He's a mean-ass drunk. Good luck tomorrow. I mean that."

"Thanks," I said, puzzled. "You sticking around for the grand finale?"

He looked skyward then back at me. "I just might."

"Then I'll take a rain check," I said, feeling bold. "You can buy me a drink when it's all over."

He smiled. "Yeah. Sounds good."

With that, he turned on his heel and headed out into the night.

Chapter 43

"WHY AREN'T THEY HERE YET?" Aubrey whispered. She sat beside me the next morning at the defense table. She was anxious to get going, though I'd explained how mundane the next hour or so might be. The judge would read a list of instructions to the jury, including legal definitions for the major issues in the case. After that, they would take the case back to the jury room and decide Aubrey's fate once and for all.

"Just be patient a little while longer," I said, finding a smile for her. "No matter what happens, I want you to know how proud I am of you."

"Proud?"

"Yes. Proud."

She cast her eyes downward. "And I want you to know if this goes bad ... I know how hard you worked. I know you've always believed in me. And I know it's nobody's fault but mine. I tried to do the right thing. I thought I was protecting my family."

"Stop," I said, taking her hand in mine. "No more looking back. Just keep your head high. Let me do my job.

We'll get a verdict. Then we'll decide if and where to fight next. Okay? One thing at a time."

She gave me a quick nod. I was going to say something else, but there was a commotion toward the back of the courtroom. The double doors stood open and Jack LaForge was in the hallway, red-faced and sweating. He looked about ready to have a stroke or a heart attack.

"Sit tight," I cautioned Aubrey. Dan and Diane sat behind me. Dan cast a wary look at me. I made a downward motion with my hand. Whatever this was, I didn't need him on my heels.

Jeanie sat beside Dan. The hallway commotion had her attention as well. As I walked to the back of the courtroom, she got up and followed.

"Do you have any idea what this does?" Jack shouted. My pulse tripped when I got close enough to see who he was shouting at. Tim Bowman stood before him, looking even worse than Jack. His suit was disheveled, his nose swollen from last night's encounter with Joe. Tim seemed sober, but barely. His eyes were bloodshot and he hadn't shaved yet. It looked like he slept in his clothes, his car, or not at all.

"It doesn't do anything. He's a drunk. A wino. The whole town knows it."

Jack tore a hand through his hair. He had a hard grip on Bowman's shoulder. In another second, I expected him to throw his own punch, shattering Bowman's nose for good.

"Something you boys need to fill me in on?" I asked. Jack reared back, startled. I'd never seen him like this. He was always cool and arrogant. He let go of Bowman.

"Just have a seat on that bench," Jack said to Bowman. "Don't fucking move."

The bench in question was right outside Castor's court-room. At the end of it sat another man just as disheveled as Tim Bowman. He looked familiar. Skinny, gray complexion. His hair was slicked back and the strong scent of Old Spice hit me. It barely masked his body odor. He could be thirty or seventy, his nose red and mottled from years of drinking.

"Whatcha doing here, Benny?" Jeanie asked, walking over to him. Benny. Shit. Benny Hyde. Long ago, he'd been a friend and drinking buddy of my father's. He was the one guy in town who was usually worse off than Joe Leary Sr. What the hell *was* he doing here?

Benny didn't answer, but gave Jeanie a nervous look. Bowman lumbered over to him and planted himself on the bench beside him.

"Cass," Jack said. "We've got a little situation. I was just coming to get you. Judge Castor is waiting for us in chambers."

"You mind telling me what the hell this is about?" I said. "I don't like walking into meetings when I don't know what they're about."

"Just come on."

Castor's secretary, Jennifer, poked her head out of his office door. She gave Jack a stern look and motioned for the two of us to come in. I shot a look at Jeanie. I'd leave her out here to figure out what Bowman and Benny had to do with any of this.

Castor was out of his robes when we walked in, wearing a blue tailored suit and a scowl. "Jack," he said. "Start talking."

We took seats on the other side of Castor's desk. Jack worked his hands together. He was still sweating. "It has come to my attention that there's a witness that had not been previously disclosed," he said. "In the park on the night of the 22nd."

"A witness to what, exactly?" Castor said, his voice rising.

"It's Benny Hyde," Jack said, exasperated. "He was

trying to sleep off a bender in the park that night. Hell, he's probably drunk right now."

"A witness to what?!" Castor and I shouted in unison.

"He says he saw Coach D on a swing by himself. He says it was 10:45."

"And just how the hell is he that specific?"

Jack dropped his head. "He says he got a phone call from his wife. He went up to the coach. Talked to him. But his phone rang and it was Dottie, trying to figure out where he was. He turned and walked out of the park."

My blood boiled. "You have got to be kidding me. Who took his statement? When?"

Jack pressed his thumb to his temple. Goddammit. I already knew the answer. "Bowman," I answered for him. "Son of a bitch. Tim Bowman. Judge, this is a Brady violation if ever there was one."

"He's a wino!" Jack said. "This guy is not reliable. He's just as likely to admit to seeing spaceships flying over the park on cross."

"That's not for you to decide!" I fumed. I rose from my chair and squared off with him. Castor gave me a warning look, but I was too far gone to care. "I can't even ... Jesus, Jack. Brady does *not* depend on whether the information is reliable. It only matters if it's exculpatory. I can't ... I don't even know what to say here. I want cell phone records. I want them right now."

Jack nodded. Castor sat back in his seat, crossing his legs. I think he was enjoying the show a little.

"We've got 'em," Jack said. "I woke the computer forensics guys in the middle of the night. I'm willing to stipulate *only* to the fact that Hyde got an incoming call from his wife at exactly 10:49 p.m. on June 22nd. It lasted three minutes."

"Let me guess," I said. "It pinged the tower near Shamrock Park too."

Jack slowly closed his eyes and sighed. "Yeah."

"I want a directed verdict," I said. "When did Bowman come to you?" My mind raced. Wray knew. It's what they were fighting about outside of Mickey's last night. He kept saying something about Bowman needing to do the right thing.

"Now hold on," Judge Castor said. "This trial isn't over yet. I can reopen proofs. Jack puts the guy on. It's unusual, but it's not unprecedented."

"No way," I said. "With all due respect, Your Honor. Let me put him on. Jack can cross. If this had been disclosed to me in the proper course, Benny would be my witness. I want him."

Castor raised a brow and looked at Jack. Jack nodded. "Fine."

But I still had a gut feeling something else was going on. I acted on it. "Jack? What else aren't you telling me?"

"Look," he said. "When this is all over, I want Bowman's badge. You can believe what you want, but I'm *telling* you, I didn't know about Hyde or the tape. Bowman called me at two in the morning. He was drunk off his ass and he got into some kind of bar fight. I don't know, I guess his conscience got to him. He says he just forgot about Hyde."

"What tape?" I asked.

Jack sighed. "He went into the office. He dug up Hyde's statement from his notes."

"Why weren't those notes part of what you turned over to me in discovery?" I asked.

"Because I didn't have them. I told you. This was Bowman's fuck-up. Not mine. He found some security footage from Beanie's Coffee Shop. He overlooked it. It was mislabeled on the property room shelf. He found it when he was looking for the rest of his notes. As much as you might want to go after him—and believe me, there will be a disciplinary investigation—this is worse for you. Your client was there at Beanie's on the 22nd. It shows her walking in at 11:03, ordering a latte, then sitting in a booth drinking it until 11:42."

My world turned upside down as I tried to process what he was saying. "You're telling me Bowman just happened to find this security footage last night?"

"Yeah," Jack said. He turned a mottled shade of green and put his head down, almost in a crash position.

"Jack," Castor started. "I don't even know what to say."

"So let me get this straight," I said. "You have access to evidence that your murder victim was alive in the park twenty minutes after my client testified she left. And he was *on the swing* just like she said he was. That information was never disclosed to the press. Not even after Aubrey's testimony. Nobody has it. There's no way Hyde could have pulled that out of thin air. He *saw* it, Jack. It happened. I don't care how drunk he was. And then, you have evidence that Aubrey was at Beanie's at 11:03. Beanie's is on the other side of town. Even in no traffic, it's going to take somebody twenty minutes to get there. She has an alibi, Jack. You drop these charges, never mind directed verdict."

Jack glared at me. "She *killed* that man. She confessed to it. You keep wanting to forget about that. And she had plenty of time to go back to that park and do what she *said* she did. The body wasn't discovered for almost an hour after she left that coffee shop."

I put my hands on the top of my head, afraid it might pop off. "Your Honor," I started.

He put a hand up to silence me. "I think our positions are clear here. You can make your motion on the record. I'll hear argument. But I'll tell you right now, as much as this stinks to high heaven, we're still dealing with fact questions, not legal ones. The jury is free to interpret all of this when they deliberate. I can't direct a verdict. You're dealing with the credibility of a potential eyewitness. You're dealing with a timeline issue."

"It's more than that," I said. "I should be able to present testimony about how long it would even take for my client to drive from Beanie's back to that park. It's not plausible."

"Your Honor," Jack said. "I've gotta live with Bowman's screw-up. But regardless of any footage, Aubrey Ames never said she was at Beanie's that night. Why is that? I'll argue it's because she knew damn well it left her enough time to go back to that park. It makes sense that she would have. She left her phone. I say that's exactly what happened. She's been lying to you, Cass. She went back looking for it and found Coach D still there. This is a mess. But it's still a murder. We aren't backing down from that."

I felt ready to murder someone myself. I just didn't know who. Jack? Tim Bowman? Or Aubrey? Jack was right about one thing. She had never once told me she'd gone to Beanie's.

"All right," Castor said. "We've got a plan here. We will reopen the evidence so Cass can call Benny Hyde to the stand. Please tell me he's here and ready to testify."

"He is," Jack said.

"Fine. You're going to stipulate to the cell phone evidence for Hyde. And you're going to stipulate to entry of the coffee shop footage."

"Your Honor, we ..." Castor's blistering glare stopped Jack cold. "Yes. We'll stipulate to the authenticity of the Beanie's tape. I have a statement from Bud Cross, the owner. He handed it over to the police the week after the murder. It was reviewed then. Bowman swore there was nothing on it. He logged it. It was part of the report you *did* get."

"Bowman swore," I muttered.

"All right, then," Castor said, rising. He grabbed his robe

from a coat rack behind him. "Let's get out there. I don't want to keep the jury waiting any longer."

Jack rose and turned to me. He opened his mouth to say something. Maybe it was an apology. More than likely, this was a bad cop's screw-up, not his. I wasn't yet in a place where I could be magnanimous.

I turned on my heel and went back into the hallway. The stunned look on Jeanie's face told me she'd already heard the bombshell from Hyde and Bowman. She was at my side as I stormed into the courtroom, ready to pick up my sword.

There wasn't time to clue Aubrey in. Judge Castor took the bench and I called Benny Hyde to the stand.

Benny was terrified, but he spoke clearly into the microphone. Once we'd gotten through the preamble, I went straight to the heart of the matter.

"Mr. Hyde, how can you be so sure it was Coach D you saw in the park that night?"

Benny cleared his throat. "I wasn't at first. It was just weird to me to see a grown ass … er … sorry, ma'am … a grown man on the swings at that time of night. So I went up to him. I been to a lot of those basketball games. It's one of the only interesting things to do in this town in the winter. I played for Delphi back in the day, you know. I mean, before that coach came in. I wasn't very good … but …"

"Mr. Hyde," I said, trying to get him back on track. "You're sure it was Larry Drazdowski you saw on the swings that night?"

"Yes, ma'am. He was wearing one of those Fighting Shamrock t-shirts. Always thought that was such a dumb phrase. Shamrocks don't fight. They're weeds mostly. Anyways, I called out 'Hey, Coach D' and he looked up at me and said hello. Well, I went over there and started to strike up a conversation. He was kind of rude. Y'know. Like he was too good for me or something. But, I mean, *he* was the one on the swings. I was going to say something about that. But that's when my phone rang. I would have ignored it, but it was my Dottie's ringer."

"What time did you receive that call?" I asked.

"Ten forty-nine," he answered.

I moved for entry of the phone records confirming it. Jack, of course, didn't object.

"Then what happened, Mr. Hyde?" I asked.

"Well, Dottie was pretty steamed. I was supposed to be home for dinner. Didn't make it. Anyway, she was hollering pretty loud and I walked away so the coach wouldn't hear it. I was only on the phone for a minute or two, but I walked toward the front of the park and kept on going. That's the last I saw of that guy until the news the next day that said he was dead."

"Mr. Hyde," I said. "Did you ever tell anyone about what you saw that night?"

"Sure did." Benny puffed out his chest. "Like I said, it was on the news the next day and they had that crime stoppers number asking for information. So I called it. They put me through to that fat detective. Bowman. I told him what I saw."

"And what did Detective Bowman do with that information?" I asked.

"Well, he was rude as fu… uh …he wasn't real nice about it. Kind of blew me off. Especially when I told him my name."

"And you never heard from Detective Bowman or the police again regarding Larry Drazdowski and what you saw that night?"

"No, ma'am," he said. "Not until last night. Bowman called me up out of the blue. Well, he was *real* interested in talking to me then. Then this here Mr. LaForge called. He brought this nice suit over to the house this morning and drove me in so I could talk to you all."

"Thank you, Mr. Hyde," I said. "I have nothing further."

Jack's cross was quick. "Mr. Hyde," he said. "How much alcohol had you consumed on the night of the 22nd?"

Benny shifted in his seat. "I had some."

"Can you be more specific? Beer? Liquor? Wine?"

"I had a few beers earlier in the day. Maybe three or four. Then I went to the liquor store. I bought a pint of bourbon."

"Did you drink the whole pint?" Jack asked.

Benny looked at his shoes. "Yeah. I did. I knew Dottie was going to be mad so I went to the park to try and sleep it off before I went home."

"I see. One more question, Mr. Hyde. Are you drunk now?"

"I had a few," he said.

"Thank you, I have nothing further," Jack said.

I rose. "Mr. Hyde? Have you told the truth as you remember it here today?"

"Yes, ma'am. You can say what you want about me. But Benny Hyde never lies."

"Thank you," I said.

"The witness may step down," Judge Castor said.

There was one thing left to do. Bowman took the stand. The members of the jury sat still as statues as I asked him about Benny's testimony.

"It was a mistake," he said. "An oversight. That's all."

Then I moved to introduce the videotape of Aubrey at Beanie's on the night of the 22nd. I hadn't yet had a chance to even talk to her about it. Jeanie had done her best to whisper and pass notes to her and her family while I was questioning Benny Hyde. I couldn't read Aubrey as the tape played and the jury gasped. The time counter on the grainy security footage ticked by. Aubrey sat alone in a yellow booth at the back of the store. She wore her Dewar's t-shirt and jeans like she did every night she worked. She sipped from a Styrofoam cup as the minutes passed. Finally, at 11:03, she put a bill on the table and walked to the front exit.

"Counsel," Castor said. "Is there anything you'd like to add to your closing statement?"

The less-is-more lesson had never been this poignant. Jack scribbled furious notes. I didn't need any for what I was about to do. I walked to the lectern and faced the jury. This was not the closing argument I had planned for. As much as my own adrenaline raced, I knew the jury's did too. They were shocked by the eleventh-hour developments and still trying to process them. A few of them had held scorn in their expressions as Tim Bowman retook the stand. I would use their shock as a weapon. The sooner I got this case to them, the better.

"Ladies and gentlemen," I said rising. "That tape speaks for itself. Aubrey Ames has an alibi. She has told you the truth. No one but the police and now the people in the court-room knew Aubrey said Coach D was on the swings when she left. Benny Hyde isn't perfect, but he's telling you the truth. I ask that you now render the only just verdict in this case. Aubrey Ames is not guilty."

Chapter 44

JUDGE CASTOR GAVE Jack LaForge fifteen minutes for a rebuttal closing. He only took two. "You cannot be swayed by defense counsel's theatrics. You cannot be swayed by your own emotions. You must review the facts alone. Even if Aubrey Ames left that park at 10:30 as she claimed and went to Beanie's as she has *not* claimed, it makes sense that she would have returned to the park and murdered Larry Drazdowski. She admitted as much. Once again, I implore you to take her at her word. There is still a thirty-seven minute gap from the time Aubrey Ames left Beanie's coffee shop to when Larry Drazdowski's body was discovered. I challenge you, ladies and gentlemen. Let thirty-seven minutes go by when you're in that deliberation room. It's an eternity. And it is ample time to commit premeditated murder. You'll be instructed by the judge on the law here in a minute. The facts are up to you. They are incontrovertible. There is *no* doubt that Aubrey Ames murdered Coach D. I ask that you return the only verdict you can. Guilty. Thank you."

Jack hesitated for a moment as if he had more to say.

Then he gathered his notes from the lectern, gave the jury a grim nod, then took his seat back at the table.

Judge Castor read the jury instructions and just before lunch, he released the case to the jury. Their faces were solemn as they filed out of the courtroom tasked with determining nineteen-year-old Aubrey Ames's fate.

As soon as the last jury member left the room, Dan Ames broke into tears behind me. "What do we do now?" Diane asked. It was the first time I'd heard her speak since the trial began.

"You go home," I said. "You be together as a family. This could take a while."

Jack had already stormed out of the courtroom. I craned my neck. The Delphi Chief of Police, Dennis Bell, stood in the hallway waiting for him. Another badged man stood beside him wearing a black suit. I'd bet money it was Tim Bowman's union rep. Good call, I thought. But that would be a fight for another day.

"Come on," Jeanie said. "Let's head down to the courthouse diner and grab lunch. You look like you could use some air."

I hugged Aubrey. She was stiff as a board and her face unnaturally white. "Honey, I need you to keep it together a little while longer. We're in a different world than we were just a couple of hours ago. I still can't promise you what this jury will do, but this fight is far from over, even if it's bad news."

"We've already started an online fundraiser," Dan offered. "Baby, you hang in there. Cass was a rock star today." For the first time since I met him, Dan Ames was actually smiling. I wanted to share his enthusiasm, but I knew juries were unpredictable. Like it or not, Jack had made some solid points on rebuttal.

"We'll take her home," Diane said. "Thank you, Cass. Thank you so much."

"Don't thank me yet," I said. "But you're welcome anyway."

With that, Dan and Diane collected their daughter and led her to the back of the courtroom.

"He's right," Jeanie said. "You were great just then."

"What's your read?" I asked.

Jeanie bit her bottom lip and shrugged. "Son of a bitch, Cass. I think we're still dealing with a coin flip. If only that kid hadn't said she did it. It makes it all too neat for the jury even with all the other stuff."

She was right. Jeanie had always been right.

"Come on," she said. "Most of their food sucks, but there's this grilled cheese sandwich that's not so bad."

I put my arm around Jeanie and headed out of the courtroom with her. It seemed like the entire Delphi police detective bureau had shown up en masse. I couldn't tell whether it was in support or condemnation for one of their own. Eric Wray had caught up with Dan Ames. He shook his hand and pulled him into a bro hug. He was a good friend to Dan and I hope he knew I appreciated it. I had a feeling I had him to thank for Bowman's recent crisis of conscience. But for now, my brain was still buzzing too badly to sort that out.

Jeanie and I shared that grilled cheese sandwich in relative peace. She watched me eat and made me drink a bottle of water. God bless Jeanie. It seemed she was always there when I felt the bottom falling out on my life.

Forty minutes later, my cell phone buzzed on the table. It was Judge Castor's clerk.

"Holy shit," Jeanie said it for me.

I picked up the phone. "They're back," the clerk said. "I've got a bailiff running down to the parking lot to head off your client. Get to the courtroom in fifteen minutes."

"You got it!" I said, my heart racing again.

Jeanie threw two twenties on the table and we ran out of the diner together. Sure enough, one of the bailiffs strode beside the Ames family as we rounded the corner. Aubrey still looked too pale for my comfort level. I got to her and put an arm around her, guiding her away from her family. Jeanie would manage Aubrey's parents.

Forty minutes. I kept repeating that over and over. It could mean anything.

Jack and his team were already at the prosecution's table as we walked in. The gallery was empty of spectators and two bailiffs guarded the courtroom entrance to keep it that way.

Judge Castor took the bench. His clerk and court reporter slid into their seats. The jury filed in.

I could hear nothing but the beat of my own heart as the bailiff ordered us to our feet. Castor said words. I watched his lips moving, but to my ears, no sound came out. The clerk handed him the verdict form. The man could be a poker champion. He turned to the jury as the foreman stood. She was a middle-aged woman. Juror number eleven. A mother of three. Homemaker. She had two years of college and her husband was a pipefitter. She nodded as she told the judge they had reached a verdict and it was unanimous.

There was a rushing sound, as if a dam broke in my head. My heart stopped.

"On count one of the complaint, murder in the first degree, we the jury find the defendant, Aubrey Ames … not guilty."

Diane Ames screamed. Dan Ames sobbed. Jack LaForge dropped his chin to his chest. And beside me, Aubrey Ames slumped to the floor in a dead faint.

Chapter 45

PANDEMONIUM. It's a word you hear, not one you really understand. But it confronted us all as I walked in front of the Ames family and took to the courthouse steps. Camera phones flashed. Microphones seemed to sprout everywhere. The *Freep* was there. All the local channels. Seven live trucks lined the street in front of the courthouse and I recognized two national cable news outlets.

I couldn't even hear the questions they asked. Before we walked through the doors, I told Aubrey and her family to let me do the talking. No comment. Not now.

"My client feels vindicated," I said, almost on auto-pilot. "This was the first step toward a much bigger fight for justice. But the truth is out. My client is innocent."

"Ms. Leary," one of the reporters shouted. "Can you comment on the attorney general's statement?"

I blinked hard. Beside me, Jeanie gave a little shrug to indicate she had no idea what that meant either. Another reporter chimed in.

"The Michigan Attorney General's office has just announced an investigation into the Delphi school district.

People are demanding answers relating to Coach Drazdowski's conduct. Can you comment for us?"

"As I said," I started. "Today was the first step toward a much bigger fight for justice. I'm happy to hear that the state is hopefully picking up that fight as well. Aubrey Ames is not the only victim here. There are many more. Larry Drazdowski can never hurt another child again. We need to make sure those who shielded him and made his conduct possible can never hurt another child either. Thank you. Please let my client and her family have their privacy."

The deputy sheriffs formed a barrier as I made my way down the stairs. Corwin's imposing form waited beside an eight-seater SUV directly across the street. As much as I hated it at the same time, I was grateful for his looming, protective presence.

"Come on," he said. "You can pick up your car later."

With that, I slid into the back seat with the Ames family as Jeanie climbed in the front. Corwin spoke into an earpiece and pulled away from the curb.

"Is it over?" Aubrey finally asked.

"It is," I said, reaching for her. "It's all over. You're free, honey. We did it."

"You did it," Dan said. He pulled me into a hug. "Praise God, you brought our baby back to us."

"He lied?" Aubrey said. "That detective lied?"

"I don't know about lied," I said. "More like withheld information. He'll be dealt with. Trust me on that."

Corwin weaved through traffic. He knew Delphi streets like the back of his hand now. He took a circuitous route, throwing any potential followers. Within five minutes, he pulled up the driveway to Dan Ames's house in the woods. I hugged Aubrey one last time.

"Get back to normal, if you can," I said. "The world

knows you're innocent. And they know you weren't lying about what Coach D did. I'm proud of you."

Her parents had already exited the car. I stood apart from them, my arms around Aubrey's shoulders. She finally looked like she was breathing again.

"It's only … I don't understand."

"What?"

"Cass … I don't want to lie. Not ever again. Not about what Coach did. Or what I did. And I didn't lie. I promise. But … I wasn't *at* Beanie's the night I met with Coach D. It's like I told you. I just drove around for a while. I was scared to go home but scared to go anywhere else. I mean, I *did* go to Beanie's. But it was the night before."

My throat ran dry. The air grew thick and it got hard to draw breath. "Aubrey, it's okay." It was. She was right. She hadn't lied. I hadn't called her back to the stand. The surveillance tape spoke for itself. I couldn't tell her to lie now.

"Maybe you just got everything jumbled up in your mind," I offered.

She gave me an absent nod, but I knew her well enough now to know she was still very much confused. "Maybe," she finally said. Something changed in her. She plastered on a smile. "Sure. Yeah. I must have got the dates jumbled. I can … I can never, ever thank you enough." She hugged me once more then, with a confident step, she walked up the porch and went inside to the waiting arms of her mother and father.

———

MY PHONE BUZZED as Corwin made his way back to my office. I opened my text messaging app. Killian's words blinked back at me.

"Congratulations, counselor." Of course news traveled quickly to Killian Thorne.

"Thank you," I texted back.

"You're welcome. I hope the favor I did for you worked out as you hoped."

I let the cursor blink for a few moments. "It did," I answered. "And now you need to recall the favor I didn't ask you for. Send Corwin home."

"He already has his orders."

I wanted to type thank you again, but it just felt like another reminder that I was in his debt for finding Vangie. I didn't know where or when, but he would collect. And I knew the price would be steep. I clicked my phone off and left his last message unanswered.

Corwin pulled into the parking lot of my office. Miranda stood at the front door waving wildly. Joe's truck was also in the driveway. I slid out. Part of me felt like I should say something to Corwin. He didn't give me a chance. He slid the windows up, obscuring his face, then slowly pulled away. Just like that, he was gone. He had his orders, after all.

Miranda rushed forward and hugged me. "The phones. They're off the hook. Oh my God, Cass. You're amazing. I can't believe it. You're in demand. Danielle Ford and Chelsea Holbrook's family. They've both called. They want to sue the school. They want you to represent them."

"Well, that ought to do wonders toward putting me in the town's good graces." I joked, but I also felt that familiar tingling excitement at the prospect of going after the bastards who covered up for Larry Drazdowski. I meant what I said on the courthouse steps. I just hadn't realized I might have the chance to fight them in a direct way again so soon.

Joe and Matty waited for me in the conference room. Joe popped the cap on sparkling grape juice in lieu of champagne. Matty was on the wagon again. With his track record, it might not last forever, but we could celebrate today.

Only Vangie was absent and my heart twisted. Matty had country music blaring from the office speakers as Joe and I took a quiet minute away.

"She left you a note," he said. "It's back at the house."

"What does it say?"

"She's good. She's going to keep in touch. She promised to come back for Christmas. By the way, you're hosting it at the lake house."

I laughed. "I figured."

"She likes her life in Indianapolis. She has friends there. A job she likes. She's thinking about going back to school."

"She should," I said. "Once I get this practice fully off the ground, I'd like to help her pay for it."

"I still don't get how you managed to find her so fast. And I can't say it doesn't worry the shit out of me."

I slid my arm around my brother's waist and rested my head on his shoulder. "I can't make you stop worrying. But I can tell you that I'm okay too. It took me a while to figure it out, but I know I'm where I'm supposed to be now."

He pulled away so he could see my face. "Do you promise? No more running. I like it better when you're here. It's good for Emma too. Josie's ... well ... she tries hard ... but she hasn't always been the most positive female role model."

"What about Katy?"

Joe shrugged. It told me all I needed to know. So they were struggling too. I only wanted him to be happy. I suppose that's all he wanted for me too. So, here we were. Trying.

"It's good to have you back," he whispered, kissing the top of my head. I felt a lump in my throat as I saw the mist in my brother's eyes. His desperate worry for me, for Vangie, for Matty, it would never go away. It wouldn't for me either. But it helped that we could face it together now.

"I love you, you big dummy," I said.

"I love you too, shrew," he answered back.

"Fine," I said. "I'll do Christmas. But that means you've got to help me get that house fixed up once and for all. The roof is leaking in the back bedroom. The water pressure is for shit. That deck is sagging. There's a damn mole tearing up the yard …"

He squeezed me hard. "Yeah, yeah. Slave driver."

"Slacker."

His whole body shook with deep, infectious laughter. And, for the first time in a long time, I felt like I was truly home.

Later, Joe took Matty home. I sat at the end of the conference table in the dark. Miranda had turned the corkboard toward the wall while the others were here. Now that it was just me, I walked over to it and slowly turned it around.

Now that Matty was gone, Miranda came in holding a bottle of wine and two glasses. Jeanie came in behind her as I stood in front of that corkboard.

"Relax," Miranda said. "Job's over." She poured the wine and held a glass out for me.

"None for you?" I asked as she handed the other to Jeanie.

"Time for me to get home. I've got cats to feed. And I'm taking the damn day off tomorrow."

Smiling, I lifted my glass to her. Miranda gave me a little salute. "Lock up when you leave," she said. "You want me to call you an uber? That tall guy was menacing as hell but he would have made an excellent designated driver for the night."

Smiling, I took a sip. "Stop worrying about me. And take more than one day off. How about I see you next Monday?"

Miranda waved over her head as she flicked off the office sign. We were closed for business.

"Come on," Jeanie said. "Let's get the hell out of here. I'm fine if I never see another picture of Larry Drazdowski's face."

His lifeless form stared at me from the top of the corkboard. Beneath it, I had head shots of every other witness in the case. Jeanie moved a push pin and stuck it right through Detective Tim Bowman's right eye.

"How the hell does he screw up like that?" she asked. "I've known Tim since he was a beat cop. He's an asshole. And he was the wrong man for this case … but … he was a good detective once upon a time. Losing alibi evidence like that? I've been in that property room. It's not like it's that big. My God, they probably would have convicted her without that tape. You know that, right?"

I raised a brow. "Gee, thanks."

Jeanie tilted her head. "Come on, you wanted me to blow smoke up your ass?"

"Well, maybe just the one puff."

Jeanie laughed then looked back at the board. "The stink of this is going to rub off on his partner, Megan Lewis," she said. "There's no help for it. Too bad. She's a good kid. Promising rookie. Man, it's such a small department to begin with. They'll have no choice but to suspend her pending an investigation. That'll just leave Wray and Knapp to handle shit for the foreseeable future. Here's hoping nobody else gets robbed or murdered in Delphi anytime soon. Never *mind* them figuring out who really killed that bastard. Jack will never get a conviction now if and when they do reopen the case."

I froze. The air grew thick just like it had when I dropped

off Aubrey earlier in the night. Jeanie was still talking but her voice blended in with the howling wind outside. I went to the corkboard and ripped Bowman's head shot off. I took another long sip of wine then stuck the picture back on the board.

I don't know how long I stood there. Long enough that Jeanie put a hand on my arm and turned me to face her, her eyes wide with concern.

"You okay?" she asked.

"What? Yeah," I said, mustering a smile. "It's just … you're right. Let's turn out the lights and go home."

Jeanie narrowed her eyes, searching my face. But whatever she saw there, she left it alone for now. Arm in arm, we left the conference room. I was the last one out. I looked back, letting Tim Bowman and Larry Drazdowski stare at me one last time before I turned out the lights.

Chapter 46

Three Weeks Later

EARLY NOVEMBER HAD BROUGHT the first light snowfall, heralding the brutal Michigan winter yet to come. On the Friday after Thanksgiving, I made the slow, winding turn to the back of Shamrock Park. Joe had just put brand-new snow tires on my Jeep. It was a lease, but I was falling in love.

He waited for me on the park bench like I asked him to, wearing a black jacket, his hands stuffed in the pockets. I followed his deep footprints in the snow. He didn't even turn when he heard the crunch of my footsteps, but he saved a space beside him on the park bench. I pulled back the hood of my down parka and sat.

The swing set stood ominously beside us, seats swaying in the slight breeze. Icicles formed at the top. A few weeks ago, there had been a makeshift shrine here. Cards, letters, candles honoring the hero they thought had died here. Construction on the commemorative statue halted. Just a few uneven bricks marked its place. Red graffiti stained those bricks, freshly painted. Drops of it dotted the snow like blood. Instead of "rest in peace" the message was now "burn in hell." It jarred my conscience just as much.

"Thanks for taking my call," I said. "I'll be honest. I wasn't sure you'd come."

He smiled at me, showing those straight, white teeth. Those pale blue eyes seemed to see right through me, reading my thoughts. I studied his face again. Dark brows, just the slightest touch of silvery gray at his temples. He had a cleft in his chin when he smiled and when he scowled.

"Sure you were," he said.

"You're right," I said. I waited a moment, not sure how to start. "They've put Kevin Sydney on administrative leave. He's going down though. The superintendent may too. They're cleaning the whole house."

He nodded. "I suppose it's about time."

"What about Bowman?"

He turned to me. He was handsome in an unassuming way that I knew drove women crazy. Like he knew, but absolutely didn't care.

"Suspension with pay for now," he said. "But he's not coming back from this."

The wind kicked up, sending a swirling cyclone of snow toward us. Then it died down just as quickly as Detective Eric Wray faced me.

"I know it's hard for you to believe this, but Tim's not a bad guy. He really did think he was doing the right thing at first. And he really did just forget about Benny Hyde. That guy, he's come in and reported shit on just about every major case we've had. Anything that makes the news, there's Benny showing up saying he saw something or heard something or knows somebody."

"It doesn't matter," I said. "And *you* may not believe it, but I don't have it out for him. I don't hold him responsible for what his idiot nephew pulled with my sister. Or what he pulled with me."

Two weeks ago, Luke Bowman had been arrested for vehicular assault. The paint scrapings on his front fender matched the car I'd been driving when he ran me off the road.

Wray grew silent. The wind howled and I shivered. "Come on," Eric said. "Whatever you wanted to talk about, we can do this in the car where it's warm."

"No," I said. "I like it here. It makes sense."

A beat passed between us. He was a good cop. A seasoned detective. Of course he could read something in my face. He swallowed hard and a muscle jumped in his jaw. He could have gotten up and left then. He could have told me to just piss off and mind my own business. Except he didn't. For a long time later, I'd wonder why he didn't or what might have happened if he had. Instead, he worked something out for himself as I stared into his eyes.

He looked down and pursed his lips. "Maybe it does."

"It's just a lucky thing someone found that surveillance footage." I kept my eyes locked with his. Eric Wray was good. Almost too good. But the corner of his mouth twitched ever so slightly, almost in a smirk as he looked back at me.

"Yeah," he said. "A very lucky thing."

It was just one thing. One tiny alteration. The date on the counter of Beanie's security tape. Someone with access and know-how could have easily changed it if they knew what they were looking for. If they knew the timeline. Aubrey had told the detectives and me she'd been there the night *before* the murder.

Eric shifted. The smile faded from his lips and his eyes grew cold and dark. I stared straight ahead, considering my

next words. "Bowman hasn't figured it out yet, has he?" I
asked. Eric looked down and cleared his throat.

"Cass … I don't know what …"

I put a hand up and made a decision. "Eric, how much
money do you have in your pocket?"

He cocked his head to the side. "I …" He let out a
breath.

"It doesn't matter," I said. "Anything will do." Again, I
think he could read something in my face. I wasn't here to
hurt him. I was only here for the truth.

He pulled his wallet out of his pocket. My breath caught.
The wallet was old and well-used with worn leather and
faded circles where he kept his change. He pulled out a
single, crisp dollar bill and held it out to me.

I was wearing black knit mittens. I pulled one off with
my teeth. The bitter cold air hit my fingers. My cheeks were
already numb. I hesitated, keeping my fingers curled near my
chest. Then I took the dollar from him and folded it into my
pocket. I slid my mitten back on.

"It's a small department," I said. "Just you and Tim.
Knapp and Lewis. Four people. Lewis might be great
someday if the fallout from this doesn't hit her too hard.
Knapp, I hear he's a good guy too. Just a year from retirement though. Not one to make waves, right?"

"Cass …"

"He loves you," I said. "Dan Ames. He trusts you. You'd
have done anything for him."

I felt the outlines of Eric Wray's dollar bill in my pocket.

"I've known Dan since kindergarten," he said, the
emotion leaving his voice. His words began to rush out of
him, as if he'd rehearsed them a thousand times in his head.
I realized with cold stillness that he probably had. "I met him
the same day I met Jack LaForge's little brother Grady. That
kid was a bully. He knocked Dan down on the playground.

Found a couple of his buddies to try and keep him there. I don't like bullies. So I punched Grady's teeth out. Wasn't much of a problem. They were loose to begin with."

I couldn't help myself. I giggled at that.

"You were a good friend to Dan," I said. "He told me that."

Eric stared at that graffiti-stained spot in the snow. "Thirty-three years. Sean is my godson. If Wendy and I ever had kids, Dan would have been the first one's godfather. We hunt together every November, except not this one, of course."

They hunted together. Bits of the trial echoed in my mind. The coroner's testimony. *A standard hunting knife.* Of course, I'd seen one just like it in Eric's belt that night at Mickey's when he disarmed Joe.

"That night," I said. "June 22nd. Dan got drunk at Mickey's. Is that when he told you about Aubrey and Coach D? He doesn't even remember it. Someday, he might."

Eric dropped his head. Unlike me, he wasn't wearing gloves. The skin over his knuckles had turned red from the cold. He squeezed his fists in his lap. Finally, his breath steady, his voice nearly toneless, he looked me straight in the eye.

"Yeah. He was going to kill him."

I took a breath. "I know."

Eric set his jaw to the side, regarding me. He didn't nod, exactly, but there was an almost twinkle in his eye. "Dan was going to kill Larry Drazdowski. He knew no one would believe Aubrey's story. He knew she was trying to figure out a way to bring him down. He was drunk out of his mind. I almost didn't believe him. But I know that man."

Eric looked back out at the snow. "He told me he bought a gun. He wouldn't listen. I promised him I'd figure out a way to help. Then …"

"You followed her," I said. "You left the bar and followed Aubrey that night?"

"No," he said. "I followed him. That fucking monster. What Dan told me ... I just lost it."

The puzzle pieces had begun to take shape the night of the verdict in my conference room. Hell, maybe even before that. It was a small department. Only a few people would have had access to the security footage on that property shelf. Then there were little snippets of things Dan had said. He'd been the one to tell me he saw Eric that night. Dan was so drunk he had no idea what he'd said.

"She didn't come home that night when she was supposed to," Eric said. "Diane called Dan. He was in no condition to drive. I couldn't let him do it. I asked him to trust me. I was going to be the one to get the evidence Aubrey needed. I promised him that."

I sat back hard against the bench.

"She wasn't home. She was supposed to come straight home. I said I'd go looking for her. I took Dan's keys and gave them to the bartender. I left him there. God, it was just dumb luck I drove by the park."

"And you saw Larry's car." My pulse skyrocketed.

"I saw Larry's car. He wasn't on the swings though. He was over there. Right by that stupid shamrock statue."

"He admitted it," I said, my tone dropping an octave.

Eric shook his head. "He didn't deny it. He actually tried to fucking shake my hand. I told him I knew who he was and what he'd done to Aubrey. I swear to God I didn't know about your sister. He stood there, smiling; he told me to my face that I'd never be able to prove a goddamn thing."

"You're done, Larry. It's over." Eric went somewhere else in those few moments. He was there beside me, but his eyes glazed over as if he saw a scene from a movie playing behind them.

Eric was tall, but even at six foot three, Drazdowski would have had a good two inches on him and maybe forty pounds. But I wagered Eric was the better fighter. He'd honed his skills against street thugs and drug dealers who actually wanted him dead back in his beat cop days.

"He got scared," Eric said. Still, he wouldn't look at me. He stared at a point in the snow. "Something changed in his face. He read mine, maybe. He knew I wasn't bullshitting. He finally faced somebody who wasn't afraid of him. God, that felt so good."

"Come on," he told me. "What the hell are these girls telling you, man? You think I'm some kind of pervert? Look, I'm no saint. But, in case you haven't checked, Aubrey Ames is nineteen years old. Yeah. Maybe it's not the smartest thing to get mixed up with her, but you know how it is. She wants it. Believe me. She begged for it. Just tonight even."

I thought I might be sick. I gripped the edge of the park bench as Eric continued.

"I've been around enough men like Larry Drazdowski. He *believed* the shit he was saying. And he'd never stop. I knew it. God. In my soul, I knew he'd have to *be* stopped. I grabbed him then. I told him if he touched that girl or any other one again … *I'll fucking end you!*"

Eric went very still but for a tiny tremor in his right hand. His fingers opened and closed. I could almost see the handle of the knife fall into his hand.

"Eric?" I said, afraid to break the spell.

Eric turned to me; his eyes had gone blood red. He blinked back tears. He continued in that odd narrative, repeating Larry's words verbatim and crossed with his own. "He said … oh God. He said … It sure as shit worked on that piece of ass you married. Wendy. She was one of the sweetest. Like a ripe peach. She begged for it too. She ever tell you that? Nah. That wouldn't have been her style. But man, the way she filled out that cheerleader skirt. Swish. Swish."

The bottom dropped out of my heart.

"The shit he said then … he said he got there before I did. He asked me to ask her how my wife spent her eighteenth birthday. And he … he knew things. She has a birthmark on her thigh. He … God, Cass, it was like my blood turned to fire. He kept talking, every word just hit me, like he was bludgeoning my mind with them."

"Kind of like a heart, right? Oooh, and those freckles near her nipples …"

I put a hand over my mouth.

"He wouldn't stop. He would never stop. Wendy. She was hurt. Crying. I found her running on the side of the road on her eighteenth birthday. She was supposed to be having a slumber party with her friends. Girl drama. That's what she said. I'd been so stupid to believe it. God, I was just a damn kid myself. Nineteen. Self-absorbed. I was trying not to flunk out of college.

"She never told me. That was almost twenty years ago and she never told. How many more girls had there been since then?"

I put a hand against his cheek. A tear fell from Eric's eye. But he was far from done.

"Larry said I couldn't do shit. He told me how he could fuck up my world and threatened to have me bounced back down to the street. He thought that even mattered to me.

"I couldn't make her happy. God. Wendy. I could never make her happy. I thought it was me. It *was* me. Why didn't I stop it? Why didn't I see it?"

"You couldn't. No more than I could with Vangie," I said, but Eric was too far gone for me to reach just then.

"He made a move on me," Eric said. "I can tell myself he was going to throw a swing. Maybe he would have. But …

I just *knew* there was only one way to stop that fucking monster from hurting another little girl again. I would *never* let him get the chance."

"Your knife," I said.

He nodded. "I always keep it with me."

He slid it out of his belt loop now; the blade gleamed in the sun.

"Eric …"

"Not this one," he said. "No one will ever find the one I ended his life with."

"Good," I said sharply.

I was too stunned to wipe away my own tears. When I looked back on it, I wasn't even sure who I was crying for. Aubrey, Vangie, Wendy Wray, or Eric himself.

"I swear to God I didn't know Aubrey had met him in the park that night," he said, his voice shaking. "I didn't know she'd sent those text messages to him. I didn't know she's the one who asked to meet him there. I got there well after she'd left."

"And after Benny Hyde saw him. How did you figure out he'd been there?"

"I ran into him a couple of nights before the trial started. He started babbling about why he wasn't going to get his big moment. I thought he was just blowing smoke like he always does. But then he said something about the swings."

"That night at Mickey's," I said. "You were confronting Bowman about it."

Eric nodded. "It kept unraveling. The more I tried to contain it, the worse it got."

"She up and confessed on us," I said, a bitter smile forming on my face.

"Yeah," he said. "She came to the same conclusion I had. Her dad was going to kill that bastard. She thought he had."

"You gambled," I said. "Jesus. The jury. You know it

could have gone either way. Eric, you let that girl twist in the wind for months?"

When he dropped his head, a tear fell from the bridge of his nose.

"I wasn't going to let that happen. I swear to God."

I believed him. I still had plenty of anger. But, I believed him.

He shook his head. "You saved her. You had the jury. What your sister said. They were *looking* for a reason to set her free. God, I'm sorry for that. I never meant to have Vangie dragged through this too. But, I was planning to step forward. I know that sounds convenient for me to say now, but it's true. If Bowman had just done his job. If he hadn't suppressed evidence… It just kept spiraling."

"Still," I said.

"I would never have let that girl go to prison for what I did. Never."

"They won't stop looking though," I said. "I put it together. Someone else might. Someone with an ax to grind, like Bowman, maybe."

Eric shook his head. "Maybe. But I don't think so. Right now, nobody wants to touch this investigation. Public opinion against Coach D has turned. Most people, including the department and the prosecutor's office think he got what he deserved. Jack LaForge wants his boss's job next election cycle. He can't afford another failure. I've seen this happen before. It's going to fade away. They're focusing on building indictments on anyone involved in the cover-up."

Silence fell between us as I considered Eric Wray's words. He was right, of course. I don't know how long it lasted, but the wind kicked up again and I couldn't feel my feet.

"I used to think right and wrong was like two sides of a coin," I said. "Then I went to Chicago. Big dreams. Big career. Big money. I was seduced by it. I mean, me, Cass

Leary, from the east side of the lake. I had everything. I *was* someone. And nobody there knew where I came from. Then one day I looked in the mirror and I didn't recognize my own face. I found myself doing things for people that I knew were wrong. And it didn't happen all at once. It happened little by little. One line crossed, then another. Until finally, the burden of it all caught up with me and I couldn't breathe. But by then, it was too late to get out. Too late to turn back. At least, that's what I thought. Until now."

"I was wrong," he said. "You don't have to tell me that."

"That's not what I'm telling you," I said. "I'm telling you that I can finally look in the mirror and know who I am again. And I can look at you and tell you I understand. I think maybe you're a good man, Detective Wray. You're not a perfect man. I'm telling you there's evil in the world and sometimes we have to touch it to end it. And I think we both know Larry Drazdowski was getting ready to move on to the next girl, and the next after that. And maybe someday, he would have been caught. But it wasn't going to happen anytime soon. The Kevin Sydneys of the world were working too hard to cover it up."

His shoulders slumped, with relief or defeat, I wasn't sure. But I did recognize the lifting of that burden. I had felt it once myself, not too long ago.

"It's what I tell her," he said.

"Who?"

"Wendy," he said. "When I sit by her bedside at Maple Valley. I don't know if she can hear me. Probably not. The doctors say she was deprived of oxygen too long. But I tell her every time. He's gone. That monster is gone. I killed him for her. And I'm so fucking sorry I wasn't there to keep him from hurting her in the first place. Everyone thinks I'm a sucker for doing it. I know what she was. What she did, sleeping around on me. It was all but over between us. But the thing of it was, it's not her fault. She was broken before she even married me. And I was broken after. This job. I wasn't there for her. I just didn't realize how far back."

I put a hand on his back. His muscles bunched, solid as granite.

"I think you did the best you could. And maybe she can hear you. No matter what those doctors say, don't stop telling her."

This time, his smile was genuine and deep. He touched my face and even in the cold, Eric Wray's skin burned through mine. As I stared into his piercing blue eyes, I believed he had the soul of a good man. I just hoped he wasn't too far gone to believe it.

"I think you did the best you could too," he said. "And I think it's time for you to get the hell out of the cold."

He rose slowly, staring down at me. "See you around, counselor."

"See you around, detective," I answered back.

Then Eric Wray made the slow walk up the hill toward his car. I slid my hand in my pocket, crunching his dollar bill in my mitten. My retainer. His assurance that his darkest truth would never leave my lips. The feel of it warmed me as I made my way out of Shamrock Park.

***

Up Next for Cass Leary

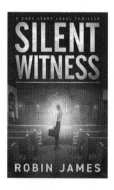

Cass takes the case that could rip her family apart. Her sister Vangie stands accused in the double homicide of an affluent, Ann Arbor couple. The only witness, is their six-year-old daughter, the child Vangie gave up for adoption. Now, the child is missing. All the physical evidence points to Vangie's guilt and Cass knows she's been keeping secrets. But, is she truly capable of murder?

Turn the page for details on how to grab a free, exclusive copy of *Crown of Thorne*, the bonus prologue to the Cass Leary Legal Thriller Series.

Newsletter Sign Up

Sign up to get notified about Robin James's latest book releases, discounts, and author news. You'll also get *Crown of Thorne* an exclusive FREE bonus prologue to the Cass Leary Legal Thriller Series just for joining. Find out what really happened on Cass Leary's last day in Chicago.

Click to Sign Up

http://www.robinjamesbooks.com/newsletter/